PENGU

NUSANTARA...

Heidi Shamsuddin was born in Malaysia, and spent part of her childhood growing up in Seattle, Washington and Petaling Jaya, Malaysia. After leaving school, she studied law at Nottingham University, obtained a postgraduate degree in corporate law, and after taking her Bar exams, eventually worked as a maritime lawyer in a London law firm. In 2007, she returned home and began to write fiction.

Heidi is now an award-winning author of stories inspired by Southeast Asia for both children and adults. Her first short story *Johan the Honey Hunter*, won the regional prize for the Eye Level Children's Literature Award in 2012. Shortly after, she signed an eight-book contract with Oyez! Books to write *The Door Under the Stairs* series for children. Since then, she has written and published short stories, readers and picture books including *The Malay Tale of the Pig King*, which is based on the Malay epic, *Hikayat Raja Babi*.

In 2017, she was invited as a speaker to the Asian Festival of Children's Content (AFCC) in Singapore to talk about the folktales of the region, and in 2018 she was invited to give a TEDx talk at University of Malaya on why we still need our fairy tales. In 2017, her screenplay for *Batik Girl* won the Intellectual Property Creators' Challenge (IPCC) Award and was made into an award-winning short animated film by R&D Studio and Tudidut Studio. *Batik Girl* has gone on to receive the Honorable Mention in Audience Favorites award at the Florida Animation Festival, Best Animated Short Film prize at the Festival de Largos y Cortos de Santiago 2019 in Chile, as well as Gold Medal in the Regional category at the 20th Digicon6 Asia in Japan.

Heidi has recently embarked on a project to collect and adapt the folklore, fairy tales, fables, myths, epics, legends, wonder and magic tales from all around the Nusantara region, with the aim of spreading and disseminating these traditional tales. As a way to reach a wider audience, she began an online project to highlight and discuss these stories on her YouTube channel (Heidi Shamsuddin) and at www.heidishamsuddin.com.

As the sun began to set, the maidens prepared to leave. One by one, they put on their flying robes so they could return home to Kayangan, where their father, the King, awaited them. However, the youngest princess could not find her magic robe. She searched the bushes nearby. She looked behind every tree. Her sisters joined her, but it was all in vain.

"Youngest sister, we will go home first and tell father to send a search party tonight. You must stay here at this waterfall."

Before the sun vanished, the six princesses of Kayangan flew up into the sky and made their way home, leaving the youngest princess all alone. She tried to be brave, but she had never been on her own before, and gradually tears flowed down her cheeks. It was at this moment, when Bayagong decided to approach her.

'My dear, what is wrong? Why are you crying?' asked Bayagong. The rough sound of Bayagong's voice startled the princess. She wanted to run away, but she did not know where to go. Without her wings, she felt completely vulnerable.

'I am lost,' she said in a very low voice.

'You are lost? Then let me help you. Let me take you home to my mother before it gets dark.'

'No, no, I must stay by the waterfall. This is where my sisters will find me,' she replied.

'You cannot stay here by yourself. Soon, it will be dark and the wild animals will come out to search for their prey. Come, you must follow me home. I promise I will take you back to the waterfall tomorrow morning.'

The princess shook her head and refused to go with Bayagong. However, the man continued to frighten her with stories of wild animals and evil spirits prowling in the jungle at night. He pestered and harassed her until she finally agreed to follow him home. They walked back to the village in the dying light of the sun. The princess tried to remember the way back to the waterfall, but it was dark and she was too distressed. It did not help that Bayagong purposely took her on a meandering route through the jungle. The youngest princess spent a restless night at Bayagong's house, and as a result, she missed the moonlight search party that had been sent by her father, the King of Kayangan.

Next morning, she looked for Bayagong to ask him to take her back to the waterfall as promised. However, the sly man was nowhere to be seen.

'Bayagong has business in the next village. He will return in three days' time, but you are welcome to stay at our house for as long as you wish. We will take care of you,' said Bayagong's mother.

Bayagong did not come home the day after, nor the day after that. By this time, the youngest princess felt as if her heart might burst. How would her sisters find her if she was not by the waterfall? When Bayagong finally returned, she begged him to take her to the waterfall.

'Of course, my dear. I will take you tomorrow as soon as it is light.'

Early the next day, the youngest princess was up and ready, but Bayagong was nowhere to be seen.

'Bayagong has gone out,' said his old mother. The youngest princess could not take it any longer and crumbled to the ground in tears.

'Do not be sad, my dear. Bayagong is a powerful man. He will take care of you if you let him.' But the youngest princess did not want Bayagong. She longed to return to her family. Day after day, she asked Bayagong to take her back, but there was always some reason, some excuse, to delay her return. This went on for so long that gradually, the youngest princess began to forget about her sisters and her home. Gradually, Bayagong wore her down until one day, she found herself married to him. She found herself bearing his two children.

And then one day, she found her magical robe.

The youngest princess was helping her child find a lost ball which had rolled under the rice urn. As she reached under the rice urn, her fingers touched something delicate and soft. Something which felt old and familiar. Gently, she pulled it out and saw her magic robe. She stroked the soft material and remembered everything.

I am the youngest daughter of the King of Kayangan.

She remembered her six sisters and how she had begged them to take her down to earth that day to play at the waterfall. She remembered singing as the sun was setting. When her sisters were ready to leave, she discovered that her robe was gone. It had vanished. At last, she realized that Bayagong had stolen her magic robes in order to force her to stay on earth. All this while, he had lied and tricked her into staying with him, into marrying him, and bearing his children.

The youngest princess felt the magic of Kayangan move through her body. Just at that moment, Bayagong returned from work and found

Nusantara: A Sea of Tales

A Collection of Folklore, Fairy Tales, Fables, Myths, Epics, Legends, Wonder and Magic Tales from the Nusantara

by

Heidi Shamsuddin

PENGUIN BOOKS

An imprint of Penguin Random House

PENGUIN BOOKS

USA | Canada | UK | Ireland | Australia
New Zealand | India | South Africa | China | Southeast Asia

Penguin Books is part of the Penguin Random House group of companies
whose addresses can be found at global.penguinrandomhouse.com

Published by Penguin Random House SEA Pte Ltd
9, Changi South Street 3, Level 08-01,
Singapore 486361

Penguin
Random House
SEA

First published in Penguin Books by Penguin Random House SEA 2021
Copyright © Heidi Shamsuddin 2021

ISBN 9789814954594

Printed at Markono Print Media Pte Ltd, Singapore

www.penguin.sg

Table of Contents

Introduction

This collection of folk tales and fairy tales from around the Nusantara was born out of a deep desire to find the meaning behind the special stories which make up the narratives of our lives. Where did these stories come from, and why do they still continue to this day?

My fascination with these traditional tales began when my father first told me the strange story of Si Tanggang, the infamous disobedient son who was punished and turned into stone. I was horrified, and yet fascinated by this cautionary tale.

Like most children around the world, I grew up on a steady diet of the *Brothers Grimm, Hans Christian Andersen,* and a smattering of *Arabian Nights.* My bedtime stories featured golden palaces, icy winter scenes, princesses with golden hair, and talking wolves. Then one day, I stumbled upon the story of *Si Tanggang* once more and it occurred to me that the stories from my own country, Malaysia, were just as rich and layered as the more popular fairy tales of the West. I began to seek out and read more of these stories, stories like *Bawang Putih Bawang Merah,* which reminded me so much of the more popular tale of *Cinderella.* The trickster tales of the brilliant mousedeer *Sang Kancil,* and the farcical tales of *Pak Pandir* and *Pak Kadok* delighted me with their subtle subversive elements. On a trip to East Malaysia, I discovered all the strange and wonderful stories by the different ethnic groups living there, complete with a cast of powerful gods and goddesses, along with a whole new universe for me to explore.

It felt like a treasure hunt. The more I read, the more I discovered that these tales had a special kind of magic which enabled them to travel long distances, moving and adapting to suit the needs of a particular society at a particular time. It was so obvious that these tales had travelled from one place to another, which is why the story of *Si Tanggang* exists not just in Malaysia, but also in Indonesia and Brunei.

This is why, instead of writing a collection of purely Malaysian traditional tales, I've decided to widen this collection to include stories from across the whole of the Nusantara. The stories chosen from this collection are mainly from East and West Malaysia, with a few tales from Singapore, Indonesia, the Philippines, Thailand, Vietnam, Madagascar, and the island of Guam. I hope that in future collections, I will be able to share stories from further afield. Located along the ancient sea routes of Southeast Asia, Nusantara is home to a multitude of wondrous tales which have originated and spread from as far away as China, India, the Middle East, Europe, and across the lands of Southeast Asia. In this collection, I use the term 'Nusantara' loosely to include countries sharing the Austronesian language such as Malaysia, Indonesia, Brunei, Philippines, Timor Leste, Madagascar, Oceania, as well as countries where Austronesian minorities are present such as Singapore, Thailand, Vietnam, and Taiwan.

The stories in this collection include both written and oral tales, and can be further categorized as folk tales, fairy tales, fables, myths, legends, epics, magic and wonder tales. Whatever you want to call them, these stories all have one thing in common: their ability to move, adapt and change through the years. These stories have been retold and reimagined countless times by writers, artists, and storytellers such as the *penglipur lara* (a beautiful word which literally means the 'soother of sorrows'). Like the seas and waterways which surround the Nusantara, these tales have ebbed and flowed without a care for national borders.

At the end of some of these stories, I have added a few thoughts about the meaning of these tales, although this is just my personal opinion and therefore, not meant to be definitive. The true meaning of a fairy tale depends on each individual person. Each one of you will extract a different message from these stories depending on your own life experiences. This is the power of fairy tales.

These notes will also contain information which I have collected during the progress of writing this book, such as whether these stories were known by other titles, where these stories originated from and where they have spread, whether there are similar stories in other countries and historical anecdotes. These tales come from a variety of both oral and written sources from around the region. Written sources used in this collection include *366 A Collection of Malaysian Folktales* (Othman Puteh and Aripin Said, Utusan Publications, 2008), *The Maiden of Many Nations: The Sky Maiden who Married a Man from Earth* (Hazel J. Wrigglesworth, 1991), *Kadazan Folklore* (Rita Lasimbang, Natural History Publications [Borneo] 1999), Sarawak Folktales (Heidi Munan, Mucow Books, 2017), *Folk-lore in Borneo, A Sketch* (William Furness, 1899), *Malay Magic* (Walter William Skeat, 1900), *Tangga Tales: A Collection of Malay Folk Tales* (Oxford University Press, 1952), *The Genealogy of Kings, Sulalat al-Salatin, Tun Seri Lanang* (translated by Prof. Muhammad Haji Salleh, Penguin Books, 2020), *Sejarah Melayu, The Malay Annals* (translated by Dr John Leyden, Silverfish Malaysian Classics, 2012), Hikayat Raja Babi (Usop Abdul Kadir, Fixi, 2015), *Stars and Keys: Folktales and Creolization in the Indian Ocean* (Lee Haring, Indiana University Press, 2007).

Although I've tried to retain the original tone of the stories, where necessary, I've trimmed and shaped the narrative to enhance the enjoyment of these tales. My goal is to provide an accessible body of work so that other artists, writers, and storytellers can reimagine and adapt these stories in their own work. These tales belong to all of us and it is my hope that they will continue to move, adapt, and live once more.

These tales contain all manners of suffering, loss, cruelty but also love, redemption, and in some cases, a 'happily ever after', all mixed in a sea of stories which form the Nusantara. I hope you will enjoy reading these tales as much as I've enjoyed rediscovering them.

Chapter 1

The Youngest Fairy Princess of Kayangan (Malaysia)

The seven fairy sisters often flew down to earth from their home beyond the skies—a place called Kayangan. They loved the lakes and pools on this green land, and enjoyed visiting a particular waterfall in the land below the wind. In this place, there lived a proud and wealthy man named Bayagong. He was rich and clever, but he was also sly and mean.

One evening, just as the sun was about to lay its weary head down on the horizon, Bayagong was walking home through the jungle when he heard singing of such beauty that it took his breath away. Entranced, he found himself walking towards the sound. Peering through the bushes, he saw seven lovely maidens bathing at the waterfall. Their skin glistened under the light of the evening sun, and their hair cascaded down their backs like flowing reeds.

The song came from the lips of the most beautiful maiden he had ever seen. His greedy heart told him that he must possess her. Bayagong realized that these maidens were not of this world, and as if to confirm his suspicion, he found seven magical robes lined up neatly by the riverside. The garments were made of the softest silver feathers, and shimmered with their own magic. Bayagong guessed that the smallest robe belonged to the youngest, most beautiful maiden—the one who had captivated his heart. He quickly snatched the smallest robe and hid it away inside the hollow trunk of a banyan tree.

his wife sitting in the back garden holding her magic robe. Bayagong opened his mouth to say something, but no words could explain away his terrible crime. Slowly, the youngest princess put on her magic robe and flew back to Kayangan.

* * *

This particular tale is also known as *Bayagong* and originates from the state of Sabah, in East Malaysia as can be seen from the reference to the 'land below the wind'. All around the world, there are different variations of this common story featuring a heavenly maiden who takes various forms; a fairy princess, *bidadari*, a djinn, a celestial or sky maiden, nymphs, apsaras, and winged birds. There are many variations of this story across the whole of the Nusantara region such as in Indonesia (*Rajapala and Ken Sulasih, The Goddess Bride, Hikayat Malim Deman*) and the Philippines (*The Seven Young Sky Women, Kimod and the Sky Maiden, The Hunter and the Seven Swimming Maidens*). There are also similar fairy tales from further afield like China (*The Cowherd and the Weaver Girl*) and Korea (*The Fairy and the Woodcutter*). The reference to 'Kayangan' is found in many other folk tales in the region, and refers to a magical heavenly realm. Some classify these tales as romance or a love story, although it is probably more appropriate to describe these as tales of deception. In spite of that, there is an element of hope in these tales when the female protagonist recovers her powers and succeeds in returning back to her heavenly abode.

Chapter 2

The Hunter and the Seven Swimming Maidens (The Philippines)

Once there was a hunter who was out hunting for wild ducks at a lake. He arrived before dawn and hid himself in the reeds so as not to be seen. Soon he heard the sound of beating wings, and assuming that his prey had arrived, got ready for the hunt. However, when the hunter peered out of the reeds he did not see any ducks but instead, he saw seven beautiful maidens who looked as if they were sisters. The hunter kept hidden and watched as the maidens laughed and frolicked in the water. He saw that the youngest maiden was the most beautiful and decided that he would trap her. The maidens soon took off their magical garments to bathe in the lake and the hunter watched carefully to see where the youngest maiden had kept her clothes. Then moving silently, he crept up to the pile and hid them away.

After the maidens had enough of swimming and playing in the lake, they got up to leave. They put on their magical garment and were about to fly off when the youngest one of them cried out, 'My garments are missing!'

The maidens searched high and low for their sister's clothes but of course, to no effect as the hunter had hidden them well. He smiled to himself.

'We will fly home first, younger sister. You can join us when you've found your clothes.' The other maidens then flew off into the heavens leaving their sister alone and at the mercy of the hunter. She began to weep.

'Why are you crying, dear maiden?' asked the hunter once he was sure that they were alone. The maiden looked up and when she saw him she narrowed her eyes.

'Someone has stolen my magic garments and because of that, I can no longer fly home.' She continued to stare suspiciously at the hunter. 'Was it you? Did you take my clothes?'

'No, I did not take your clothes. Why should I?' he said.

'I do not believe you. Return my clothes now so that I can go home,' she demanded. However, the hunter insisted that he was innocent and instead invited her back to his home. 'I will help you look for your clothes tomorrow.'

As it turned out, the hunter never helped the maiden look for her magical garments. Instead, he married her and after three years, they had two children—a boy and a girl. One day when the hunter was out, the children were playing in the house when they suddenly called out to their mother, 'Mother! Mother! We found some beautiful clothes. Do these clothes belong to you?'

All this time, the heavenly maiden had suspected that her husband had stolen her magical clothes and here at last, was the proof. She looked at her two children and told them, 'Children, tell your father that if he wants to find me, I will be at the place "east of the sun and west of the moon".' She then put on her magical garments and flew home.

When the hunter came home, the children told their father what had happened. He told his children to stay home and be safe, and then he set off to look for his wife. He brought some of his children's clothes to prove that he was indeed, the husband of the heavenly maiden. He travelled a long way and followed the river downstream until it reached the sea where he met an old man who happened to be the owner of all the birds on earth. The hunter asked the old man, 'Do you know how I can get to the place east of the sun and west of the moon?'

'I will ask my birds,' replied the old man, and so he summoned all the birds on earth. 'Do you know how to get to the place which is east of the sun and west of the moon?'

'We do not,' twittered the birds.

'I'm sorry, hunter. I cannot help you. Why don't you ask the owner of all the fish in the world? He should know how to get to the place,' said the old man.

Once again, the hunter set off on his journey. This time, he sailed across the sea and climbed seven hills, until he reached another sea. This journey took him seven long years. When he reached the sea he finally found the owner of all the fish in the world.

'I have been searching for my wife for seven years but I have not found her yet. She is in the place which is east of the sun and west of the moon. Do you know where I can find this place?' he asked the old man.

'Maybe it is far. Maybe it is near,' replied the old man, which was not very helpful. 'I will ask my fish.' The old man called out to the fish in the sea, and as they waited for all the fish to arrive, one of the fish swam towards the hunter and said to him, 'That old man is the father of your wife. You should ask him where he lives for that is where you will find your wife.'

The hunter turned towards the old man and asked if he could come to his house. 'I am the husband of your daughter.' To prove that the maiden was his wife, the hunter brought out his children's clothes. 'My wife's thumbprints are on these clothes which she has sewn for our children.'

The old man agreed to take the hunter to his house, which was east of the sun and west of the moon. There, he was reunited with his wife who finally agreed to marry him again because he had successfully found her east of the sun and west of the moon. They brought their children to this magical place and lived happily ever after.

* * *

This oral tale from the Philippines was collected from the Manobo people and is contained in the book *The Maiden of Many Nations* (Hazel J. Wrigglesworth). In this tale, the Sky Maiden escapes and returns to her heavenly abode, but she is pursued by her husband who goes on a perilous journey and faces many hardships to win her love. In this regard, even though the man initially deceived the maiden into staying on earth, his earlier wrong doing is somewhat mitigated by the fact that he goes out to prove his worthiness. It is interesting to note that this particular story describes this magical realm as 'east of the sun and west of the moon'—a title borrowed from a Norwegian fairy tale about a search for a lost husband.

Chapter 3

The Tanjung Blossom Fairy
Puteri Bunga Tanjung
(Malaysia)

Once upon a beautiful moonlit night, a fairy princess from the land of Kayangan flew down to earth to visit her favourite lake. She often came here to enjoy a swim in the cool waters and as usual, left her clothes and her flying garment at the foot of a tree which grew by the side of the lake.

After relaxing in the cool waters, she stepped out of the lake only to discover that her clothes were gone. She was particularly distressed about her missing flying garment for without it, she could not return to Kayangan. The fairy princess fell to the foot of the tree and began to sob.

An old woman living in a nearby hut heard the sound of a girl crying. Moving slowly, the old woman shuffled out the front door and followed the sound of the sobs until she came to the girl.

'My dear, whatever is the matter?' she asked. 'Where are your clothes?'

The fairy princess looked at the old lady and explained that someone had stolen her clothes. 'I cannot return home without them.'

'There, there my dear. Do not worry too much. I am sure your clothes will turn up soon. In the meantime, you are welcome to stay with me in my little hut. It is not much to look at. The roof leaks and we have rats, but it is comfortable and you will be safe there.'

The fairy princess was grateful and followed the old woman home. The next day, the old woman came out to look for firewood. As she walked towards the tree where she had found the girl, she was suddenly surrounded by a strong sweet fragrance. She looked down at her feet and saw thousands of beautiful yellow flowers spread out under the tree like a carpet. Looking up she saw that the flowers came from the tree.

'How odd. This tree has never flowered before,' she thought to herself. She looked down at the beautiful flowers and was struck by a wonderful idea.

'If we collect enough flowers, we can sell them at the market and get money to buy food and clothes,' said the old woman to the girl. The girl helped the old woman gather the flowers, and together they made their way to the market. The flowers sold well and soon the old woman's purse was full of coins. She jiggled her purse and smiled at the girl, but the girl was still feeling sad.

That night the girl went to the tree to look for her flying garment, but it was nowhere to be seen. 'Oh, what will I do?' She sat under the tree and began to sob again.

The next day, the old woman came out of her hut and to her surprise, saw that the tree had produced even more flowers. The old woman and the girl once again gathered the flowers and brought them to the market to sell and this time, the old woman filled two of her purses with coins. She was very happy but the girl was as sad as ever.

That night the girl came to the tree once more to look for her flying garment. She was not expecting to find anything and had resigned herself to another night of tears, but when she arrived at the tree, she found a small bundle on the ground. The girl opened the bundle and found her flying garment. She was so happy she could have wept out of joy, but she thought that perhaps she had done enough crying.

The girl went back to the hut to tell the old woman who was happy to hear the good news, but sad that she would not have any more flowers to sell.

'Tell me my child, what is the name of this flower?' she asked.

'This flower is called bunga tanjung, the tanjung flower. It is the symbol of my home, Kayangan. My father must have seen the flowers and sent my magic garment down to me.'

'How lovely. I think I will call you Puteri Bunga Tanjung, Princess Bunga Tanjung.'

The girl kissed the old lady's hands. 'To thank you, I will return every season and make the tree bear these beautiful flowers just for you.' The old lady was overjoyed and true to her word, the fairy princess returned every season to shed her tears in order to make the beautiful flowers grow.

* * *

This story originates from Malaysia and is commonly known as the story of *Puteri Bunga Tanjung*. *Puteri* means 'princess', and *Bunga Tanjung* refers to the 'flower or blossom of the bullet wood tree' (*mimusops elengi*). This fairy tale seems to be about the importance of caring for one another and the unexpected rewards we get for our good deeds.

This story shares some similarities with the other Kayangan fairy stories like the fairy's fondness of flying to earth to bathe in a lake or river. However, there is no deception in this particular tale. This story is more about how the kind deeds of the old woman is repaid with the flowering of the bullet wood tree and in this regard, this fairy tale could also easily fall under the category of origin stories (the origin of this particular tree). The bullet wood is a tropical tree which grows in the forest of Southeast Asia and South Asia. This tree is held in high esteem and has appeared in many other folk tales, for example the Thai folk tale *Phikul Thong*. The bark, flower, seeds, and fruit of this tree are commonly used for medicinal purposes. In addition, the flowers can be dried and made into tea, the fruits are edible, and the wood is extremely hard and strong.

Chapter 4

The Magic Rice Grains
(Malaysia)

Once upon a time, there lived a king called Raja Cahaya Santaka who ruled over Kayangan, a land full of fairies and magic. Raja Cahaya had seven daughters who loved to fly down to earth to play by a beautiful stream.

'Oh please, Papa. Can you take us to our special stream today?' asked the youngest princess.

Although Raja Cahaya was a busy king, he loved his family and always made time for his daughters. 'Yes, why not? Let's all fly down and have a picnic at the stream. Go and tell your sisters to meet us in the garden. We will fly down together.'

When the princess told her sisters, they were all excited and quickly put on their magic coats—an enchanted garment that enabled them to fly wherever they wanted. The youngest princess decided to bring her magic pouch which contained some golden grains of rice.

When they were ready, the girls met the king and queen in the garden. The king's magic coat was trimmed with shiny dragon scales and lined with the softest feathers from the garuda bird. The queen's coat shimmered with moonlight and was trimmed with rubies. In her hand, she held a small basket filled with the most delicious treats for their picnic.

'Are you all ready, my daughters?' asked the king. The girls laughed and reached out to hold their parents' hands. They had travelled using their magic coats so often, that all they had to do was close their eyes and think of their special stream and a short while later, the family arrived at their destination.

It was a beautiful day. The sun was shining in a sky full of white clouds. There was a gentle breeze which brought the scent of wild flowers from a nearby field and the river sang and hummed a cheery tune.

The king spread out a woven mat under the ara tree and the queen took out the cakes and little parcels of food from the picnic basket and after that, there was nothing much to do but settle down for a lovely afternoon.

As her sisters were bathing in the stream, the youngest princess decided to play with her pouch of rice. She slowly poured the golden grains of rice onto a big rock and watched as the rice settled into the deep cracks. The grains glittered and made her smile.

'Come and swim with us,' said her sisters. Excited, the youngest princess left her rice to join her sisters in the stream. They played and laughed, and had a wonderful picnic, and soon it was time to go.

'Make sure you take home everything you've brought here. Nothing from our land should remain on earth,' warned the king. The youngest princess suddenly remembered her grains of golden rice but when she went to the rock, the rice was all gone. She looked around and checked the ground, but could not find a single grain.

'Papa, I'm sorry but I've lost my golden rice,' she said to the king who became worried. 'My child, you must stay here and find every grain of rice. Until you do, I'm afraid you may not return to Kayangan.'

The youngest princess agreed to stay behind and said goodbye to her sisters and her parents. She promised she would find every last grain of rice. Next morning, she went down to the river to wash herself. As she bent down, she saw tiny shoots growing in the cracks of the rocks. Every day, the shoots grew taller and taller, and soon spread until it covered the whole bank of the river. The shoots grew into plants which started to produce rice. The youngest princess stayed near her rice field and tended her crops from morning till evening and soon, people from all around came to her for the seeds. She gave them the seeds and soon, this rice was grown all over the land. The youngest princess decided to stay on earth

to make sure her rice fields were always bountiful and provide seeds for
those who needed it.

* * *

This tale is also known as *The Golden Rice* and originates from Malaysia.
Once again, we are introduced to Kayangan, a celestial place inhabited
by fairies who are fond of flying down to earth. This time, however, a
whole family descend to earth to enjoy a picnic by the stream. As with the
story of *The Tanjung Blossom Fairy,* there is no element of deception by a
man in this tale. In fact, this story seems to be another origin story—that
is, the origin of rice. This is only obvious and understandable since rice
is the staple food of this region and each culture has its own story about
rice. In the story of *The Magic Grains of Rice*, the youngest princess
became the goddess who gave the gift of rice to humankind.

Chapter 5

The Legend of Ulek Mayang
(Malaysia)

For as long as the tides of the South China Sea ebbed and flowed, the fishermen of the east coast would take their nets far into the vast sea to bring back its bounty. One morning, a group of men set out in the usual way, laughing and praying for good fortune. The sun warmed their backs and they gave thanks to the clear sky and calm waters. However, shortly after the fishermen left the land, blue skies turned grey, and a fierce wind churned the waves.

'We must turn back. The sea spirits are dancing under the waves,' said the oldest fisherman on the boat. He could read the sea and knew that they were not welcome there.

'Let us stay awhile longer please. I need a good catch to feed my family,' said the youngest fisherman. He was young and lacked the experience of the others, but he had a charming way about him. The others agreed to stay awhile longer in order to help the young fisherman.

Unfortunately, within three breaths, a dark cloud blocked the sun, turning day into night. The wind lashed, rocking and swaying the tiny boat, and then a giant wave fell upon the boat and swallowed the men, pulling them deep into the churning sea. They sank under the water like stone. Although they were strong swimmers, cold invisible fingers clutched at their ankles, dragging them down to the bottom of the sea.

A haunting melody played around the men and in the distance, they saw six beautiful maidens dancing under the waves, coming closer and closer to them. Gracefully, the maidens twirled and danced, their long hair floating in the water.

By some miracle, the bodies of these fishermen washed up on shore the next day. All were fit and fine, except for the youngest, who lay on the sand with a dreamy smile upon his lips. It seemed that nothing could awaken him from his sweet slumber.

'His body is here, but his soul has been captured by the sea spirits,' announced the bomoh, the village medicine man. The eldest fishermen nodded and described how they were pulled under the water by the sea spirits.

'We saw them dancing under the waves. There were six beautiful sea princesses, wearing gowns of gold and carrying yellow sashes.'

The bomoh ordered the villagers to bring him three items; incense to burn, rice dyed by turmeric, and mayang pinang—strings of the coconut palm blossom. The villagers hurried to gather these items, and placed them near the unconscious body of the young fisherman. Soon the ritual began.

The bomoh placed a hand on the sleeping young man and closed his eyes. Soon, the bomoh fell into a deep trance as his mind entered the world under the sea.

The land below the waves was cool and tinged with hazy blues and greens. From time to time, he felt the slippery fins of passing sea creatures. His mind delved deeper and deeper under the sea until he saw two figures in the distance. The young man was in the arms of the youngest sea princess, a beautiful marine spirit. She had cast a love spell on the young man, and if she did not release him soon, he would be lost forever.

In the land above, the bomoh pleaded with the youngest sea princess to let the man go, but she would not hear of it. Furious, she called upon two of her older sisters to challenge the bomoh. The three sisters began a haunting dance, moving and swaying in the water to the strains of music. A strange magic surrounded the bomoh, and he felt something powerful pressing upon his chest.

On the beach, a deafening clap of thunder echoed through the sky and a flash of lightning set the tops of the palm trees on fire. The villagers cowered together and prayed.

The bomoh fought and resisted the three sisters, and so the youngest sister called upon another two sisters. Now, there were five sea princesses moving and swaying under the waves. Their yellow sashes swirled round and round, making his head spin. Closer and closer they came as the music grew louder and louder. He closed his eyes and tried to calm his racing heart. Once again, the bomoh called out for the release of the young fisherman.

Up above, black clouds covered the sun and a fierce wind blew away the rooftops of the houses in the village. All five sisters twirled and whirled, working their magic on the bomoh. Then, another sister joined in the eerie dance, and so now there were six princesses casting their magic in the churning water. The bomoh held on tight even though he could feel the waves trying to push him away into the darkness.

On the beach, the earth shook and a wall of water came hurtling towards the village ready to destroy everything in its path. It was then that the eldest and seventh sister intervened, for she was the wisest of them all. With a wave of her hand, she ordered her six sisters to stop their enchantment.

The wall of water gently melted back into the sea and the earth stopped shaking.

'Let those from the sea return to the sea, and those from the land return to the land.' With those words, the oldest sea princess released the young man from her sister's spell.

On the shore, the young man's eyes fluttered open. He had finally returned to the place where he belonged. Feeling grateful, the villagers presented gifts of incense, turmeric rice, and mayang to the sea spirits and always, always they remembered the words of the eldest sea princess. 'Let those from the sea return to the sea, and those from the land return to the land.'

* * *

Ulek Mayang or Ulik Mayang is a classical Malay dance from the east coast of Malaysia. '*Ulek*' means 'to entreat, to beg, or plead'. '*Mayang*' refers to the 'coconut palm blossom' which is traditionally used to chase away spirits in this region. The story of Ulek Mayang is thought to originate from the state of Terengganu, on the east coast of Malaysia.

The most interesting aspect of this fairy tale is that it takes the form of a ritualistic dance performed to appease the spirits of the sea. Ulek Mayang is performed by seven female dancers, each dressed in an elaborate costume with a regal headdress and flowing yellow sashes. Three to four male dancers perform the role of the fishermen and the bomoh. During the performance, the male dancers fall into trance until they are healed by the bomoh who engages in a tug-of-war battle with the sea spirits until they finally release the man. The source of this fairy tale comes from the lyrics of the song itself. The lyrics are provided below in both Malay and English.

Ulek mayang ku ulek
Ulek dengan jala jemala
Ulek mayang diulek
Ulek dengan tuannya puteri
Ulek mayang diulek
Ulek dengan jala jemala
Ulek mayang diulek
Ulek dengan puterinya dua

Puteri dua berbaju serong
Puteri dua bersanggol sendeng
Puteri dua bersubang gading
Puteri dua berselendang kuning
Umbok mayang diumbok
Umbok dengan jala jemala
Nok ulek mayang diulek
Ulek dengan puterinya empat

Puteri empat berbaju serong
Puteri empat bersanggol sendeng
Puteri empat bersubang gading
Puteri empat berselendang kuning
Umbok mayang diumbok
Umbok dengan jala jemala

Nok ulek mayang diulek
Ulek dengan puterinya enam

Puteri enam berbaju serong
Puteri enam bersanggol sendeng
Puteri enam bersubang gading
Puteri enam berselendang kuning
Umbok mayang diumbok
Umbok dengan jala jemala
Nok ulek mayang diulek
Ulek dengan puterinya tujuh

Puteri tujuh berbaju serong
Puteri tujuh bersanggol sendeng
Puteri tujuh bersubang gading
Puteri tujuh berselendang kuning
Umbok mayang diumbok
Umbok dengan jala jemala
Nok ulek mayang diulek
Ulek dengan tuannya puteri

Tuan puteri berbaju serong
Tuan puteri bersanggol sendeng
Tuan puteri bersubang gading
Tuan puteri berselendang kuning
Umbok mayang diumbok
Umbok dengan jala jemala
Nok ulek mayang diulek
Ulek dengan tuannya puteri

Ku tahu asal usul mu
Yang laut balik ke laut
Yang darat balik ke darat
Nasi berwarna hamba sembahkan
Umbok mayang ku umbok

Umbok dengan jala jemala
Pulih mayang ku pulih
Pulih balik sedia kala

I entreat the mayang
Entreat with shining nets
Entreat the mayang
Singing with her highness the princess
Entreat the mayang
Entreat it with shining nets
Entreat the mayang
Singing together with the second princess

Second princess wears a slanted blouse
Second princess with a slanted hair knot
Second princess wears ivory earrings
Second princess has a yellow scarf
Persuading the mayang
Persuade it with shining nets
Entreating the mayang
Singing with the fourth princess

Fourth princess wears a slanted blouse
Fourth princess with a slanted hairknot
Fourth princess wears ivory earrings
Fourth princess has a yellow scarf on
Persuading the mayang
Persuade it with shining nets
Entreating the mayang
Singing with the sixth princess

Sixth princess wears a slanted blouse
Sixth princess with a slanted hairknot
Sixth princess wears ivory earrings
Sixth princess has a yellow scarf

Persuading the mayang
Persuade it with shining nets
Entreating the mayang
Singing with the seventh princess

Seventh princess wears a slanted blouse
Seventh princess with the slanted hairknot
Seventh princess wears ivory earrings
Seventh princess has a yellow scarf
Persuading the mayang
Persuade it with shining nets
Entreating the mayang
Singing with her highness the princess

Her highness the princess wears a slanted blouse
Her highness the princess with a slanted hairknot
Her highness the princess wears ivory earrings
Her highness the princess has a yellow scarf
Persuading the mayang
Persuade it with nets
Entreating the mayang
Singing with her highness the princess

I know your origins
Let those from the sea return to the sea
Let those from the land return to the land
I present the coloured rice
I persuade the mayang
Persuade it with shining nets
I heal with mayang
Bringing back to health

Chapter 6

The Tale of The Biggest Basket in the World (Malaysia)

Once there was a girl who was too lazy to be bothered to wash her face or brush her hair. She never helped out around the house, preferring instead to daydream as she gazed up at the sky.

'You really are the laziest girl in the world,' said her mother one day as she was busy husking the paddy. 'Why don't you help me instead of staring out of the window?' The girl shrugged her shoulders and wandered into the garden to continue daydreaming.

'You really are the laziest girl in the world,' said her father as he was repairing the roof of their house. 'Why don't you help me fix this roof?' The girl smiled and wandered off to the river to stare at the water as it flowed over the rocks.

As the days, weeks, months, and years passed by, the girl grew into a young lady but still remained the laziest girl in the world. Her parents had no choice but to let her go. 'If she cannot be useful to the family, then she must go,' said the father. The mother who was rather fond of the girl was sad, but she reluctantly agreed. The family could not afford to keep such a lazy daughter.

The next day, the father brought the girl to the other side of the village where he had built a small hut for her to live in. 'This is your new house, daughter. There is a little food and water, and a blanket to keep you warm at night. You are almost an adult now and will have to fend for yourself from now on.' The girl understood. Although she would have preferred to live at home, she realised that it was unfair of her to burden her parents.

'Take this. It's a knife to protect yourself from wild animals and any strangers who may come wandering here at night,' said the father. The girl took the knife and entered her hut. As it was already quite late, she crawled under her blanket and went to bed.

The next morning, she was awoken by a loud voice coming from inside the hut. 'Girl! Girl! It's time to wake up.' She sat up and looked around, but she could not see who had spoken.

'Who's there? Are you a ghost?' she asked in a frightened voice.

'I am most certainly not a ghost, silly girl. Now get up, you have a lot of work to do,' said the voice.

The girl saw that the voice had come from the big knife her father had given to her.

'Big Knife? Is that you? How is it possible that you can speak to me?'

'Get up! Get up! The sun is high in the sky and there is much to do. First, you must go to the river and wash yourself,' said Big Knife. Since there was nothing else to do, the girl got up. She went to the river to wash herself. She discovered that it felt good to be clean.

'Now, you must clean your teeth and brush your hair,' ordered Big Knife. Since there was not much else to do, the girl did as she was told and cleaned her teeth and brushed her hair. She found that it was also quite pleasant to have clean teeth and shiny, soft hair.

'Now, you must wash your clothes and clean your hut,' ordered Big Knife. Once again, the girl did as she was ordered. She liked wearing clean clothes and having a clean hut to live in.

'Very good,' said Big Knife. 'Now you must use me to cut up the pandan leaves growing by the side of the river. You will be weaving the biggest basket in the world,' ordered Big Knife.

'A basket? I do not know how to weave a basket,' she said.

'Of course you don't. You have been an idle child all your life and have not learned how to do anything useful. Do not worry, I will show you how to weave a basket,' said Big Knife.

Once again, the girl did as she was told. She took knife and began to cut up long strips of the pandan leaf. Even though the sharp leaves hurt her fingers, the girl worked diligently. Big Knife then showed her how to use fire to clean and whiten the leaves. After that, Big Knife taught her how to weave the basket.

The girl worked on her basket every day. At first, she worked inside her hut, but soon the basket was too big for the hut. She worked outside the hut and one day, the basket was even bigger than the hut.

'What are we going to do with this enormous basket?' asked the girl.

'I will use this basket to find you a good husband,' replied Big Knife.

The next day, Big Knife went to town to visit the king and his son, the prince, who was coincidentally looking for a wife to marry.

'Are you looking for a good wife, Prince?'

'Yes, I am. However, I'm looking for someone who is hardworking. Do you know anyone like that?' asked the prince.

'Yes, I know the perfect person. Ask your servants to prepare a feast for the wedding banquet. I will fetch your bride,' said Big Knife. The prince ordered his servants to cook up a feast for his wedding, but he was still unsure of his new bride. *I will wait and see her first. If she is indeed hardworking and good, I will marry her,* said the prince to himself.

Soon the food was ready but there was so much food that it could not fit into any of the baskets in the palace.

'How will we get all this food to the wedding?' asked the prince.

Just at that moment, Big Knife appeared at the palace. 'Do not worry, someone has woven the biggest basket in the world.' The prince was surprised to see the biggest basket in the world. *The person who has made this basket must be very hardworking indeed*, thought the prince to himself.

'Tell me Big Knife, who made this basket?' 'I would like to marry her.'

'Why, it is your bride, of course,' said the Big Knife, as he presented the girl who was no longer the laziest girl in the world. Her dress was sparkling clean and her face and hair shone brightly under the sun. She had just woven the biggest basket in the world.

* * *

This Malaysian tale is known as *The Biggest Basket in the World* and is contained in a book titled, *Tangga Tales: A Collection of Malay Folk Tales*

(Oxford University Press, 1952). This tale is unusual because unlike many of the fairy tales from the West, there do not appear many stories featuring a talking inanimate object.

This story focuses on the issue of change and transformation and in that sense, it is a metaphor for growing up. Big Knife represents a kind of self-regulatory instinct which the girl uses in order to improve herself and her future prospects. However, Big Knife doesn't stop at merely improving the self-discipline of this girl. He goes further than that by rewarding her effort at the end. Once the girl has finished weaving the biggest basket in the world, Big Knife uses that to attract a good mate in order to secure the girl's future. In this regard, this is not the usual fairy tale where the princess simply waits for her 'prince charming'. This girl, with the help of her magical knife, takes an active step in shaping her own future.

Chapter 7

The Magic Crossbow
The story of Trọng Thủy and Mỵ Châu
(Vietnam)

Once there was a great king called An Dương Vương who established a powerful new kingdom called Âu Lạc. In order to keep his kingdom safe from invaders, the king ordered a fortified citadel to be built around his city. However, for some mysterious reason, all the work which had been completed during the day would be destroyed overnight. The walls would crumble to the ground and the men would have to start again the very next day. It was believed that this was caused by a group of spirits from the descendants of the previous empire who were seeking revenge. The evil spirits were led by a thousand-year-old white chicken who was perched on top of Mount Tam Dao.

The king decided to burn incense, make offerings, and pray to the gods for help. In reply, the gods sent a golden magic turtle who was able to subdue the white chicken. As soon as the magic turtle was in the city of Âu Lạc, the king found that the walls did not crumble down as it did before, and the citadel fortress was soon completed. The magic turtle was summoned back to the gods, but as a token to the king, he gave one of his claws and instructed the king to use it as a trigger for his royal crossbow. 'This will keep your kingdom safe and make you invincible.'

With the help of this magic weapon, the king became a powerful ruler and managed to repel many attacks from other kingdoms. The magic

Turtle Claw and crossbow was able to kill hundreds of people in a single shot.

A Chinese warlord by the name of Triệu Đà had tried to take over the Kingdom of Âu Lạc for many years, but failed until finally, Triệu Đà decided to try a different tactic. He suspected that the King must have a secret, and decided that he would negotiate peace and send his son to spy on the king. Triệu Đà sent his son, Trọng Thủy, to the king's court to ask for the hand of Princess Mỵ Châu.

The two were wed and even though their families were mortal enemies, Trọng Thủy and Mỵ Châu fell in love with each other. Trọng Thủy convinced his new wife to reveal the secret of the king's success and one night, she showed him the magic turtle claw.

'This is the secret to my father's power,' she whispered to her husband. Trọng Thủy secretly replaced the magic claw with a fake claw and then made an excuse and sought permission to return back to his father. However, before he left, he made a promise to his wife that if war broke out, he would come and find her. Mỵ Châu told her husband that she would leave a trail of goose feathers as a clue from her blanket so that he could easily find her.

As soon as Triệu Đà had the magic claw, he gathered his great army together and launched another attack on Âu Lạc. Although the king was disappointed, he calmly faced the attack knowing that he had his magical weapon and crossbow. When the enemy appeared at the gates of his great fortress, the king took his magic crossbow and aimed it at his enemies but to his dismay, nothing happened. It was then, that the king realised that his magic turtle claw was gone.

He fled the city with his army and his daughter trailing behind him. As she promised, Mỵ Châu left a trail of goose feathers from her blanket so that her husband could find her. When they reached the shore, they found that there were no ships to take them, so the king called once more on the gods for their help. The golden turtle appeared out of the water.

'Please, help me,' said the king. The magic turtle turned towards the king and said, 'You must destroy your enemy first before I can save you. The enemy is behind you.'

The king looked back and saw his daughter, Mỵ Châu, with a trail of white feathers scattered on the ground. Furious, the king drew his sword and struck down his own daughter. The magic turtle then took the king below the waters and vanished.

Meanwhile, Trọng Thủy had followed the trail of goose feathers to the shore and was shocked to find his wife lying in a pool of blood. The blood flowed into the ocean and was swallowed by the oysters transforming them into pearls. Feeling distraught and guilty, Trọng Thủy took his life and drowned himself in order to be reunited with his wife.

* * *

This tale is also known as *An Old Vietnam Tale of Trọng Thủy and Mỵ Châu*. This Vietnamese folk tale is a heroic story and is said to be based on true events which happened during the 3rd century BCE King An Dương Vương established the capital of Âu Lạc, where a fortified citadel known as Cổ Loa was constructed. It was the first political centre of the Vietnamese civilisation and has one of the largest prehistoric settlement sites in Southeast Asia. The events surrounding the construction of this spiral-shaped citadel have been depicted in this particular tale.

King An Dương Vương was also said to have commissioned a famous Vietnamese weaponry engineer to construct a crossbow, and named it, 'Saintly Crossbow of the Supernaturally Luminous Golden Claw'. According to historians, the trigger mechanism for the crossbow was capable of withstanding high pressure and of releasing arrows with more force than any other bow.

Chapter 8

The Origins of Akinabalu
(Malaysia)

Long ago, there was nothing in this world. There were no vast lands with deserts and jungles, no immense blue seas teeming with sea creatures, and no animals roaming on the earth. There were certainly no humans to be found.

There was nothing. Nothing except for a strange, round rock which stood at the centre of the world. It was that way for many long years, until one day, the rock lit up with a silvery glow and began to hum and sing. It split, and out of it emerged two beautiful children.

A boy called Kinohiringan, and a girl called Umunsumundu.

The two children grew up and eventually created the world.

One day, Kinohiringan saw a light from above. He heard a soft song in the air and felt a light breeze caress his cheeks. A heavenly scent wafted towards him and he held his hand up in the air, as if to catch it. He brought the scent to his nose and tasted it with his tongue. It was a shadow of the sky, an idea of it, and it tasted like wind and freedom.

And then, Kinohiringan knew that he had to create the sky, and so he raised his hands and made a small piece of clear blue sky. Satisfied, he twirled his fingers and made white fluffy clouds which he sent up to live in the sky. Kinohiringan was rather proud of his sky and carried on with his work.

Around the same time, Umunsumundu was sitting down when she suddenly caught the scent of wet earth and green grass. She put her head down and felt a strong vibration under her cheeks and she suddenly knew she had to create the land, the soil, and the earth. She began her work at once, kneading, moulding, and rolling the soil in her hands until she created a small patch of land that she laid down under her feet. She patted the land down and made another piece which she placed next to it. On and on she worked.

Together, the two gods toiled night and day.

Kinohiringan waved his hands and made clear skies in some places; and in other places he created pink, sun-tinged heavens. High up in the atmosphere, his skies were dark and full of dancing stars. In the far north, they were blindingly white and cold. Kinohiringan then decided to make the wind and the breeze, so that his skies could move around freely. The clouds he created began to gather water and would sometimes pour rain from their bellies.

Umunsumundu, on the other hand, gathered the soil in her hands before kneading and rolling it out to create vast, flat fields. Inside the soil, she carefully placed tiny seeds which would one day grow into grass, plants, flowers, trees, and huge jungles. She made soft, white sand with the tips of her fingers, dotting it around here and there on a whim. Some of the earth was wet and fertile, and some of the soil was dry. She mixed it up and laid it down, working steadily through night and day.

The two gods did not stop to rest. One creating the sky above and the other, the land below. They laboured on, cultivating and building until the land grew bigger and bigger, and the sky above it multiplied.

One night, Kinohiringan felt lightheaded and dizzy for he had been working for many, many days without rest. He lowered his arms and decided to take a short nap. As soon as he lay his head down, sleep came and took him.

Umunsumundu, however, continued to work, steadily kneading and rolling, and laying out pieces of land, one by one. She had not realized that Kinohiringan had stopped his work until she saw that her land was far bigger than his sky. Annoyed, she woke Kinohiringan up.

'See here, Kinohiringan! My land is bigger than your sky. You must continue your work.'

Kinohiringan rubbed his tired eyes and grumbled, but went back to work and made more sky to cover the land. However, after a while, his eyes grew heavy once more, so he stopped and fell into a deep slumber. Umunsumundu continued to work on the land until her land was a hundred, a thousand, a million times bigger than his sky. When she noticed this, she woke him up again.

'Kinohiringan! Look what has happened. My land is so vast now, I do not see how your sky can cover it all.'

'That is impossible! I will go down to the land and see for myself.'

And with that, Kinohiringan went down and walked the earth. He saw beautiful, fertile land and growing upon it, the first blossoming shoots of plants and flowers.

Kinohiringan tilted his head up to look at his creation—the majestic sky. What a sight to behold. The colours shimmered and changed as the wind blew the clouds across the sky. Kinohiringan smiled, happy that he had created something so beautiful. He walked and followed the sky till he came to the very edge of it. Beyond the edge, there was nothing but emptiness. He looked down at the land and found that it stretched as far as the eye could see.

Umunsumundu was right. There was not enough sky to cover the land.

'This will not do.' And so, Kinohiringan bent down and began to push and pile up the land creating hills, valleys, and mountains. He shoved and thrust the soil until all the earth could fit under his sky. At one point, there was so much land that he pushed and pushed with all his might until all of the land piled up so high that it reached his sky. It was only then that all the land lay under the sky.

Kinohiringan looked up at the majestic mountain he had created and was happy that his sky and Umunsumundu's land were together. He knew that this was to be a sacred place, and so he gave the mountain a special name—Akinabalu.

And this is how Akinabalu, or Mount Kinabalu was created.

* * *

This folk tale is also known as *The Origin of the World* and comes from the Kadazan-Dusun people of Sabah, Malaysia. Mount Kinabalu or Akinabalu is the tallest peak in Southeast Asia standing at more than 4,000 metres. Due to this special distinction, there are many myths and legends which attempt to explain the origin of this special mountain.

This folk tale also falls under the category of geomythical stories; stories which explain the connection between changing landscape, and local myths and folk tales. In geology, the explanation of the connection between landscape, active and natural phenomena such as earthquakes, floods, and volcanoes, and local myths are known as geomythology. The term 'geomythology' was coined in 1968 by Dorothy Vitaliano, a geologist from Indiana University, who argued that some of these folk tales could prove that people in the past had witnessed these geological events. This particular tale seeks to explain the existence of Mount Kinabalu in a way which venerates the two Gods, Kinohiringan and Umunsumundu.

Chapter 9

The World on the Tip of a Buffalo's Horn
(Malaysia)

A long, long time ago, people did not understand how the world came into existence. They did not know whether the world was flat or round. They did not understand how the sun moved across the sky and disappeared at the end of each day. When earthquakes shook the ground, volcanoes erupted, and huge waves destroyed the land, people would explain this by telling a story.

'There is a dragon inside the mountain breathing fire and causing the earth shake.'

'The water spirits are angry when they make the waves destroy the land.'

'The sun is being chased by the moon. That is why it moves across the sky.'

A long time ago, there was a story about how the earth moved and why there were earthquakes, volcanoes, and tsunamis. According to this story, the world was round and lay on the tip of the horn of an enormous buffalo.

In this mysterious universe, there is a colossal buffalo standing alone on an island. On the very tip of one of its horns, the buffalo carries our earth and keeps it there safe and sound. However, after a while, the buffalo gets tired of carrying the earth on that horn. When this happens, the huge buffalo simply tosses up the earth and catches it upon the tip of his other horn.

When the earth gets lobbed up in the air in such a manner, you can just imagine what sorts of things might happen. Earthquakes shake the ground and bring down tall mountains, giant waves swallow up whole villages by the seaside, volcanoes spit out fire, smoke, and hot lava. Sometimes, when the earth flies up in the air like that, it shakes things up so much that everyone thinks the world is going to end. However, this huge buffalo is very good, and eventually catches the earth on his other horn and there it will stay, safe and sound. That is, until he gets tired again and decides to move the earth back to the other horn.

It is said that the world-buffalo walks around an island in the midst of the Nether ocean eating and foraging the delicious grass there. This island and the whole universe is surrounded by an immense dragon called Ular Naga, who feeds upon his own tail. A long time ago, this is the story people told to explain the position and movement of earth and our universe.

* * *

This story is contained in the book, *Malay Magic* (Walter William Skeat, 1900) and originates from Malaysia, although the tale is probably based on Hindu mythology. Walter William Skeat (1866–1953) was an English anthropologist who studied and wrote about the ethnography of the Malay Peninsula in the 19th century. According to the endnotes of this book, in other variations, the world-buffalo stands on the back of a tortoise, turtle, or a fish called 'Nun'. This concept of the world balanced on the back of a tortoise or turtle, can be traced to Hindu mythology, and also exists in Chinese and North American mythology. This tale seeks to explain the movements of the earth and natural phenomenon such as earthquakes, volcanoes, and tsunamis. In order to make sense of these natural events, our ancestors created stories to pass on to the next generation.

Chapter 10

What Kop the Frog Said to the Kayan (Malaysia)

The Kayan people of Sarawak live in the rainforest and are known for being skilled warriors, blacksmiths, boat builders, and farmers. The Kayans not only grow rice, but also sago, corn, yam, and pumpkins. Each tribe has their own longhouse and because they live in such a harsh environment, it has been important for each tribe to work together in order to survive and thrive. Each longhouse has had to defend themselves from their enemies in order to protect their families, their livelihood, and their honour. After each war raid, the usual practice was to take the hair of their enemy as a trophy.

It was said that a long time ago, Kop the Frog spoke to the Kayan people. He told their chief, a man named Tokong, that after a raid, it was not enough to take just the hair of their enemies as a trophy.

'In order to bring blessings upon your people, you must take the whole head of your enemies,' declared Kop the Frog.

At first, Tokong was angry and refused to carry out such an act. Shortly after, Tokong's longhouse was plagued with a spell of bad luck. For several long months, their crops died and the hunters returned home empty-handed. His people were struck by a mysterious illness and were dying. His men pleaded with Chief Tokong to follow the advice of Kop the Frog.

Finally, the chief agreed and after the next raid on their enemies, Tokong and his men did not just take the hair of their enemies, they took the whole heads. They prayed that this would help put an end to their bad luck.

After the raid, the men retreated to the river to the place where they had left their damaged war boats and to their surprise, they found that their boats had been repaired and were all in good shape. What more, the current of the river had reversed itself making it easy for the war party to return to their longhouse.

When the men returned home, they discovered that during the fifteen days they had been away, their crops of rice had grown, ripened, and was ready to be harvested. Those who had been ill were now fit and healthy once more. The blind could see, and the lame could walk. Finally, the bad luck had been lifted from their longhouse.

That day onwards, Tokong and his men followed the advice of Kop the Frog and took the heads of their enemies to ensure the prosperity of their people. This was the way of the Kayan people.

* * *

This short tale is contained in a book titled *Folk-lore in Borneo, A Sketch* (William Furness, 1899), which gives a brief monograph into the different folk tales found amongst the various ethnic groups in Borneo. William Furness was an American physician, ethnographer, and author and was one of the first to study and photograph the Kayan people of Borneo. This book was first published in 1899, and is therefore somewhat outdated. However, it does contain some interesting stories from the Kayan people, including the origin of headhunting. Headhunting is no longer practiced, of course, but its existence and importance in the past cannot be ignored. The practice was thought to be essential for the survival of the various different ethnic groups living mainly in Borneo and forms part of their religious and spiritual beliefs.

Chapter 11

The Tale of Gamong
(Malaysia)

A long time ago in a Kayan longhouse deep in the rainforest of Borneo, there lived a young man named Gamong. Gamong was like any ordinary young man. He loved to spend his time with his friends hunting and catching fish. Most of the other young men from the longhouse were already warriors and had gone on the war path to prove their bravery. However, Gamong was not interested in fighting other men, preferring instead to hunt and fish for his family.

'You are a young man now, Gamong,' said his father. 'When will you go on the warpath with the other warriors?'

'There is plenty of time for that, father. I will go with them next time,' replied Gamong with a smile on his face.

One day, when Gamong was out hunting, he was struck by a sudden sharp pain in the middle of his forehead. It felt as if a hot knife had sliced through his head. Gamong crumbled to the ground and was later discovered by his friends who brought him back to the longhouse. The medicine man worked all day and night but it was too late— Gamong was dying.

He could feel his body slipping away. He knew that soon his soul would leave his body and go on a journey to the afterlife, but Gamong was stubborn and refused to accept his fate. After all, he was still a young man and had not yet proven his bravery. He had not gone on a warpath and had not brought honour upon his family.

He desperately wanted a second chance to live his life. Gamong knew he had not much choice in the matter, but he thought that at the very least, he could do his best to cheat death. Calling his family and friends to his aid, he made them promise to dress him in his war clothes. Gamong asked his family not to bury him for three days, and instead place him in a sitting position with his sword and spear in his hands.

His family protested, but he reassured them by saying that he would return from the dead in three days' time. Gamong's pleas won the day and his family did as he requested.

Finally, Gamong died and for three days, his body sat upright in the middle of the longhouse. Three days later, Gamong drew in a deep shuddering breath and opened his eyes once more. As he promised, he came back to life much to the surprise of the people in his longhouse. When they asked him what had happened, this was his story:

'When my spirit left my body, I found myself walking down a path towards the great tree trunk, Bintang Sikopa. That was when I saw *him*,' began Gamong.

'Him? Do you mean the great demon Maligang?' asked his neighbour.

'Yes, Maligang was waiting for me on the fallen tree trunk. He wanted to account for my bravery.'

Maligang lived in the Kayan underworld and was the gatekeeper to the land of the spirits. Each departed soul had to walk across the fallen tree trunk called Bintang Sikopa, above a deep ditch filled with devouring worms. Maligang's task was to challenge all newcomers to the underworld. If they had no record of bravery, he would shake the tree trunk until they fell into the ditch and were devoured by the worms.

Gamong explained that Maligang, whose arms were as big as his whole body, began to shake the tree trunk.

'Who are you? What have you done in your life? Account for yourself!' commanded Maligang.

I replied, 'I am Gamong, the great warrior and you must not shake the tree while I cross.'

Maligang then consulted the pegs which speaks the truth and contains the records of the deeds of men. 'You are no warrior. I have no record of your bravery, Gamong.'

'As soon as the demon uttered these words, I raised my sword and gave out a battle cry so fierce that it echoed through the underworld, taking Maligang by surprise. I ran into the great demon's home. In his home, I smashed his possessions and overturned the great jars of rice-toddy,' said Gamong.

Maligang had never encountered such a departed soul and was taken aback. For the first time since the beginning of the afterlife, the demon abandoned his post at the tree trunk shouting to Gamong. 'I have not got you now Gamong, but in seven years' time you will return to me.'

'I returned home following the same path, and now here I am,' announced Gamong.

Gamong lived on for exactly seven more years until he finally succumbed to the will of Maligang. Unfortunately for Gamong, he wasted those seven years and never achieved glory for his family or longhouse and as a result, it is presumed that he was shaken off the tree trunk and his soul was devoured in the pit of worms.

* * *

This folktale originates from the Kayan people of Sarawak, Malaysia. This story is contained in the book *Folk-lore in Borneo, A Sketch* (William Furness, 1899) which describe the Kayan afterworld as being underground. The entrance is through a ditch filled with devouring worms. The souls of the dead must cross over this ditch by means of a fallen tree trunk called Bintang Sikopa, guarded by the great demon, Maligang. If there is no record of bravery (by taking part in war or by taking a head, for example), the demon shakes the tree trunk until the soul falls into the ditch where they are devoured by the worms.

Those who pass the test are assigned to their proper places by Laki Tenangan, who presides over the land of sprits which is divided into different areas. The land of 'Apo Leggan' is for those who die of sickness or old age. The most ideal level of the afterlife is the land of 'Long Julan', which contains the souls of those who have died a violent or sudden death either on the battlefield or in their farmsteads. Most Kayans will strive to reach this level of afterlife. 'Tak Tekkan' is the place for those who have committed the sin of suicide. In this wretched place, the departed souls wander about in the jungle eating what roots and fruits they can find. 'Tenyu Lalu' is assigned to the spirits of stillborn children. These souls do not feel pain or experience danger in this world. 'Ling Yang' is the abode of those who have died by drowning and lies below the river beds. It is this division of afterlife that provides motivation for the Kayan people to live their life in a certain way so as to achieve a more favourable place for their souls.

Chapter 12

Si Jura's Trip to Pleiades
(Malaysia)

A long time ago when the world was young and the only things to eat were fruit and the fungus growing around the roots of the trees, a party of Dayaks set forth in their boats to seek new types of sustenance. Among this party of adventurers was a young boy called Si Jura.

They sailed for many long months until one day, they came to a place in the sea where the roar of the water could be heard from miles around. The water swirled into a gigantic whirlpool and in the middle of it grew an enormous tree. The tree was upside down, its roots were anchored to the clouds above, and its branches touched the sea water.

The men could see ripe fruit growing within the branches of the tree and they asked Si Jura to climb down to retrieve this new type of fruit. They were naturally excited about the prospect of finding something new to eat.

Si Jura climbed down into the bough of the tree to pick the fruit, but once he was there, he looked up at the tree and was overcome with curiosity. *How could a tree grow here in the middle of the sea?*

Si Jura decided to find out and he slowly began to climb the tree up to the sky, to its roots. Higher and higher he climbed until he reached right to the top of the tree where he found long, thick roots meandering through the white clouds. Si Jura looked down at his friends, but saw that the boat was sailing away without him. Since he had no other place to go, Si Jura decided to continue his journey up the strange tree.

Si Jura found himself in a country which, he later learned, was called Pleiades, or the 'Seven Chained Stars.' Si Jura began to wander around the country until at last, he came upon another being, much like himself.

'My name is Si Kira. Please follow me to my house where you can eat and rest.' At Si Kira's house, Si Jura was served a bowl of soft white grains which he mistook to be maggots at first.

'This is rice,' explained Si Kira. 'I will show you how to plant and harvest this special grain for your people to eat.' Si Jura stayed and learned all he could about how to plant and harvest rice. Si Jura was given instruction on the planting, weeding, reaping, husking, and boiling of rice.

One day, when Si Kira and his wife were out, Si Jura noticed that there was a beautiful huge jar standing in the corner of the kitchen. Feeling curious, Si Jura slowly lifted the lid of the jar and peeped inside. To his surprise, he saw his father's house, and all his brothers and sisters sitting in the garden laughing and talking. He saw his little dog playing with a stick and he became homesick.

When Si Kira returned and saw how sad Si Jura was, he told the boy that he must return home. 'Here are three different grains of rice for your people. I have already taught you how to clear the land and read the omens from the birds before planting. You must instruct your people to hold a feast at the end of harvest time. Do you understand?' Si Jura promised to do what was asked.

'You will return home through this jar. Get in,' said Si Kira. Si Jura climbed into the big jar and was lowered down to his father's house by a long rope. As soon as he arrived home, Si Jura told his family and all the villagers about his adventures in Pleaides, and about the rice he would grow to feed the people. That time onwards, the Dayaks had the knowledge to grow and harvest their own rice.

* * *

This folk tale originates from the Dayak or Iban people of Sarawak, Malaysia. The Iban are the largest of Sarawak's ethnic groups and had a fearsome reputation as a strong and successful warring tribe. There are many stories from East Malaysia which feature a heavenly country above the clouds (something similar to the concept of Kayangan) accessible by climbing up vines or trees. Comparisons can be drawn with the popular European tale of *Jack and the Beanstalk* although in this tale, Si Jura meets a magical being who doesn't wish to eat him up, instead helps him by teaching him how to grow and cultivate rice. The theme of *Si Jura's Trip to the Pleaides* therefore includes both the origin of rice, and tales of magical beings since Si Kira lives in a magical realm and has magical powers.

Pleaides, which is also known as the 'Seven Sisters', is an open cluster of stars. The reference to Pleaides (which the Iban people call 'Seven Chained Stars') is important because the position of these stars informs the Iban people when to begin farming, when to cut down the jungle, and when to burn, plant, and reap paddy.

Chapter 13

Mat Chinchang and Mat Raya
(Malaysia)

A long time ago, giants lived on the island of Langkawi. According to the legends, there was a village of giants who lived quite peacefully and harmoniously most of the time. However, sometimes a fight would break out and when that happened, the whole of the island changed.

In this village of giants, there were two friends called Mat Chinchang and Mat Raya who were also the two best fighters on the island. They had a friend called Mat Sawar, and the three friends grew up together and were like brothers from the same mother. When Mat Chinchang's son announced that he would like to marry Mat Raya's daughter, the two giants were overjoyed.

'We will not only be best friends, we will also be in-laws,' said Mat Chinchang to Mat Raya. Everyone in the village was happy that the two families were to be united and they were looking forward to a joyful wedding celebration. All the villagers got together to help prepare for the wedding feast. The women cooked a huge pot of gravy and rice, while the men made a beautiful ring for the bride. Everyone was excited for the big day.

The whole village dressed up in their finest clothes to attend the wedding of the children of Mat Raya and Mat Chinchang. The bride looked beautiful and the groom was the most handsome man in the village that day. After exchanging their vows, the groom suddenly disappeared.

'Where is my husband? It is time to sit down for the feast,' said Mat Raya's daughter.

'Do not worry, daughter. I will look for my new son-in-law,' said Mat Raya. Mat Raya looked inside the house, but could not find the groom. He searched the kitchen and the garden, but the groom was nowhere to be seen. Suddenly, he heard the sound of laughter coming from behind a bush.

'Son-in-law, is that you? Come and follow me. It is time to begin the feast,' said Mat Raya. When he looked behind the bush, he was shocked to see his new son-in-law flirting and laughing with another maiden. The groom's face grew pale as he came face-to-face with his angry father-in-law.

'What is the meaning of this? How dare you!' shouted Mat Raya. His face had turned a deep angry red, and the veins throbbed across his temple. Mat Raya's booming voice came to the attention of Mat Chinchang who ran towards him.

'What is it Mat Raya? Has something happened?' asked Mat Chinchang.

Mat Raya's flaming eyes turned towards his friend. 'Your son is wicked and shameless! How can he do this to our daughter?' shouted Mat Raya.

'How dare you say that about my precious son! I do not believe you. You are lying!' shouted Mat Chinchang.

'I never should have agreed to marry my daughter to your useless son,' said Mat Raya.

'Hah! My son is too good for your daughter,' said Mat Chinchang.

Soon, a crowd gathered around the two men. Mat Raya's family were enraged that Mat Chinchang's son was caught with another maiden at his own wedding. Mat Chinchang's family did not believe the allegations and insisted that the groom was innocent.

The bride burst into tears and when Mat Raya saw his daughter crying, he flung himself at Mat Chinchang. All the men from both families started to kick and punch each other. The women from both families screamed and tore at each other's hair and clothes.

All the pots and pans used for the wedding were flung about and a huge copper pot was split into two. The place where the pot landed is now known as Kampung Belanga Pecah, or 'the village of the broken pot'.

A cauldron of boiling water was overturned and the hot water seeped into the ground. The place where this happened is now called Ayer Hangat, or the Ayer Hangat hot springs.

The 'kuah' (gravy) from the main dish spilled out and became the main town of Langkawi which is called 'Kuah'.

The bride's engagement ring was flung into the air and fell to a place which is now known as Tanjung Cincin, or 'ring headland'.

The fight between the giants also frightened some of the animals such as the lion, the snake, and water buffaloes, who all fled from the main island and were turned into smaller islands. The lion or 'singa' turned into Pulau Singa, the snake or 'ular' turned into Pulau Ular and the water buffaloes turned into Kubang Darat and Kubang Laut, which is where the water buffaloes wallow.

The battle between Mat Chinchang and Mat Raya changed the landscape of the island, and went on and on until the skies were filled with thunder and lightning. Finally, Mat Sawar, who was friends with both Mat Raya and Mat Chinchang, decided to step in. He pleaded with his two friends to stop their fight before they destroyed the island. Feeling guilty, the two giants agreed to turn themselves into mountains.

Mat Raya was transformed into Gunung Raya, which is the tallest mountain on Langkawi, and Mat Chinchang got transformed into Gunung Machinchang. Lying right in between these two mountains is a small hill called Bukit Sawar, who is there to make sure that the two giants never fight again.

* * *

This oral folk tale originates from the island of Langkawi, Malaysia. Like most oral tales, there are many versions of this story and in some versions, Mat Chinchang and Mat Raya were not giants, but ordinary people with superhuman strength.

This is a classic geomythical tale as it attempts to explain the geological landscape of the island and the names of the places here. Langkawi's geological landscape is made up of five key rock formations known as Machinchang, Setul, Singa, Chuping, and the igneous rock of Gunung Raya. The Machinchang formation is said to be one of the oldest rocks in Southeast Asia (550 million years old). This formation has been exposed to a series of tectonic events such as folding and faults, and as a result, it has produced a landscape which looks as if it's been beaten up, and has inspired the myth of the fight between the two giants, Mat Chinchang and Mat Raya. The peak of Machinchang is part of the Machinchang Cambrian Geoforest Park geotrail and is a main tourist attraction with a 360-degree viewpoint that can be accessed via the world's steepest cable car.

This folk tale also addresses the names of places on the island. The tectonic movements in the earth caused rocks to be crushed to pieces and in Langkawi, this site is known as Belanga Pecah, which literally means 'broken pot'. In addition, because the fault lines lie deep under the earth where it is hot, it has resulted in hot springs, and the place where this occurs is called Ayer Hangat, which means 'hot water'. The folds also leave numerous patterns on the rock and in the case of Langkawi, the symmetrical fold is like the shank of a well-formed ring at *Tanjung Chinchin*, meaning 'ring headland'.

The following stories are two different versions of the story of The Lake of the Pregnant Maiden, with a general commentary at the end of this section.

Chapter 14

Mambang Sari and the Lake of the Pregnant Maiden
(Malaysia)

Once upon a time, there was a beautiful fairy princess from the land of Kayangan, called Mambang Sari. One day, Mambang Sari decided to visit her favourite lake on earth with her court ladies. She loved to swim and bathe in its crystal clear water and listen to the birds singing nearby.

As she floated in the water, she began to sing an enchanting song which attracted the attention of a djinn walking nearby. Mesmerized, the djinn, who was called Mat Teja, made his way to the lake and was surprised to find the most beautiful fairy he had ever seen. Mat Teja could not help but fall for her. He overheard the court ladies talk and discovered that the lovely fairy was called Mambang Sari. Mat Teja spent the whole day admiring the Kayangan princess and was sad to see her leave when the sun began to set.

'I must find a way to win her heart,' thought Mat Teja to himself. He decided to go see the local wise woman, called Tok Dian.

'Tok Dian, please help me win the heart of Mambang Sari, the fairy princess from Kayangan,' asked Mat Teja.

'I do not have time to help you with your love life,' grumbled Tok Dian. 'Go away.' However, Mat Teja did not give up. He sat in front of Tok Dian's house for days, pleading for help until the old woman finally relented.

'Oh, very well. If you want to win her heart, I will tell you how.' Mat Teja listened carefully.

'You must wipe your face with the tears of a mermaid,' said Tok Dian.

Mat Teja smiled and thanked Tok Dian. He left her house and headed towards the sea. He managed to catch a mermaid and used her tears to wipe his face.

As predicted by Tok Dian, Mambang Sari fell in love with Mat Teja as soon as she saw him. She decided to marry Mat Teja and stay on earth near the lake. Soon after, Mambang Sari found that she was going to have a child. The couple were overjoyed by the news and spent many happy months by the lake. Their happiness was complete when their baby son was born but sadly, this did not last. Just seven days after the boy was born, he died. According to local legend, the baby turned into a white crocodile and became the guardian of the lake.

Mambang Sari and Mat Teja were heartbroken as they buried their son by the lake. Mambang Sari had never felt such grief and did not want any other woman to feel this pain, and so she blessed the waters of the lake. 'Any woman who drinks or bathes in this lake will have a child born to them,' she whispered. From that moment onwards, people believed that bathing in this lake would help them conceive a child.

. . .

Chapter 15

The Lake of The Pregnant Maiden
The Tale of Telani and Telanai
(Malaysia)

The king loved to hunt on the islands of Langkawi. Before the start of each hunt, he, along with the princes and their courtiers would gather together for a feast that lasted throughout the night. It was during one of these festivities, when a beautiful court lady by the name of Telani stole away to meet Prince Telanai, the king's son.

The next day, the sky was bright and clear and the king was looking forward to some good hunting. Court Lady Telani who was with the hunting party, suddenly felt a great thirst and bent down to drink the waters of the lake. As she drank, the sky turned grey and a terrible storm appeared out of nowhere. When the king saw this change, he took it as a bad omen and called off the hunting trip.

Shortly after, the kingdom was hit by a severe drought which brought hunger and death to the people of the land. The king feared that the ancient god Sang Kelambai had been displeased and when he heard the news that the court lady Telani was with child, he called his son Telanai who confessed that he was the father of Telani's child. In order to appease Sang Kelambai, the king banished Telani to a deserted island in the middle of a beautiful lake. There, she gave birth to her baby.

Prince Telanai was distraught and he searched everywhere for Telani. One day, as Prince Telanai's boat was approaching Telani's island, a clap of thunder woke up the sleeping baby who fell into the lake and turned into a white crocodile. Telani rushed forward, but the baby was gone. Grief-stricken, Telani froze in her tracks and wept. A mist descended upon her island and when it lifted, Telani had turned to stone.

Prince Telanai never reached his beloved Telani and his son. Instead, he was transformed into an island. It is said that their son, the white crocodile, swims between the rock which locals call Batu Dayang or 'damsel rock', and the island, which is called the Isle of Tajai. According to local lore, water from his particular lake or tasik will help those who have trouble conceiving.

* * *

This tale is known locally as *Tasik Dayang Bunting* and originates from the island of Langkawi, Malaysia. Since this story was spread orally, there are many different versions as can be seen from the two versions included above. The version with the fairy from Kayangan shares similar traits to the story of *The Youngest Fairy Princess of Kayangan*.

Another interesting aspect of this tale is that it falls in the category of geomythical stories. Tasik Dayang Bunting literally means the 'lake of the pregnant maiden'. Today, this lake is a popular tourist attraction in Langkawi, and many still believe that if they swim in this lake, they will be blessed with a child. The landscape in this area is formed by running water and rain which erodes the limestone rock and shapes the hills into a combination of rounded, cone-like, sharp peaks. In one particular area, this landscape looks like the profile of a pregnant lady lying on her back.

Chapter 16

The Maidens Who Saved Guam
(Guam)

For some reason, the middle of Guam island was shrinking. The fishermen in Hagatna Bay and Pago Bay noticed that every morning their bay was getting larger and larger, and the land was getting smaller and smaller. Sometimes at night, the earth shook and if you listened carefully, you could hear a gnawing sound, as if something was eating up the earth below.

The clan leader was worried. If something was not done soon, their big island would be cut in halves and become two smaller islands. Throughout the land, people came together to try to solve the problem, but no one knew what to do. Then one night, a fisherman discovered why their land was shrinking. A gigantic fish was eating its way through the middle of the island.

'It is the most frightening creature I have ever seen. Instead of scales, it is covered with hard rock and when it opened its jaws, I saw a thousand sharp teeth. Its eyes glowed in the dark.'

'How big was it?'

'It was as big as an island.'

'How fast was it?'

'It was as fast as lightning.'

'Tell us fisherman, what was this terrible creature doing?'

'What do you think it was doing? It was eating the middle of our island! This is the reason why our land is shrinking,' exclaimed the fisherman.

'Then it is clear what we must do. We must kill the monster,' declared the leader. The people of Guam were angry that such a vile creature was destroying their homeland. The men of the island gathered their spears and daggers, they sharpened their bamboo poles, and before the sun rose the next morning, they sailed into the bay to hunt the loathsome creature. The canoes of every man on the island were used to search the waters around the bay, but there was no sign of the monster.

'It is a clever thing. Hiding, and bidding its time. We must stay in the water and find the monster. We will not stop until we kill it.'

While the men were hard at work, hunting down the creature, the women of Guam were also busy trying to find a solution. Even though the women were not as strong as the men, they were wise and clever.

News of the hunt travelled around the island and reached the ears of the young maidens of Hagatna Springs. These maidens were known for their long, beautiful, and incredibly strong hair. Every day, they came to the springs to wash their hair in fresh water scented with lemons. When they left, the pool was filled with lemon peels which floated on the surface like little golden boats. One day, a girl from Pago Bay, which was on the other side of the island, found these floating lemon peels.

'My cousin in Hagatna told me about these lemon peels. The maidens there love to go to the fresh spring to wash their hair with these fruits. But how did the lemon peels float all the way around the island to arrive here?' she wondered. It did not make sense and it bothered her for days, and so she decided she would visit her cousin at Hagatna Bay to find out.

'How did your lemon peels arrive in our bay across the island? How did it arrive on my beach in Pago Bay?' asked the girl, when she arrived in Hagatna Bay.

'How indeed? It is mysterious,' replied her cousin.

The maidens sat at the beach wondering how the lemon peels had travelled around the island. As they sat, they could see the boats of the men out at sea hunting the monster fish. The answer came to them as the waves crashed at their feet.

'The monster...'

'Yes, it must be the monster. I heard that it is big and has huge teeth sharp enough to eat our island.'

'The men have been searching for the monster for days, but it has vanished.'

'Then the monster must be…'

'Hiding underneath our island! It must have eaten its way underneath the island causing a tunnel of water to flow from Hagatna Bay to Pago Bay. This is how your lemon peels arrived at my beach!' said the girl from Pago Bay.

'We must catch the monster. Come, let us weave a strong net made of our hair. The lemon wash we use makes our hair thick and strong and if we work together, we can catch the monster.'

The maidens cut off their long hair and worked all day to weave the strands into a net and by the time the sun had set, they were ready to go fishing. Working together, the maidens swam out to sea with their net of hair and sang an enchanting song to attract the fish. The fish heard the song and swam straight towards the maidens.

'Here he comes! Get ready.'

Working together the maidens threw their net over the fish. The monster struggled and bit at the net, but it was of no use. The net was too strong. The men in the boats could not believe their eyes when they saw that the monster had been caught by the brave, clever maidens of Hagatna and Pago Bay.

* * *

This folk tale from Guam is also known as *The Folk Tale of Pago Bay* and *The Legend of the Young Women That Saved Guam*. Guam is a small Micronesian island east of the Philippines. It is a U.S. territory and is the southernmost and largest member of the Mariana Islands archipelago. According to historians, Guam was discovered and populated by Austronesian peoples around 4,000 years ago.

The indigenous people of Guam are the Chamorros, who are related to other Austronesian natives of the Philippines, Taiwan, and Eastern Indonesia. The Chamorro language lies within the Malayo-Polynesian subgroup which is why this story is included within my broad umbrella of Nusantara tales. This folk tale is interesting because not only does it attempt to explain the shape of the island (in that it looks as if something has taken a big bite out of the land), it also highlights the important contribution of the female members of this island. In order to defeat the sea monster, the maidens use their intelligence, their strong sense of communication, and their beauty in the form of their super strong hair. This folk tale highlights the agency of the wise, brave female figures from the island, and is therefore a good example of a folk tale with strong female characters.

Chapter 17

Cencewi and Puteri Manis
(Malaysia)

Once there lived a mysterious woman named Cencewi. Cencewi was the most beautiful woman in the village, but for some reason, no one could remember when she first arrived and how long she'd lived among them.

Cencewi never changed. She never grew old. As time passed, the other men and women in the village became old and haggard. Their smooth skin became wrinkled and lost the glow of youth. Their bodies became bent and soft, and they lost their energy and vitality. All the men and women of the village went through this usual rite of passage, but not Cencewi. Time seemed to defy her. She remained as fresh-faced and youthful as the day she arrived in the village. Her skin was as smooth as a rose petal, her hair as dark as the night. She walked with the light gait of a young woman. Everyone was puzzled as to how Cencewi could still remain young and beautiful. They did not know that she had a secret.

All the men in the village wanted to marry Cencewi, but she always refused saying that no man could ever be good enough for her. She preferred to live alone and sell her herbal oils and poultices she was famous for. She had a remedy for every type of aches and pains and if you asked her nicely, she could brew you a love potion or sell you something to mend a broken heart. This was why the villagers left her alone because they depended on her medicine.

One day, Cencewi was in the woods looking for her special herbs when she heard the sound of a child crying. She followed the sound to the river and was astonished to find a baby lying on a rock by the side of the river. Cencewi took the baby home and named her Puteri Manis, or 'Sweet Princess'. Cencewi took care of the baby but she kept it a secret. None of the other villagers knew that she had secretly adopted a child. When the girl was bigger, Cencewi forced the girl to live in a small room under her house which contained a small kitchen.

'You must stay in this room forever, Puteri Manis,' said Cencewi. 'You are only allowed to come out to cook and clean the house.' Since Puteri Manis did not know any other life, she thought this was perfectly normal and continued to live in her cramped little room under the house.

Many years passed. One day, three merchants arrived in the village to sell their wares. Cencewi invited the three merchants into her home and after some bargaining and haggling, she bought many fine things from them such as fine silks, beautiful beads, and exotic spices. By then, the sun had set and it was getting dark, and so Cencewi invited the merchants to stay for dinner.

'Please, sit and rest. I will prepare a special meal for all of you,' she said. The merchants accepted Cencewi's kind invitation and sat down as she began to prepare their meal in the kitchen. She did not realize that the merchants were watching her cook in the kitchen.

First, Cencewi took a big fish and began to clean and slice it up into smaller pieces. However, after that she did something quite peculiar. Instead of throwing out the fish bones, she put the bones into a pot, and then she took the flesh of the fish and dropped it into a small hole in her kitchen floor. Next, Cencewi broke some eggs and once again, she put the egg shells into the pot, but she poured the eggs into the same hole in her kitchen floor. Finally, Cencewi took a small sack of rice and once again, poured the rice into the hole in her kitchen floor. The merchants, who were secretly watching her, were puzzled, but did not say anything.

'It is ready. Please, come and eat,' she said, once the meal was ready.

The merchants watched in awe as a plate of freshly fried fish appeared out of the hole in the floor. This was followed by a plate of fried eggs, and a big bowl of freshly cooked rice. The merchants ate the food, thanked Cencewi, and quickly left the house feeling a bit uneasy. However, they were curious to see who had prepared their meal.

Later that night, the merchants snuck under Cencewi's house and were shocked to find a girl who was locked up in a small room. Inside the room, they could see the kitchen where she had prepared their meal.

'Who are you? Why are you living underneath Cencewi's house?' asked one of the merchants.

'My name is Puteri Manis. I am the one who prepared your meal,' she said. Puteri Manis told the merchants how she was found by Cencewi in the woods and how she had been living underneath the house all her life. The merchants were shocked by the cruelty of Cencewi and immediately rescued Puteri Manis.

Cencewi was angry that Puteri Manis had run away, but she did not pursue her adopted daughter. She stayed in the village and remained as beautiful as ever for the next few years until one day, the villagers discovered her dead in her house. After her death, they were shocked to find that Cencewi had turned old and ugly. Some believe that she had used black magic to look young and beautiful but once she died, her true face finally emerged.

* * *

This tale is also known as *Puteri Manis and Cencewi* and is said to originate from the state of Kelantan on the east coast of Malaysia. This chilling story is actually contained in a children's book and bears some resemblance to the European tale of Rapunzel in that there is an imprisoned girl. It is quite possible that Cencewi used black magic in order to retain her youth and vitality. In Malay society, the use of black magic is looked down upon and can be said to lead to other harmful activities. The fact that Cencewi secretly adopted a child in order to turn her into a servant illustrates how Cencewi's morality had fallen.

Chapter 18

Timun Mas
(Indonesia)

Mbok Srini lived alone in a small village at the edge of a vast jungle. She made a living growing vegetables in her little garden and for many years, she was content with her simple life. However, as time passed, she grew lonely and longed for a child to love.

Mbok had heard that there was an ogre, a *raksaksa* named Bhuto Ijo who lived in a cave deep in the jungle. According to the villagers, Bhuto Ijo could grant wishes. Mbok decided to find the raksaksa and ask him to give her a child. The next day, Mbok set off into the jungle. The journey was long and difficult but finally at dusk, Mbok reached her destination and entered the wide gaping mouth of the cave. Inside, the cave was cold and silent. Mbok was glad it was dark for she did not want to see the victims of the *raksaksa*.

'Greetings, Bhuto Ijo,' she whispered as she stood inside the cave. It was so dark, she could not even see her own hand in front. However, she could hear something slithering around her. A deep, low growl greeted her.

'I am Mbok Srini. I am here to ask you to grant me a wish,' she said, her voice shaking. Slowly, a dim light illuminated the darkness. Mbok gasped as she saw candles floating in the air. When her eyes adjusted to the light, she saw that she was standing in front of a gigantic throne made of human bones, and sitting on top was a monster so hideous and huge, his head almost touched the ceiling of the cave. He growled and bent down to look at Mbok with eyes glowing red in the dim light.

'You have come here to ask for a wish? Are you sure?' asked Bhuto Ijo in a low voice.

'Yes, I wish for a child of my own.' She blurted the words out quickly before she could change her mind.

Bhuto Iio closed his eyes and smiled. 'I can grant your wish, but there is a price to pay.'

'I will pay the price,' replied Mbok.

'Very well. You must raise this child, but on her seventeenth birthday I will come and find you. On that day, you must give your daughter to me to do with her as I wish.'

Mbok began to shake. The term of the agreement was too cruel, but Mbok knew she had no other choice for she had already fallen in love with the child who was yet to be born.

'I promise to give you my child on her seventeenth birthday.'

The raksaksa gave her a tiny golden seed. 'Plant this magic seed in your garden and take care of it. Soon, your wish will come true.'

As soon as Mbok got home, she planted the magic seed in the best spot in her garden. She used the best soil and every day, she made sure the seed had just enough water and just enough sunlight. Soon the seed sprouted and grew into a tiny shoot, which then grew into a beautiful cucumber plant. Mbok looked after the precious plant protecting it from insects and birds. She spoke to the plant and sang songs. For seven days, the woman did not eat or sleep, and was constantly in her garden.

Then, on the seventh day, something miraculous happened. As Mbok walked through her garden, she noticed that hanging on a branch of her precious plant was a single, beautiful golden cucumber. Mbok admired the fruit and noticed that it began to move on its own. The fruit turned and twisted on its vine until it finally detached itself and fell straight into Mbok's outstretched hands. She watched as the two halves of the golden cucumber slowly opened to reveal the most beautiful baby girl she had ever seen nestled inside. The baby opened her eyes and smiled at Mbok.

'Oh, you are mine and I will love you forever,' said the woman to the child. 'I will call you Timun Mas after this golden cucumber.' Mbok covered the baby in kisses and said a prayer of thanks.

Mbok cared for and loved her daughter who grew up to become a clever, kind, beautiful girl. Mbok knew that one day she would have to give Timun Mas back to the *raksaksa*, but that day seemed so far off that whenever the thought entered her mind, she banished it away.

The years passed too quickly until finally it was the eve of her daughter's seventeenth year. Mbok was filled with dread at the thought of giving up her beloved child to Bhuto Ijo.

'Please, I cannot give up my precious Timun Mas. My heart would break and I would die,' she prayed.

That night she dreamed that she must gather four items in order to protect Timun Mas. These were cucumber seeds, needles, salt, and a clump of soil. As soon as she woke up, she gathered these four items and placed them into four small pouches. Mbok finally told Timun Mas how she was born and the promise Mbok had made to Bhuto Ijo. She told Timun Mas that the *raksaksa* was coming to get her that day as it was her seventeenth birthday.

'You must run away. If he catches you, throw these items at him to protect yourself.' Timun Mas was shocked and frightened, but she was determined to escape from the raksaksa.

'Ibu, I will find a way to survive,' said Timun Mas. She was trying hard to be brave but deep inside, she was shaking with a fear. She could not see how the cucumber seeds, needles, salt, and soil could save her, but she had faith in her mother. They embraced one last time, and then Timun Mas ran out through the back door to escape from the raksaksa.

As promised, Bhuto Ijo arrived at Mbok's house and knocked on the door. 'I am here for your daughter. You must fulfil your promise, Mbok Srini.' She opened the door and almost fainted at the sight of the terrifying raksaksa.

'I will give Timun Mas to you as promised but I'm afraid she is not here.'

Bhuto Ijo roared and smashed the door with his fists. He looked into the house and saw that the back door was opened. 'She has run away but no matter, I will soon catch her. She cannot escape from me.' He sniffed the air and ran to catch up with Timun Mas.

'Come here, Timun Mas. You belong to me!' Timun Mas looked over her shoulder and saw the raksaksa gaining up on her. She grabbed the first pouch of cucumber seeds and threw it at him. As soon as the seeds hit the ground, they grew into a gigantic cucumber patch with ripe, delicious cucumbers. Butho Ijo was momentarily distracted and he actually stopped to eat the fruit. However, when he had devoured all of the cucumbers, he got up and began to pursue Timun Mas once again.

'Timun Mas, you cannot escape from me,' he bellowed. The girl looked back and saw the raksaksa just a few feet away. She took out the second pouch, the one containing the needles. She waited for the monster to come closer before she threw the needles at his feet. Once again, the needles sunk into the ground and grew into a thick bamboo forest surrounding Bhuto Ijo. The bamboo had sharp edges which tore through his flesh making him roar in pain. However, he was so strong that he managed to crash his way out of the bamboo forest. This time, he was bloodied and injured by the sharp ends.

Timun Mas ran along the river towards the waterfall and soon she heard the sound of his thumping steps behind her. She stopped in front of the waterfall and waited. She took out the third pouch, the one containing salt, and got ready.

'Timun Mas!' roared the raksaksa. This time she did not wait and flung the salt into the water which immediately churned and rose up into the air in a gigantic wave and crashed down onto the Raksaksa flinging him into the river. Timun Mas climbed up the cliff using the rocks and thick vines. She had one last pouch to use, the one with a clump of soil.

Down below, the raksaksa fought the waves which threatened to drown him, but still emerged out of the water triumphant. It seemed like nothing could bring down the powerful ogre. Timun Mas finally reached the top of the waterfall and waited.

'Please, protect me,' she prayed as she threw the last pouch full of soil to the raksaksa.

Down below, Bhuto Ijo was climbing the cliff ready to kill the girl who dared to defy him. In his rage, he did not hear the low rumbling coming from the earth, he did not see the avalanche of rocks and soil as it fell, pushing him off the side of the cliff onto the ground. The rock kept piling on top of Bhuto Ijo, pounding him under the ground until he was completely submerged, and still it did not stop. More and more rocks fell until the raksaksa was buried deep under the ground. At last, the earth stopped moving to reveal the final resting place of Bhuto Ijo.

Timun Mas turned her gaze towards the sky and said a prayer. Then the girl who came out of a magic cucumber got to her feet and began the journey back home.

* * *

This famous folktale is also known as *Timun Emas,* and originates from Java, Indonesia. *Timun* means 'cucumber' and *emas* means 'gold', and this is a story about a girl who was named after a golden cucumber. This story is an example of a successful Nusantara folk tale that has spread and has been adapted into different forms (books, animated movies, and dramas) especially in Indonesia.

Essentially, this story is about the issue of childlessness and the desperate measures people go through in order to conceive a child. Srini's yearning for a child is so extreme that she is willing to agree to the unfair term set by the ogre. This is a common theme found in fairy tales and is a reflection of people's biological need to pass on their genes to the next generation.

Another theme which crops up in this story is the usage of the natural environment in the narrative. Perhaps due to the circumstances surrounding her birth, Timun Mas appears to have a powerful connection to nature and is able to manipulate the environment using ordinary objects in order to escape from the ogre. These objects are found in the ground or in the sea and includes objects such as cucumber seeds, needles (made of metal), salt, and soil. In other versions of this story, other objects are used including shrimp paste or 'terasi'.

There is a similar theme in Giambatistta Basile's version of *Rapunzel,* called *Petrosinella,* contained in his book, *Pentamerone* or *The Tale of Tales,* which was written in 1634. In this version, the heroine, Petrosinella, escapes from the ogress by throwing three magical gallnuts. The first nut turns into a Corsican hound, the second into a ferocious lion, and the third nut into a wolf which swallows up the ogress at last.

Chapter 19

The Tale of The Blind Man and
The Lame Man
Si Buta and Si Tempang
(Malaysia)

Once there was a blind man called Si Buta, and a lame man called Si Tempang. The two men knew that they could not always depend on the charity of others, and so they decided to help each other out. One day, they left their small dwelling on the edge of the jungle to find food.

Si Tempang, who could not walk properly, sat on the back of Si Buta, who could not see, in order to guide him. Along the way, Si Tempang saw various items and asked Si Buta to stop to collect them.

First, he saw a thick piece of rope. 'Stop! We should take that piece of rope. It may be useful to us,' said Si Tempang.

Next, Si Tempang saw an axe lying on the ground. 'Stop! We should take that axe. It may be useful to us.'

Finally, Si Tempang saw a turtle on the ground. 'Stop! We should take that turtle. It may be useful to us,' said Si Tempang.

Si Buta was not convinced that either the rope, the axe, or the turtle could be of any use. It was nearly lunch time and his stomach was grumbling and yet, they had not found anything to eat. Si Buta was getting annoyed at having to carry Si Tempang on his back and the odd items he collected added weight to his load, but he continued to walk and did not complain.

After a while, lulled by the swaying movements of Si Buta's back, Si Tempang fell asleep. Without any eyes to guide him, Si Buta walked into the wall of a house and both men fell to the ground.

'Hey Si Buta! How could you not see that big house,' complained Si Tempang, not realizing that what he said did not make any sense. However, Si Buta was not listening for he could smell food which made his stomach grumble even louder. The two men entered the house and Si Tempang gasped.

'Look at that table. It is as big as a buffalo,' said Si Tempang.

'Tell me more,' said Si Buta.

'There is a plate on the table as big as a goat,' said Si Tempang.

'And food? Is there any food?' asked Si Buta rubbing his stomach.

Si Tempang was just about to have a look when the floor and wall of the house began to shake. They could hear the sound of giant people approaching.

'This house belongs to a giant! Come, we must hide,' said Si Tempang as he guided Si Buta up a ladder to the loft. Up in the loft, Si Tempang found a huge jar and helped Si Buta climb into the jar where they found a ripe, tasty banana.

'Ah, finally, some lunch,' said Si Buta. He peeled the skin of the banana and began to eat the fruit.

In the meantime, the giants, a man and his wife, entered the house and sat at their table.

'I'm hungry, wife. Let us eat the banana we have been saving.'

'Very well, I will fetch it from the loft and then you can cut it up for us,' said the wife.

When Si Buta and Si Tempang heard this, they began to shake and shiver.

'What will we do?' whispered Si Buta. Si Tempang looked down at the items he had found in the jungle: the rope, the axe and the turtle. He closed his eyes and tried to think.

'I have an idea, my friend,' smiled Si Tempang.

They could hear the female giant climbing the ladder up to the loft.

'Stop!' shouted Si Tempang.

'Who's there?' asked the female giant.

'I am the biggest, most powerful giant in this country. I have come here to challenge you,' cried out Si Tempang in a loud voice. When the male giant heard this, he stood up and roared.

'I accept your challenge!' said the male giant.

'Throw me a strand of your hair,' ordered Si Tempang. The giant pulled a strand of his hair which was as thick as a man's finger and threw it up to the loft. Si Tempang threw down the coil of rope. The giant picked up the rope and saw that it was as thick as a man's wrist.

'Now, show me your head lice,' ordered Si Tempang. The giant reached up and plucked a big, black louse from his head and threw it into the loft. It was as big as a mouse. Si Tempang took the turtle and threw it down to the giant. The giant picked up the turtle, impressed at the size of the head lice.

'Now, show me your tooth,' ordered Si Tempang. The giant pulled out one of his teeth and threw it up into the loft. It was the size of a man's big toe. Laughing, Si Tempang threw down the metal head of the axe which clanged onto the floor.

When the two giants saw the size of their enemy's teeth, they ran out of their front door and never returned.

Si Buta and Si Tempang climbed down from the loft and began to eat the giant's food. Si Tempang saw a pile of gold in the corner and the two men filled their pockets, but gradually they argued over who would get the bigger share.

They fought. Si Buta kicked Si Tempang in the knee which fixed his bad leg. Si Tempang hit Si Buta in the eye and restored his sight. Laughing at their good fortune, the two friends made peace and lived happily ever after.

* * *

This story is known as *Si Buta and Si Tempang*, and originates from Sabah, Malaysia. *Buta* means 'blind' and *tempang* means 'lame'. In this tale, two men who have their own individual ailments decide to live and work together in order to overcome their shortcomings. Like any relationship, the two men initially have difficulties adjusting to each other's personalities, resulting in conflict. However, once they are confronted with danger, the two work seamlessly together for their benefit. It's interesting to note how at the end of the story, the two men are 'cured' of their disabilities. Many folk tales about those with disabilities tend to focus on a cure, whereas it might be more beneficial to the reader if these characters could find a way to live with their disabilities.

Chapter 20

The Crocodile's Wife
(Malaysia)

The Crocodile King was on the hunt for a wife. He had been searching for a worthy companion for years, but the gods were not on his side, and he wondered whether he would remain alone for the rest of his life. The maidens he encountered on the banks of the River Barito had not stirred a ripple in his cold heart and he found that he could not even bear to look at them.

All this changed one beautiful morning when the sun shone down and made the water sparkle. The light dappled on the leaves and danced on the river. As the Crocodile King floated in the water contemplating another tedious day, she appeared out of nowhere—the Crocodile's Bride. Her name was Galuh Bungas and she was the daughter of the village head.

'Today is her wedding day,' said the tortoise to the crocodile. 'She is going to marry the brave warrior, Apai.'

The Crocodile King watched as the wedding raft decorated with dangling vines and flowers of every colour floated past his hiding spot near the roots of a mangrove tree. The Crocodile King drank in her dark eyes, her smooth skin, her beautiful long hair, and when she suddenly smiled, he knew that she was the one for him.

The wedding festivities lasted all day with music and drums playing, and children laughing. The men drank to the couple's health and the women came together to whisper and gossip of the wedding night.

All day, the Crocodile King waited for his chance to take his bride. Finally, after the last guest had left the festivities and the sun was about to set over the river, Galuh Bungas appeared once more, this time alone. She had gone further upstream in an enclosed bend to bathe.

Moving as silently as the setting sun, the Crocodile King swam towards her. The ripples under the water brought to him the movement of her body and he could smell her skin. Surfacing, he watched as his bride hummed a tune to a passing mynah bird.

'She is moving away to her husband's longhouse tomorrow,' said a passing fish. 'If you want her, you must take her now.'

The Crocodile King decided to act. His bride was in front of him, he had waited years for her and this was his only chance. Moving silently, the Crocodile King dived under the water and in an instant, took his bride. Galuh Bungas did not even have a chance to scream and all that was left were the ripples in the empty water.

When word reached Ajai that his young bride was missing, the warrior went mad. He searched the longhouse and the surrounding areas. Tok Dukun, the medicine man, was called in to help locate Galuh Bungas. They searched everywhere but there was no sign of her. Galuh Bungas had vanished into thin air. Finally, in the early hours of the morning, Tok Dukun, who had been in a trance since Galuh's disappearance, opened his eyes.

'I am afraid Galuh Bungas is now the bride of the Crocodile King,' he declared. The chief sprang to his feet and his wife fainted. If this was true, then their daughter was as good as dead.

'No, I will not let him take her. I will find her,' said Ajai clutching his knife. 'Tok Dukun, you must help me get her back.'

'She is still alive and there may be a way to save her. We must go down to the river and negotiate with the Crocodile King,' said Tok Dukun. Ajai waited to hear more.

'Listen carefully, Ajai. The Crocodile King will offer some kind of payment as compensation for the loss of your wife. You must accept whatever the Crocodile King offers to you, even if the thing he offers is not your wife' said Tok Dukun.

'I will do whatever it takes,' replied Ajai.

The two men then made their way to the place where Galuh Bungas was last seen. Kneeling down, Tok Dukun began to chant and offer prayers to the spirit of the river. After a while, the water began to bubble, and out of it emerged the enormous head of the Crocodile King.

'You have taken my wife. Please, return her to me,' said Ajai in a low voice.

'She is the bride I have been searching for all my life,' replied the Crocodile. 'She will stay with me.'

Ajai could feel the blood rising in his body. *How dare this creature take his beloved wife away from him?* 'Never! Return Galuh Bungas to me now.'

For a while, the Crocodile King said nothing and simply closed the three lids of his eyes as if in deep contemplation.

'As payment for Galuh Bungas, I offer you this young goat,' said the Crocodile King and from out of nowhere, a white goat appeared threshing about in the river. Tok Dukun reached out to grab the goat but in a fit of anger, Ajai leaped into the river and pushed away the goat.

'I do not want this wretched goat! Return my wife to me now,' shouted Ajai.

'Fine, if you do not want this goat, I shall take her now,' said the Crocodile King.

'No!' cried out Tuk Dukun who jumped into the river and tried to grab the goat. He managed to grab the goat's leg and pulled away a small object, but the Crocodile King was too strong. In the blink of an eye, the goat and the Crocodile King vanished under the churning waters of the Barito River.

Tok Dukun was furious with Ajai for breaking his promise to accept the Crocodile King's conditions. 'See, what you have done!'.

Tok Dukun held up the small object he had pulled from the goat— it was the wedding ring of Galuh Bungas. With a sinking heart, Ajai realized what he had done. He had rejected the offer of the Crocodile King and had condemned Galuh Bungas to become the wife of the Crocodile King.

That day onwards, Ajai sat at the edge of the river pining for his beloved bride. Over time, the great warrior's body turned to stone and became Ajai Rock, and according to the people living nearby, any water that washes over the rock turns red.

* * *

This tale is also known as *The Crocodile's Captive* and originates from Sabah, Malaysia. East Malaysia has many crocodile-infested rivers and waterways which may explain why there are so many folk tales and stories about crocodiles from this area. In these places, the river forms an important part of people's lives as it is their main source of food and transportation.

In many of these tales, the crocodile is a shapeshifter and is able to take human form once he has left his domain. The people living in Sabah usually tell these stories to warn children of the dangers lurking in the rivers. These stories are therefore considered to be cautionary tales.

Chapter 21

The Tale of Man and the Crocodile (Malaysia)

Many moons ago, a young Melanau prince wandered along the edge of the wild river and came across a girl so beautiful he could not help but fall in love. He asked the girl to marry him but she could not tell him where she came from or who her parents were. No matter, the prince took her to his palace and the two were wed in a great celebration.

The king and the queen were happy that their son was in love, but they had some misgivings about their new daughter-in-law. She was a strange sort of girl, keeping to herself and not saying much. She would disappear for hours and when the prince finally found her, she was usually by the river staring into its murky depths.

One night, she woke up and whispered to her sleeping husband. 'I must go home now. Take care of our child and release him into the river when he's ready.' In the morning, the girl had vanished leaving behind a tiny egg.

'I knew there was something wrong with that girl,' said the queen to the king.

'I am glad we got rid of her,' replied the king.

But the prince was heartbroken and took to carrying the egg around with him everywhere. One day while he was sitting by the river, the egg twitched and moved, and finally cracked open. Out of it popped a tiny creature with beautiful green scales that glittered under the sun. It blinked at the prince.

'You have your mother's eyes,' said the prince to his son. The prince gently released the creature into the water, and watched as his son swam away. This magical creature was the first of its kind; half-human and half-crocodile. Some people call them were-crocodiles.

Many, many moons later, two young crocodile brothers named Radin and Bujang decided to go on land to explore what life had to offer. The brothers were following a sampan boat when they heard its owner speak of a big wedding at the longhouse.

'The wedding is tomorrow evening and will last for three days. There will be music and dancing and lots of food and drink,' said the first voice.

The crocodile brothers were intrigued and decided to go to the wedding. The next evening, they crawled out of the river and slipped off their crocodile skins. They were afraid that someone would steal their skins and so they looked for a suitable hiding place.

'Here, let us hide our skins under this bush,' said Radin. They hid the skins, put on their rich woven garments, and casually strolled to the longhouse where the wedding was being held. The arrival of the two handsome brothers caused quite a stir amongst the guests at the wedding.

'Who are those two rich men?' asked the old ladies of the longhouse, for the brothers had brought gifts of precious stones.

'Who are those two strong men?' asked the men of the longhouse for the brothers had helped to carry the firewood out to the pit.

'Who are those two handsome men?' asked the young ladies of the longhouse, for the brothers had danced beautifully to the beat of the gong.

Everyone wanted to know who the two brothers were, but was too afraid to ask. Radin and Bujang spent the evening dancing and eating, and admiring the pretty girls. They had such a wonderful time that they decided to return the following evening.

The next evening, Radin and Bujang crawled out of the river once more, took off their crocodile skins and dressed in their rich garments. However, this time, they were seen by a man named Lueng.

'Greetings,' said Radin bowing to Lueng.

'We are going to the wedding at the longhouse but we are afraid that our skins will be stolen. Could you look after our skins for us?' he asked. Lueng was so scared that all he could do was nod.

'Thank you. We will of course pay you for your good deed,' said Bujang, and the two brothers set off to enjoy themselves at the wedding. After the party, the brothers returned to the river to find Lueng guarding their skins.

'Thank you,' said Radin. 'Here is a little gift for you for your kindness.' Radin gave Lueng a small yellow rock and then the two brothers changed and slipped back into the river.

When Lueng arrived home, he told this story to his neighbour, Ngareng.

'Well, what did they give you?' asked the nosy neighbour. Lueng held out the yellow rock which glittered in his palm.

'Why, it's gold! Those two brothers have gold,' exclaimed Ngareng.

The next evening, Ngareng went to the river and waited for the two brothers to arrive. Sure enough, two enormous crocodiles crawled out of the river and took off their skins to get ready for the wedding.

'Oii! Who are you and what are you doing here?' asked Ngareng trying his best to sound brave.

'Greetings,' said Radin bowing to Ngareng. 'We are going to the wedding at the longhouse, but we are afraid that our skins will be stolen. Could you look after our skins for us?'

'Yes, yes. Go to the wedding but make sure you don't come back too late, you hear?' said Ngareng. The two brothers smiled and set off to make merry at the longhouse. After they left, Ngareng did an evil thing. He gathered the crocodile skins and placed it on some dry leaves and twigs. He set fire to the skins and watched as it burned. The smell of it attracted the other crocodiles in the river. They swam towards Ngareng but merely watched and waited.

Later that night, Radin and Bujang returned to the river having had a wonderful time at the wedding.

'Thank you for looking after our skins,' said Bujang to Ngareng.

'I want my payment. I want my gold,' said Ngareng in a surly tone. It was then that Radin noticed the smell of smoke and charred skin.

Bujang saw a pile of burnt leaves and twigs and a call from the river told the brothers what had happened.

'You want gold?' asked Bujang.

'Yes. Give me the gold first and then I will return your skins,' replied Ngareng.

'Well, if it is gold that you want, you are welcome to have it. There are piles and piles of gold in our house at the bottom of the river. All you need to do is dive down and get it,' said Radin.

Ngareng was so consumed with greed that he did not notice the look on the two brothers' faces. He did not see the ripples in the river and the bulging eyes breaking the surface of the water. Ngareng dived into the river and was torn to pieces for his treachery. Unfortunately for Bujang and Radin, they could no longer transform into their crocodile selves again. And from that time onwards, crocodile and man became enemies.

* * *

This folk tale is also known as *The Crocodile Princes* and comes from the Melanau people of Sarawak, East Malaysia. The Melanau are an ethnic group who live in the swampy deltas where the river meets the sea. Stories of shape-shifting animals are common in this part of the world, and this particular folk tale seeks to trace the origin of the were-crocodile; a crocodile who can transform itself into human form. This tale is interesting because it is told in two parts. In the first half, we discover how the were-crocodiles first came into existence. In the second half, we find out why there is war between man and crocodiles. According to some myths, once a were-crocodile skin has been burned, the creature will remain trapped in the body of a human forever.

Chapter 22

Danjai and the Weretiger's Sister
(Malaysia)

To show his new bride how much he cherished her, Danjai needed to bring home a human head. This was the way of his people.

And so Danjai, the great chief and protector of his village, went down to the river with his men to build his war-boats. Danjai was so determined to finish his task that he left early one morning without taking his morning meal. His new bride decided she would bring him some food and prepared a bundle of cloth filled with rice, fish, and salt.

Danjai's bride was new to the land and had never been out in the jungle alone, but she was not afraid for in the distance she could hear the sound of men chopping wood. As she walked through the jungle path, she came upon a peculiar sight. On a low stump of a tree, was a basket of sibau fruit.

'Oh, how wonderful! Did Danjai leave this fruit here for me?'

Without thinking, she reached out and took the fruit, twisting the tough skin to reveal the pale juicy flesh inside. She popped it into her mouth and savoured the sweet, tangy taste of the fruit. Feeling happy, she picked up the basket and walked on till she reached her husband who was chopping wood by the river. When he saw the basket of sibau fruit, he asked her about it.

'I found it on a stump of a tree on the way here. Did you leave it there for me? The fruit is sweet and delicious.'

As soon as Danjai heard his wife's words, his face turned as pale as the flesh of the sibau fruit itself, and his hands began to tremble. Quickly, Danjai's eyes searched the jungle.

'We must not linger here any longer. Come, my wife, I must get you home now.'

She did not understand why Danjai was suddenly so frightened. What could scare the bravest man she knew?

'Danjai, what has happened? Please tell me.'

'Wife, you have taken food belonging to the were-tiger who is feared by all. He lays his fruit along the path in the jungle to tempt us. We never touch it because we know what will happen if we do.'

She could feel the blood drain from her face.

'Tell me, Danjai. What will the were-tiger do to the person who has taken his fruit?'

'He will come and have his revenge. He will come and take your head.'

Her legs gave way and she almost fell, such was the shock of this revelation.

'I am sorry I did not warn you, my wife. You are a stranger to our land and you did not know. This is all my fault.'

His wife had turned as white as the frangipani flowers in their garden. She opened her mouth to speak, but no words came out. Danjai brought her home and asked his servants to hide her beneath some mats in the room. Then he ordered his men to stand guard outside his house. Twelve strong men stood with swords, guarding her hiding place.

As night approached, they waited for the were-tiger. They knew the creature would come and they had to be ready. They waited and waited and then, just when the night sky was at its darkest hour, the creature appeared. Just beyond the trees, came the low growling of a tiger on the hunt. The nervous men standing outside the house could hear it moving through the grass, coming closer. They could feel its stare, but they could not see the were-tiger for it had made itself invisible.

Soft and as silent as the night, the were-tiger climbed up the tall fig tree which grew near the house and with a graceful leap, landed onto the thatched roof and fell into the house. There was a great disturbance as Danjai and his twelve men tried to kill the invisible creature, but it was all in vain. Moments later, a great roar of triumph was heard in the distance.

Danjai raced to his wife's hiding place and lifted up the mats. His wife was dead, her headless body still warm from the onslaught of the attack. Danjai fell to the floor and felt his world crashing around him. He had lost his beloved wife. He vowed he would avenge her death and made a promise that night that he would kill the were-tiger.

Early the next morning, the hunt began. Danjai tracked the were-tiger by its footprints and the drops of his wife's blood trailing the jungle floor. The bloody trail led him up a mountain. On and on he climbed until he came to the entrance of a cave he had never seen before. He entered and immediately saw another opening at the far end of the cave. He raced towards it and when he looked out, he saw a land filled with rows and rows of the ripe yellow stalks of sugarcane topped with flowering green leaves.

Slowly, Danjai followed a path down from the mountain through the sugarcane plantation. The trail of blood ended at the bottom of a carved ladder which led up to a big wooden house on stilts. This was where he would find his wife's murderer. Danjai began to climb. There were men sitting on the open veranda, but Danjai ignored them and walked straight into the house. A girl greeted him inside.

'Danjai! We had not expected you to come so soon. Please sit down and make yourself comfortable.' Confused, Danjai sat as the girl brought him a beautiful brass box. 'My brother is out at his sugarcane plantation, but he should return home soon. Please rest here and chew on some betel nut.'

She left Danjai alone to gather his thoughts. He wondered how she knew his name and why they had expected him to come. A short while later, the were-tiger arrived home carrying a bundle of sugarcane over his shoulder but this time, he had shape-shifted into his human form. He was tall, strong and handsome, but Danjai noticed something sinister hidden behind his eyes.

'Welcome to my home, Danjai. I am happy to see you. Please, help yourself to some sugarcane.' He placed the pile of sugarcane down and invited Danjai to try some. Once more, Danjai was surprised that the were-tiger knew his name and was being so courteous. He reached out and took a stick of sugarcane.

'Thank you. That's very kind of you.'

'You will eat with me tonight and stay here awhile, yes?' asked the were-tiger. Danjai had no choice but to agree. At least, it would give him a chance to avenge his wife's death. The were-tiger nodded and then headed down to the river to bathe. As soon as he left the house, the girl came back and spoke to Danjai.

'Danjai, I know what my brother has done to you and I am very sorry for your loss. I want to help you. If you want to stay alive, you must listen carefully.'

'Why are you helping me?' asked Danjai. He did not trust the girl for he knew that she, too, was a weretiger.

The girl sighed and gazed at the floor. 'My brother is cruel and evil. All our people hate him, but none are brave enough to fight him.' Danjai nodded.

'What must I do?' he asked.

'Presently, I will serve you and my brother some food. Do not take the plate he offers for it is sure to contain poison.' Danjai nodded.

'Later when you retire for the night, do not sleep on the mat he offers, but sleep elsewhere. Place the wooden mortar for pounding paddy on that mat instead. On the second night, do the same, but this time use the wooden mill for husking paddy, and on the third night, place a roll of coarse matting used for treading paddy. If his three attempts at killing you are unsuccessful, he will be under your power and will do what you command.'

Just then, they heard the were-tiger climbing the ladder. His sister gave Danjai one last look and returned to the kitchen to bring out the food.

'Come Danjai, let us have our evening meal, my sister is a wonderful cook.'

All that the sister foretold happened. Danjai did not take the plate of rice that was offered to him, but merely picked on some pieces of fish and vegetables. After their meal, the two men sat by the fire on the veranda. Danjai looked up at the rafters and saw the skulls of human heads staring down at him. Once again, he felt the intensity of the loss of his wife.

'What grieves you, Danjai? Have you lost someone you love?' The were-tiger's words felt like a sword in his heart. That he could tease and taunt him so, made Danjai's blood boil.

'I am not aggrieved, my friend,' lied Danjai. 'The smoke from this fire is making my eyes sore.'

'Well then, let us go in and retire for the night,' said the were-tiger. Once again, the sister's forewarning came true. The were-tiger placed a mat on the floor and invited Danjai to sleep there. Danjai pretended to be asleep but later in the night, he got up and placed the wooden mortar on his mat and covered it with a sheet. He hid behind a big urn and waited.

Not long after, the were-tiger stood up and unsheathed his sword. Moving silently, he made three vicious cuts into the wooden mortar. Under the light of the moon shining in from the window, Danjai could see his cruel smile. From his hiding place, Danjai called out.

'What is that noise? What has happened?'

The were-tiger frowned, and then put his false smile back on. 'Oh Danjai, it is you. Thank goodness you were not sleeping on this mat for surely you would have been killed by my sword. I am prone to bad dreams and sleepwalking, you see. Come, let us go back to sleep and put this behind us.'

Danjai's heart burned with vengeance, but he remembered the sister's words. If the were-tiger failed to kill him thrice, he would be under Danjai's control.

On the following two nights, the were-tiger attempted to kill Danjai, but each time he failed as Danjai followed the advice of the sister. He used the wooden mill on the second night, and the roll of coarse matting on the third night. Each time, the were-tiger used the same excuse for his strange behaviour.

On the morning of the fourth day, the were-tiger left the house early to catch some fish in the river. His sister came to Danjai and whispered the last of her instructions. He nodded and waited for the were-tiger to return. After breakfast, Danjai thanked the were-tiger for his generosity and said that he must return home.

'I will accompany you to the border,' said the weretiger, and together they left for the cave. Once they reached the far end of the sugarcane plantation, Danjai asked the were-tiger if he could eat some of his delicious sugarcane one last time. He cut a few stalks and handed them to Danjai, for he was under his command.

'May I borrow your sword to cut this, for mine is quite blunt.' Without thinking, the were-tiger handed Danjai his sword. Danjai took the sword and in one swift motion cut off the head of the weretiger. He remembered what the sister had whispered to him that morning.

'The were-tiger can only be killed by his own sword.'

Danjai picked up the head and walked back to the were-tiger's house and as he approached, he saw the sister standing on the veranda waiting for him. In her hand, she carried the head of his late wife. The two exchanged heads.

'Thank you,' he said. 'I would have been killed without your help.'

'Thank you, Danjai. You have rid my people of a cruel leader.'

Danjai returned home but he could not forget the were-tiger's sister and not long after, he returned for her. She agreed to marry him on one condition—that he must warn his people not to ever take food they might find lying in the jungle, on a rock, or a stump of a tree. This must be remembered from one generation to another.

* * *

This is a folk tale from the Iban or Dayak people of Sarawak, Malaysia and was collected in a book titled *Seventeen Years Among the Sea Dyaks of Borneo* by Edwin H. Gomez in 1904. This tale falls under many categories including tales of shape-shifters (in this case, were-tigers), and tales which seek to explain the origin of a particular custom (in this case, the taboo of taking something from the wild). It appears to be a cautionary tale designed to warn children about the dangers of eating things from the wild, which is not surprising, bearing in mind that there are many fruits, berries, and mushrooms which are not only harmful, but also poisonous. However, there seems to be more to this story which taps into the culture of the Iban people.

According to Iban beliefs, certain items found in the wild are considered as a form of bait or 'taju'. The bait found on land is called 'taju remaung' (spirit tiger's bait) and the bait found near the water is called 'taju baya' (spirit crocodile's bait). It is thought that if someone were to take this bait, they would soon be taken and killed by either a tiger or crocodile, which is why till today, children are warned not to take anything outside their longhouse that catches their eye.

Chapter 23

The Cloth Merchant of Tanjung Rimau
(Malaysia)

Once there was a cloth merchant who had a deep dark secret—he looked like an ordinary man most of the time, but no one knew that he had a magic tail which he often used to turn himself into a tiger.

The cloth merchant loved the taste of human flesh and in order to hunt, he travelled from village to village pretending to sell silks and satins. He would hide in the shadows until he was sure that all the men were out working in the fields or in their fishing boats. Once the men were gone, he would come out to look for his next victim: the wives and daughters who were left at home to take care of the house.

'Hello my dear, would you like to see my wares? I have silks and satins, cotton and lace. Something pretty for one as lovely as you?' He charmed the ladies with his sweet smile and gentle eyes. When the ladies looked at him, they saw a small man who walked with a limp and they did not feel threatened or afraid. They saw his bales of cotton and thought that perhaps it wouldn't be a bad idea to get a little something for themselves.

'Would you like to see some fine silk from China, my dear? It just came off a ship today. I can give you a special offer.' He licked his lips and smiled, and if the ladies had been paying attention, they would've noticed his teeth which were a little bit too sharp, and the look of hunger hiding just behind his eyes. But the ladies never took any notice of the cloth merchant. They were too preoccupied with the beautiful silks and satins he carried on his back. They invited him in and made him tea as he spread out the cloth on their wooden floors.

'Look at this fine workmanship, Puan. Look how this pink silk brightens your eyes.'

As the ladies fell under the charm of his beautiful cloth, they did not notice the merchant looking down at the floor as if searching for something. Always, his head moved hither, thither looking and searching until at last, he found it – a floorboard with a small hole in the floor. Once he located this special place, he would sit down and slowly, slowly unfurl his long yellow tail into the hole.

'Puan, this print is perfect for you. Your husband will love you even more when he sees you wearing this,' he would say, as he sipped his cup of tea and stroked his reddish-brown beard. As he sat on top of the floorboard with the hole, his tail would grow longer and longer. Slowly he could feel the tiger in him rise to his chest. He closed his eyes and waited.

By this time, the ladies were so mesmerized by his merchandise that they would pay him no attention. Slowly, the transformation would take place as his human body changed into that of a tiger. A low growl, a powerful lunge, and it was all over. All that was left was blood splattered over the beautiful materials laid out on the floor.

Soon, people began to look out for the cloth merchant who was killing the women in the area. The men decided to lay a trap and waited under the biggest house in the next village. As usual, the cloth merchant appeared when the sun was high in the sky. The village was quiet and he could see that all the men were away at work. This was the perfect time for a hunt.

He approached the biggest house which belonged to the Penghulu, the chief. Inside, he could hear a young girl singing to herself and he licked his lips in anticipation. The girl was the daughter of the chief who had volunteered to lure the were-tiger into her home.

When the cloth merchant called out to her, she appeared at the door and smiled. 'Good morning Cik, I have some beautiful cloth for a sweet girl like you. Can I come in and show you?' he asked.

'Why not, of course, please come in,' she said, smiling sweetly. The merchant walked in and immediately saw the perfect spot to sit;

near the window was a small hole in the floorboards. He licked his lips and sat down. Slowly, his tail began to unfurl and fall through the crack in the floor.

Unfortunately for the cloth merchant, the chief was waiting under the house with ten strong men from the village. They watched as the were-tiger's tail began to fall through the hole in the floor above. With a smile and a nod to the other men, the chief grabbed hold of the tiger's tail and pulled.

The cloth merchant felt a pain as he had never felt before. *What was this?* He looked down at the floor and tried to retrieve his tail. Feeling surprised, he looked up and saw that the girl was smiling at him.

'We have you now, tiger,' she said. The cloth merchant immediately changed into his tiger form to escape, but the men under the house held onto his tail with an iron grip and refused to let go. The tiger let out a ferocious roar and leapt up, but his tail remained inside the crack. Unable to stand it, the tiger lunged out of the open window and fled into the jungle, leaving his severed tail behind. Under the house, there was much triumphant shouting as the men celebrated their victory.

Without his magic tail, the cloth merchant was forced to remain in his tiger body forever, and roamed around the nearby jungle alone and tailless.

* * *

This tale is also known as *The Story of Tanjung Rimau* and is said to have taken place in Tanjung Rimau, or Cape Rimau in the state Melaka, Malaysia. 'Rimau' is the short form of 'harimau', which means tiger. In the past there were many wild tigers in Malaysia and these kinds of stories were used to remind and warn people of the dangers lurking in the jungle. As we have seen, were-tigers feature prominently in the folk tales and fairy tales from the Nusantara (see for example, *Danjai and the Were-tiger's Sister*), but this particular were-tiger has taken it to another level by using trickery and deceit in order to kill his victims. In that sense, this tale could also be a warning to be careful of strangers as well as tigers.

Chapter 24

The Mosquito Queen's Lost Earring
(Malaysia)

The hunter could sense his prey up ahead on the hill, weak and injured from his dart. It was close to death, yet it wandered deeper and deeper into the jungle, clinging to an impossible hope of survival. He admired this and allowed his prey its final, precious few hours of life.

This was what the hunter lived for; following the drops of blood, stalking his prey, and the final kill. His family would eat well tonight. Before the hunter struck his final blow, he said a prayer of thanks to the spirit of the jungle for providing him with this bounty. The hunter slung the small prey over his shoulder and started the long walk home. He had not realized how late it was until he saw the long shadows cast by the sinking sun. He knew he would not make it home that night for it was dangerous to move through the jungle once darkness descended. And so, he settled himself on a high branch of a banyan tree and watched as the sun sank into the horizon. The sky at first shimmered with tinges of pinks and purples, but now melted into a dark inky blue. It was the hunter's favourite time of the day.

Exhausted, the young man soon fell into a deep slumber filled with dreams of the hunt. At rest, his stern features softened to reveal a smooth, handsome face, a face which soon attracted some curious creatures of the night. A scourge of mosquitoes flew by. Lured by the sweet-smelling blood of the hunter, they hovered above him and prepared for a feast. Even in the deepest of sleep, he could hear the buzzing of mosquitoes. He stirred.

Just then, the queen of the mosquitoes caught sight of the handsome young man and entranced by his fine looks, ordered her mosquitoes away. Under the light of the moon, using magic as old as the jungle itself, the queen transformed herself from a small mosquito into a beautiful maiden. Her long dark hair reached her lower back and she wore a black dress studded with colourful beads that shimmered under the light of the moon.

The queen raised her arms and floated up to the branch where the hunter slept, all the while buzzing softly. Gently, she serenaded the hunter with a strange song, tracing her fingers down his cheeks. He woke up with a start and reached for his dagger, but stopped when he saw the beautiful maiden.

'You are tired and hungry,' she smiled. 'Please, come to my palace and rest awhile. The jungle is no place for one such as you.' The queen took his hand and led him down the banyan tree. Intrigued, the man followed the queen and her servants until they came upon a stunning palace made of gold and jewels. He wondered why she had built such a magnificent palace in the middle of the jungle.

She invited him to sit and eat at her table, laid with golden plates and crystal glasses. Out of nowhere, platters of rice, vegetables cooked in coconut, and roasted meat appeared, and the crystal glasses filled with a dark red sparkling drink. The hunter put the glass up to his lips and tasted the drink. He did not care for the rusty, strong taste, but he pretended to drink. As the night wore on, the queen and her subjects became more and more euphoric. They drank and ate and danced and twirled, until finally all fell into a deep slumber.

When the queen and her subjects had fallen asleep, the hunter got up to explore the strange palace. The polished floors in the main hall were covered with the finest silk rugs. On the wall, hung beautiful and ornate wood carvings. He looked up at the ceiling and was surprised to see that it was made of something clear and that he could see the stars dancing in the night sky. What an extraordinary palace this was.

The hunter wandered further into the palace and at the very far end of a dark hallway, he found himself drawn to a closed door. It was made of carved solid wood and seemed to hum at him. Slowly, he opened the door and entered a room which was completely empty except for a table that held seven jars. Curious, the hunter opened one of the jars and found that it contained a thick, red liquid. He held it under his nose and the smell of it made his stomach lurch. It was human blood.

All the jars were filled with the blood of humans and that was when he remembered the sound of buzzing in his ears just before the queen woke him up. It was the sound of mosquitoes.

His heart, always steady, began to beat faster as the hunter realized that the beautiful queen was not human. *The queen of the mosquitoes.* He had heard stories of her as a child. She was able to transform into a beautiful woman in order to lure people into her golden palace where she would entice them with fine food and wine. The hunter realized that she was planning to kill him and drain his blood to feed her mosquitoes.

With his heart beating like thunder, the hunter turned around to flee that cursed place. He retraced his steps back to the main hall and just before he got to the front door, he saw the queen sleeping on her side, a beautiful gold earring dangling from the lobe of her left ear.

The hunter felt a sudden fire rage through his body. Moving silently, he crept up to the sleeping queen, reached out, and slipped off her precious gold earring. He escaped from the palace and vanished into the night.

The queen awoke to find that her guest had disappeared along with one of her gold earrings. Incensed, the she ordered all her mosquitoes to search the land and the seas for the hunter.

'Do not come back until you find him, and my earring,' she ordered.

The mosquito army flew across the land besieging villages and homes in search of the hunter and the lost earring, but by then, the hunter had disappeared. More and more mosquitoes were sent across the mountains and the seas, always looking and searching.

Whenever the scourge of mosquitoes came close to any humans, they would immediately fly to the person's ear to look for their queen's earring, buzzing and humming. They searched on and on, and they are still searching till this day.

* * *

This folktale is also known as *Why the Mosquito Makes a Buzzing Sound in Our Ears* and comes from the Kadazan-Dusun people of Sabah,

Malaysia. This story is contained in a book titled *Kadazan Folklore* by Rita Lasimbang, and published in association with the Kadazandusun Language Foundation. Although small, mosquitoes can spread dangerous disease among the population and as such, there are many cautionary tales warning people to be careful when dealing with this insect. These folk tales fall under the category of tales of shape-shifters (since the mosquitoes are able to change into human form), but it is also a story that seeks to explain the annoying trait of mosquitoes—their buzzing in our ears.

Chapter 25

The Sembilang Curse
(Malaysia)

Cik Sambi has been living in the village for a while now, and although the rice was delicious and plentiful, her delicate stomach could not take the salted fish everyone seemed to devour. She desired something fresh and tender. As she worked in the paddy field next to her neighbour Nenek, she gazed out onto the waters of the clear lake and imagined the bounty lying under. Closing her eyes, she could almost taste the delicate, sweet flavour of fresh fish in her mouth.

Nenek saw the look of longing on Cik Sambi's face and frowned.

'Cik Sambi, you seem to like the lake in our village. It is beautiful, isn't it ?' asked Nenek. Cik Sambi nodded and smiled at her elderly neighbour.

'Yes, and there are so many fish in the lake. Tell me Nenek, why do the villagers continue to eat salted fish when there is plenty of fresh fish in the lake?'

'You are new in this village, my child. You do not know the old stories.'

And it was true, Cik Sambi was a young widow who arrived in the village a few weeks ago. The Penghulu was kind enough to allow the young woman to live and work there on one condition: she must never ever catch, or eat the fish in the lake.

'The fish in that lake does not belong to us, Cik Sambi. Our rice fields flourish and we have plenty of fresh water because we respect this rule. The fish in that lake belong to the guardians of the lake.'

The young woman's brow crinkled faintly. She did not believe in such things.

'It seems such a waste, Nenek,' said the young woman. 'The lake is brimming with beautiful fish, I can see them just under the surface.' When she spoke, her mouth watered and her heart beat faster.

'Cik Sambi, if you take the fish from the lake, something awful will happen not just to you, but to this whole village.'

Cik Sambi smiled at Nenek and nodded, but in her heart, she thought the old woman was being foolish. How much harm could one fish do?

Weary from a long day at work, Cik Sambi returned to her tiny hut by the edge of the forest. She took off her straw hat and sat at the veranda overlooking the lake. How peaceful it was. The evening was so still and quiet that she thought she could hear the fish swimming and moving through the water. She thought she could even hear them whispering. Reluctantly, she tore her eyes away and busied herself by making her usual evening meal—rice with salted fish. And even though she was hungry, the sight of her dinner turned her stomach.

Exhausted, Cik Sambi got ready for bed but her craving would not allow her any rest. Slowly, she got up from her mat and looked out the window. Night had descended and the dark sky was lit up by a million glittering stars. The moon, full and round, cast its silvery light over the lake, painting the surface of the water with its glow.

The young woman longed to go to the lake and look at the fish, and before she knew what she was doing, Cik Sambi found herself standing at its edge looking down into the clear water. She saw hundreds of fish dancing under the lake, their silvery backs luminous under the night sky.

And then, the strangest thing happened. Cik Sambi felt something small, cupped in her palm. She brought up her hand and opened her fingers to find some grains of rice. How did it get there? Had she brought the rice with her down to the lake?

Just then, two beautiful fish jumped out of the water and without a second thought, Cik Sambi threw the grains of rice into the lake. Almost immediately, the lake came alive with dancing fish, swimming and jumping towards Cik Sambi. She laughed and with her heart thundering in her chest, the young woman caught a fish with her bare hands. And then she caught another, and another, until there were nine splendid fish lying by the side of the lake. Exhilarated, Cik Sambi gathered her catch in her sarong and ran home.

It was late and the village was deep in slumber, but Cik Sambi was busy. She gathered wood and made a fire. Then she prepared the fish and roasted it over the fire.

With shaking hands, Cik Sambi picked up a piece of fish and placed it in her mouth. It was just how she imagined it would be—fresh, slightly nutty, with a sweetness at the end of each bite. It was the most delicious thing she had ever tasted in her life, and she wanted more. Such was her greed and desire that she ate all nine fish, leaving nothing but bones scattered near the fire.

Cik Sambi could not remember what happened next, but somehow she found herself back on her mat and fast asleep.

The next morning, Cik Sambi was awoken by a twisting pain in her stomach, as if a million sharp daggers were stabbing the insides of her body. She opened her eyes expecting to see herself cut open and bleeding, but she was still whole. Moving slowly, Cik Sambi got up and dragged herself to the veranda of her house to call for help, but by the time she reached the front door, the pain was too much to bear. She let out a piercing scream and fainted.

Next door, Nenek heard the scream and dropped her bowl of rice. Worried, she hurried over to Cik Sambi's house to see the young woman sprawled on the floor clutching her stomach. Her face was pale, her body trembling.

'Cik Sambi! What has happened?'

Even in the deepest clutches of pain, Cik Sambi would not admit her crime.

'I am fine, Nenek. I have just a little stomach pain…' A blunt knife stabbed her somewhere inside her stomach and turned and twisted, making Cik Sambi writhe.

'Cik Sambi!' Nenek hurried to her neighbour and that was when she saw the scattered fish bones near the embers of the fire. Nenek knew what had happened and sighed.

The transformation happened a short while later. Slowly, gradually, the skin on Cik Sambi's legs became wet and slippery. Her light-brown skin darkened into a silvery-grey colour. A burning pain spread through her body and she screamed and grabbed Nenek's arm.

'What is happening to me?'

'I am sorry my child, but you took what was forbidden. And this is your punishment.'

Cik Sambi's legs drew together and began to merge until it transformed into a gigantic fishtail. Her skin burned like fire and she screamed again.

'Please, please help me,' she begged.

Nenek felt sorry for the woman, but there was nothing she could do. The silvery-grey skin gradually spread to her stomach, onto her chest and down her arms, which then turned into fins.

'Nenek! I am turning into a fish!' The pain was unbearable, but the sheer terror of what fate awaited her was more than she could take. Cik Sambi had a sudden terrifying thought.

'Nenek, please don't put me in the lake when I turn into a fish. The other fish will kill me for what I have done.'

Nenek promised. The transformation was almost complete. With one last scream, the slippery fish skin spread up to Cik Sambi's face, gills appeared on her cheeks, and Cik Sambi's fish-body shrunk until it was the size of a normal fish. Nenek quickly scooped up the fish and took it to the river.

Cik Sambi, the fish was dazed and confused as she swam towards the sea. She wanted to get as far away as possible from the enchanted lake. However, when Cik Sambi reached the open sea, she became dizzy and ill. She found that she was not able to tolerate the salt water.

Not knowing what else to do, she swam back up the river but when she reached the lake, she discovered that it had dried up. Such was the curse that she had inflicted upon the village. Cik Sambi stayed in the river until the day the people of the village turned the old lake into a paddy field. Reluctantly, Cik Sambi swam into the paddy field and there she lived for the rest of her life.

Today, the state where this tale originates is called Negeri Sembilan after the 'sembilan', or nine fish Cik Sambi caught. Within the borders of that state, there is a town called Kampung Kuala Sawah, which means paddy fields. It is said that the enchanted lake used to be located in Kampung Kuala Sawah, and in the paddy fields of this town lives a colony of sembilang fish.

* * *

This folktale is also known as *Sembilang* and originates from the state of Negeri Sembilan, Malaysia. *Sembilang* refers to 'cat fish', commonly found living in rice fields. The word 'sembilang' sounds similar to the word 'sembilan' which means the 'number nine', and is the name of the state where this story comes from (Negeri Sembilan).

This tale is essentially about a community who have thrived by working together and following certain rules, the most important of which is not to take any fish from the lake. There is a social aspect to this story in that everyone in the village works together to earn a living off the land. Perhaps the lake was a valuable source of fresh water for the people and irrigation for the paddy fields. In any event, Cik Sambi was advised and warned not to misuse the lake which she chose to ignore only to face some dire consequences.

Chapter 26

The Curse of Mahsuri
(Malaysia)

Once upon a time on the island of Langkawi, there lived an old couple, Pandak Maya and Mak Andam, who longed for a child. One day, Mak Andam was in the paddy field when she heard the sound of a baby crying. When she looked closer, she saw that the sound came from a crust of rice. Mak Andam took that home and because she was hungry, she ate it. Shortly after, Mak Andam discovered that she was going to have a baby.

The couple were overjoyed when they were blessed with a perfect baby girl, whom they named Mahsuri. Mahsuri was adored by her parents and was raised with love. She grew into a charming, bright young woman who was kind and always cheerful. She was also quite lovely and soon became the most beautiful maiden on the island of Langkawi. Mahsuri had hair the colour of the deepest part of the night, skin as fine as the silk, and a heart filled only with love and kindness. Mahsuri stole the hearts of those around her. Men from across the island and many from beyond, came to court her, but Mahsuri only had eyes for her one true love. He was the brave warrior, Wan Derus. The couple soon married and were excited to set off on their adventure of living happily ever after. Sadly, this was not to be.

After the wedding, the island declared war on the kingdom of Siam. Wan Derus, the best and most skilled warrior, was called away to fulfil his duty to the Sultan. Mahsuri was sad to see her husband go off to war. She moved back to her parent's house and waited for Wan Derus to return.

During this time, a peculiar thing happened. Every time Mahsuri thought of her husband, she would grow more and more beautiful. Her skin glowed with the blush of true love, her eyes brightened at the thought of Wan Derus, and she bloomed until she became the envy of all the women on the island. The village chief's wife and Mahsuri's sister-in-law, Wan Mahura, was particularly jealous of Mahsuri's beauty and grace.

One day, a travelling poet by the name of Deramang arrived on the island searching for work. With the blessings of Mahsuri's parents, Deramang moved into their home and taught Mahsuri to recite poetry. This made Wan Mahura even more jealous and after Mahsuri had given birth to a son, Wan Mahura began to spread malicious rumours about Mahsuri.

The rumours began to spread across the island like wildfire until one day, it could no longer be ignored. Deramang and Mahsuri, unaware of the grave accusation made against them, were hauled up to the middle of the village for a trial. Mahsuri was accused of being unfaithful to her husband. The village chief called the first witness, Wan Mahura, who claimed that Mahsuri was unfaithful to her husband.

Mahsuri could not believe that Wan Mahura would utter such horrible words.

'I love my husband and I would never betray him.' As Mahsuri spoke, the ground seemed to tremble and a breeze fluttered the fronds on the coconut trees. The accusation was like a burning arrow to Mahsuri's heart. Mahsuri turned and looked at the faces of the other villagers and saw that they believed the lies.

'Mahsuri and Deramang, I find you both guilty. You will both be executed immediately,' declared the village chief. There was a gasp from the crowd as the men grabbed Mahsuri and tied her to a tree. Mahsuri looked calm, but a fire was burning behind her eyes.

'You will regret what you have done today. I am innocent and all will come to know of it. Listen carefully, I curse the island of Langkawi. I curse all that I see before me, and I curse your descendants for the next seven generations.'

No one spoke, but they could all feel something rippling in the air and under their feet. A man stepped forward with a keris dagger which belonged to Mahsuri's family, and stabbed her in the heart. Wan Mahura smiled as she watched Mahsuri die.

Mahsuri did not cry out. Her head fell to her chest, but as she slowly raised it, everyone saw the impossible. The blood which flowed from Mahsuri's chest was not red. The blood which flowed was pure white and it was gleaming under the evening sun. It was then that they realized that Mahsuri was telling the truth, for only those who speak the truth have blood this pure flowing through their veins. Above them, the sky had turned black with angry clouds, and a sudden wind blew in from the sea bringing with it the smell of Mahsuri's curse.

Mahsuri perished from her wounds that day, but the village and the island were cursed for the next seven generations. No matter how hard the people worked, the island was plagued with bad luck. No crops grew on the previously fertile soil, animals died of unknown diseases, and babies slept, never to wake up again. For the next seven generations, the people of Langkawi floundered and festered under the curse of the beautiful Mahsuri.

* * *

This story is known as *Mahsuri* and is the most famous folk tale from Langkawi, Malaysia. The story of Mahsuri falls under the category of a legend because it includes an element of truth but has some mythical qualities. Legends usually involve heroic characters or fantastical places, and often encompass the spiritual beliefs of the culture from where they originate.

According to the information at Mahsuri's tomb (Makam Mahsuri, which is located in the village of Mawat), Mahsuri binti Pandak Maya was the daughter of Pandak Maya and Mak Andam. She was born in the 18th century in Ulu Melaka village, Langkawi, and died in 1819. Soon after her death, Langkawi was attacked by Siam (Thailand today) and when a battle broke out between Langkawi and the Siamese in the Pancur Straits in 1821, the chief of Langkawi's army, Dato Kemboja, ordered the villagers to poison their wells and collect all the paddy stocks, and burn it in a hole dug up in the compound of a house owned by Ku Halim bin Ku Hasan in Kampung Raja, the king then. Unfortunately, Siam was still able to capture and hold Langkawi. Today, you can visit this place which is called Beras Terbakar (or the Field of Burnt Rice) in Padang Matsirat. The evidence of this burning can still be seen today, 200 years later, as charred and blackened rice grains surface from the ground especially after it rains heavily.

This legend is one of the most gruesome tales from Malaysia and encompasses a variety of themes: polygamy (in some versions Mahsuri is the second wife), jealousy, revenge, mob violence by the villagers who believed in Wan Mahura's allegations, class struggle between an ordinary village girl and those in authority, oppression of the marginalized, slander, breach of justice, and cold-blooded murder. This is a classic tale of the injustice faced by the oppressed from those in power. This legend reflects the patriarchal values and feudalistic social order in a Malay community in the 18th–19th century.

Chapter 27

Awang with the Watery Eyes
(Malaysia)

A long time ago, there was a woman called Bidan Tok who lived in a small village called Kampung Bakung with her son Awang. Even though Awang was a kind, gentle boy, everyone hated him because of his eyes were always inflamed and watery. They were disgusted by Awang and did not want to be near the boy.

As Awang grew older, the teasing and jeering increased. The children in the village called him a dirty dog and threw stones at the poor boy. The children's parents thought the boy had an infectious disease and warned their children not to go near Awang. As time passed, some villagers even thought that Awang was cursed. Poor Awang was so lonely that he tried to make friends even with the animals.

'Here kitty, come here and I'll share my fish with you,' said Awang to the old tabby cat who lived under his house. The cat hissed at him and walked away, but not before it grabbed the fish from Awang's hands.

'Come little birdies! I have some rice for you,' said Awang as he flung the grains of rice into the air. The birds flew towards the grain of rice but they took one look at Awang's red, watery eyes, squawked in disgust, and took off. No meal was worth being close to such a hideous creature, thought the birds.

Poor Awang. The only person who loved him was his mother who tried her best to care for him. As he grew older, he realized that he was a terrible burden on his mother. In the past, the villagers would flock to Bidan Tok's house to purchase all kinds of herbs and poultices to cure their aches and pains but for some time now, the villagers began to question Bidan Tok's expertise. Why should they go to her for medical help when she could not even cure her son's diseased eyes? Some of the villagers even thought that Bidan Tok was a fraud.

'Oh Awang,' she cried one night. 'I do not know how long we can live here. My customers refuse to consult me anymore. Soon we will run out of money and we will be destitute.' Awang hung his head down in shame for he knew he was the cause of his mother's troubles. That night Awang cried himself to sleep which of course made his eyes water even more, but at least there was no one around to tease him.

That night he had a strange dream; an old man reached out to touch his eyelids. The old man was so small that he had to stand on his toes to reach Awang's face. Awang knew this must be a dream because no one had ever dared touch his eyes before.

'Your eyes are disgusting boy,' said the old man rather unhelpfully. Even in his dream, the boy was tormented.

'Do you want to know how to cure your ailment?' asked the man.

Awang looked at the old man who now seemed to tower over him. He wondered how the small man had suddenly grown taller.

'Well, do you want to know the secret?' he asked again.

'Yes, please. If you know how to cure my eyes, please tell me Tok,' replied Awang.

'Listen carefully. First, you must find the most beautiful white frangipani flower.' Awang nodded.

'Then, you must find the perfect wild coconut. It must be as round as the moon.'

'Yes,' said Awang.

'Soak the frangipani flower in the coconut water. Once the flower is thoroughly soaked, use the flower to rub and clean your eyes. Do this for seven days in a row and your eyes will be cured.'

Awang was so happy, he felt that his heart might burst inside his chest. A short while later, he woke up and before he could forget the instructions of the old man, Awang sprung out of bed and told his mother everything.

'There are no frangipani trees in our village, Awang. And the wild coconuts only grow on the island. I know! We will ask someone to take you to Pulau Mandul.' Awang thought this was a splendid idea, and so mother and son ran to the top of their road and began to knock on their neighbours' doors.

'Please, help us. Awang needs to go to Pulau Mandul and we have no boat. Please can you take Awang there?' pleaded Tok Bidan.

'Go away! Why would I take that cursed boy on my boat?' said the fisherman slamming the door in her face.

'He will probably sink my boat. No, is the answer!' said trader.

'Get lost,' said the farmer.

On and on it went until they came to the final house at the bottom of the road. The house belonged to a man called Jurangan Boyok who was sitting on his porch watching Tok Bidan and Awang making their way from house to house. Jurangan felt a little sorry for them and decided that if no one would take Awang, he would. After all, he wasn't doing anything important that morning.

'Oh thank you, Jurangan,' said Tok Bidan. They walked to his sampan and after a hasty goodbye, Awang and Jurangan set off to Pulau Mandul.

Pulau Mandul was not far away but a short while after they had left land, the boat sprung a leak.

'Ah... I knew I had forgotten something,' said Jurangan scratching his head. He had meant to fix the leak in his boat but never got around to it. He looked around his boat for a rag or something to stuff into the small hole at the bottom of the boat.

'What's happening, Pak Jurangan?' asked Awang who noticed that the small sampan was slowly filling up with seawater.

'What do you think is happening, boy? Look, we have a leak and if we do not plug it up, we will sink here in the middle of the sea and you will never reach your precious Pulau Mandul.'

Awang was determined to reach his destination and in a stroke of genius he used the only thing he had plenty of, the crusty discharge oozing from his eyes. He scooped it out and used it to stuff the hole and lo and behold, the boat stopped leaking.

Jurongan bent down and examined the plugged-up hole at the bottom of his sampan. 'Well,' he said looking impressed. 'I see that eye of yours has some uses.' And with a grunt and a hint of a smile on his lips, Jurongan sailed towards Pulau Mandul. He left the boy on the island with a promise to collect him in seven days' time.

A week passed and true to his word, Jurangan appeared in his little sampan which was still seaworthy from the crust of Awang's eyes. This time, he had brought Tok Bidan who was anxious to meet her son. As they landed on the beach, Tok Bidan saw that her son had transformed into a bright-eyed handsome boy. He ran towards her and kissed his mother's hands.

'Mother, I found a village here willing to accept us. Come let us leave Kampung Bakung and make a new life on this island,' said Awang. And that is exactly what they did.

* * *

This folk tale is also known as *Awang—the Boy with the Watery Eyes,* and originates from Malaysia. This is an interesting tale which features someone with a disability affecting his personal appearance. The main character, Awang, is ostracized by all the other people in his community who think he is under a curse, and as a result, searches for a cure. The 'curse' in this story is possibly an illness or allergy, and the search for the cure seems to be more of a wish-fulfilment dream. Awang will only be happy once he has cured his eyes. However, at the end of the day, his faulty eyes only proved to be useful saving the boat from sinking.

Chapter 28

The Squirrel Princess
(Malaysia)

Once there was a prince from a land called Kampung Negeri Berasap. The prince loved nothing more than to go hunting in the wild jungles near his kingdom. One day, he ventured forth on such an excursion and travelled all the way to a place called Antah Berantah but unfortunately, he did not spot a bird or an animal all day.

Frustrated, the prince settled down under a tree to rest and cool off before heading home. His eyes were about to close when he spotted movement in the branches above. He saw a squirrel, the most magnificent squirrel he had ever seen. It had dark brown eyes, a shiny coat of fur, and on its head was a strand of silver hair running down its back. After casting a long look at the prince, the squirrel leaped gracefully away onto another tree.

The prince grabbed his bow and arrow, and followed the animal as it led him deeper and deeper into the jungle. The squirrel jumped from tree to tree until it finally dropped to the ground and approached a big ara tree which stood in a clearing near the river. It turned its head once more to look at the prince as if to make sure he was still there, and then entered the gnarly bark of the tree.

Up above, the sun was about to set. The prince took a step towards the tree but froze when he heard laughter like the sound of crackling leaves. He crept closer and peered into the bark, and was surprised to see a tiny old man sitting cross-legged inside the tree speaking to the squirrel.

'My dear, every morning you escape from me but my curse brings you back every night,' cackled the old man. 'This is your father's fault, Princess. If he had not banished me, I would not have cursed you.' The old man leaned back and smiled to himself.

'And here you will stay forever Princess Gemalai Suri, for the curse will only be broken if another speaks your name.' The Squirrel Princess looked down at her paws and a tiny teardrop fell on her cheeks.

The prince decided to spend the night nearby. The next morning, he was up before the break of dawn and hid behind a bush near the ara tree. As soon as the sky brightened, the squirrel leaped out of the tree and headed towards the river. The prince followed, making sure to stay hidden.

The squirrel stopped by the edge of the river and began to scoop up water into her tiny paws to drink. Just then, the prince stepped out from behind a boulder.

'Please, do not be afraid. I am a prince from a neighbouring land.' The squirrel inclined her head and looked at the prince.

'I believe that you are a special squirrel,' he continued. The Squirrel Princess stood up straighter and slowly approached the prince.

'Could it be that your name is, Princess Gemalai Suri?' said the prince with a small smile.

Almost immediately, a white mist surrounded the squirrel and when it cleared, there stood before him a girl who shared the same dark eyes as the squirrel. Running through her long dark hair was a strand of silver.

The Princess closed her eyes and smiled. 'You have spoken my name and lifted the terrible curse from me. I thank you with all my heart.'

The prince was enchanted by the princess and stepped forward to take her hand. He led her out of the jungle and back to his kingdom where eventually, the two lived happily ever after.

* * *

This fairy tale originates from Malaysia and falls under the category of stories about curses inflicted on someone. It's an interesting story for a variety of reasons. Firstly, the use of a name to break a spell is reminiscent of the European fairy tale of Rumpelstiltskin. Secondly, the names of the places used in this tale such as Kampung Negeri Berasap (which literally means 'the village of the smoky country') and the country of Antah Berantah (which means 'in the middle of nowhere') are commonly used names for imaginary places in Malay mythology. These names can be found in other folk tales as well.

Chapter 29

The Tale of Chi Wi
(Malaysia)

Once there was a princess who had itchy feet and could not keep still. Every day she ran about the palace gardens, climbing trees, falling into ditches, and getting into trouble. Her mother, the queen, was fraught with worry for they lived near the sea and she had a great fear that her daughter would one day vanish into the water. In her nightmares, a strange creature called Chi Wi came and took away her precious daughter. As a result, the princess was never allowed to bathe or swim in the sea or the river. The servants had to carry great big pots of water from the river in order to bathe her.

Years passed and the little princess grew up to become a beautiful and clever young lady. Unfortunately, growing up did little to cure her of her itchy feet. She still could not sit still and loved to run off to discover new places.

'Daughter, promise me you will not go near the sea. Do not even step foot into the water for if you do, Chi Wi will come and get you. He looks for young ladies to catch, and when he catches them, he takes them away and they are never seen again.'

'What does he do to them?' asked the Princess.

'I do not know, but it cannot be good. Maybe he eats them. You don't want to be eaten, do you?' said the queen trying to scare her daughter.

'No, I do not want to be eaten. What shall I do if I meet Chi Wi, mother?' asked the princess. The queen looked thoughtful for a while and then answered, 'Tell him that he must release you because you know his name. Once you know a thing's name, you have power over it. That's what my mother used to tell me.'

The princess promised her mother that she would never, ever go into the sea. However, she was such a forgetful girl and prone to excitement that she soon forgot her mother's warning. One hot sweltering day, the princess found herself alone on the shore. The sun was beating down on her and she felt terribly warm and flustered.

'Wouldn't it be nice to dip my toes into the sea, just for a little while?' she said to herself. 'It couldn't do any harm. I will not go to the deep end.' And so the princess took off her slippers and began to wade into the edge of the water. The water was so cool and refreshing, and soon her toes began to feel refreshed.

'Ah, I think I will go in a little more. The water is calm and there is no danger here,' she said to herself as she walked further into the sea. The salty breeze blew on her face and the princess felt happy. She didn't realize that she was walking further and further into the sea until the water reached up to her neck, and the strands of her dark hair began to float around her head.

Suddenly, a cloud covered the warm rays of the sun and it became dark. The waves lapped at her cheeks and she felt her body sinking deeper into the sea. The princess became frightened and immediately tried to swim back to the shore, but she found that she could not move her legs. Something, which felt like a fishing net, had wrapped itself around her legs, trapping them. The net moved up her body until it held her tight. At first, the princess was frightened, but as the net began to tighten its hold around her body, she could feel herself getting angry.

'Who are you? How dare you hold me against my will! Release me at once,' she commanded. The net-like creature stopped moving as if it was surprised by her words. Its other victims had never spoken to him like this before.

'Are you not frightened of me, princess?' asked the creature in a low, dangerous voice.

'Of course, I'm frightened, but that does not give you the right to hold me against my will. You must release me for I know your name,' she replied, remembering what her mother had told her.

'You know my name, Princess?' said the voice which was now sounding less sure of itself.

'Yes, I do. You must release me at once.'

'No, tell me my name first,' replied the voice.

'Your name is Chi Wi.'

All at once, the net-like hold on her body vanished and the princess found that she could float freely in the water once more. Around her, the water began to churn and in front of her, a whirlpool appeared. A spray of water exploded out of the centre of the whirlpool and a moment later, a head popped out of the sea. A handsome man with dark eyes smiled at her. He could not stop smiling at the princess and she soon began to feel a little flustered.

'Who are you? Why are you smiling at me in such a way? Where is Chi Wi?' she asked.

'I was Chi Wi, but you have broken the curse put on me by an evil sorcerer. I am a man once more, thanks to you,' said the man.

'So, you're not going to take me away and eat me?' she asked a little uncertainly. The man laughed.

'I won't eat you,' he said, still smiling.

'Well, if that's the case then we should go back to the palace so you can meet my mother. I would like to introduce her to you .' The princess took the man back to the palace to show her mother that Chi-Wi was no longer a frightening creature. The princess thought that she quite liked the handsome man and they eventually married and live happily ever after.

* * *

This fairy tale is also known as *The Chi Wi* and comes from Malaysia. It is contained in the book, *Tangga Tales: A Collection of Malay Folk Tales* (Oxford University Press, 1952) and is told within a frame story of a grandmother telling stories from the 'tangga', or steps of her house. Like the story of *The Squirrel Princess,* the curse is broken by saying the name of the person under the curse. This time, it is the princess who breaks the curse. In the original story, Chi Wi takes the princess back to his country, marries her, and they live happily ever after.

Chapter 30

Si Tanggang
(Malaysia)

Si Tanggang was the much-loved son of Si Dalang and Si Deruma who lived in a ramshackle hut by the sea. Si Dalang and Si Deruma were true people of the land, working and tilling the soil from dawn to dusk, but their young son was different. He was destined for a greater life. Every day the boy would stare out at the open waters with a longing he could not understand. The blue water, the sound of the waves crashing onto the shore, and the smell of salt in the air seemed to call out to him, beckoning him to its watery arms.

'When I am older, I shall go out to the sea, Mama. I will make my fortune there.' Si Deruma frowned at her young son. Like everyone else in the village, she had a deep mistrust of the open waters.

'We are people of the land, my son. We work on the land and grow our rice to feed our families. This is how we have always lived. The sea provides us with some bounty, but it is not a place for people like us.'

Si Tanggang listened to his mother and nodded obediently, but deep in his heart he could not believe that something so beautiful could be such an awful thing. He saw how difficult it was to make a living from the land; the long, back-breaking hours working under the sun to grow grains of rice. There must be a better way of living, he thought to himself.

Although Si Dalang and Si Deruma were poor, they felt like the wealthiest couple in the world for they were blessed with their beloved son who soon grew up into a handsome, strong, young man. As soon as he was old enough, he joined his parents and the other villagers on the paddy field. Every day, even before the sun was up, Si Tanggang would be out on the field, tending to the crops, laying traps for the mice and birds that threatened the harvest, and harvesting the paddy and turning it into rice once the paddy was ready. He was a hard-worker and respected by the other villagers, but he was unhappy. Each evening, as the sun set over the sea, he would stare out and wonder what his life would be like on the sea.

One sunny day, a big ship appeared in the horizon and anchored in their bay. Si Tanggang could not believe his eyes for ships of that size rarely came to their small village. With his heart thundering in his chest, Si Tanggang ran to the harbour with the other curious villagers to watch as sailors from the vessel climbed down into rowing boats and made their way to the shore.

'Welcome to our village,' said the Penghulu, the head of the village. The sailors smiled and greeted everyone with a cheerful wave as the villagers came forward to inspect the exotic and wonderful items brought by them, like salt, spices, and rolls of batik cloth from lands unknown.

One of the sailors noticed Si Tanggang staring at the big ship anchored in the harbour. The boy had a far-off look in his eye which the sailor immediately recognized. He approached Si Tanggang and noticed that the boy was sturdy and tall.

'You seem to like our big ship,' said the sailor.

'It is truly a thing of beauty. Please sir, could you tell me how something so huge can move like the wind on the water?' The sailor stared at Si Tanggang, surprised by his words. And then he burst into laughter for he knew that the boy had the sea in his veins. 'Well, if you really want to find out, then you must come and sail with us, son.' Si Tanggang almost fell down when he heard these words.

'Would you take someone like me? I mean, would it be possible for me to work on the ship?' he asked, his voice quavering with excitement.

'You look fit and strong, and eager to learn. Why not? My captain has asked me to recruit some young men to come work with him.

You are more than welcome to join us.' The sailor looked at Si Tanggang. 'Settle your business and meet me here tomorrow at dawn. That is when we will row back to the big ship and sail away.'

For the first time in a long while, Si Tanggang felt a lightness in his heart. This was what he had desired all his life—to go out to sea and earn a living in the deep blue. He ran home to seek permission from his parents. He knew this would make them unhappy, but it was the one thing he desired most. Surely they would understand.

'You both know it has always been my dream to sail the open seas. Please give me permission to join the crew. I promise I will make you proud. I will make my fortune and you will never have to work on the paddy field again.' His parents could see that their son had already made up his mind, and with a heavy heart gave their blessings. That night Si Deruma cried silent tears.

Just before dawn, Si Tanggang kissed his father's hands and embraced his mother. He gathered a few precious items and ran back to the shore to join the other sailors making their way back to the big ship.

Once he was on board, Si Tanggang was overcome by the feeling that he had finally found the place where he belonged. He loved the sway of the ship over the waves, the wind in his hair, and the smell of the salt in the air. Here, he felt truly free.

Si Tanggang was quick and eager to learn everything about life on the ship. He scrubbed the wooden planks, cooked the meals, washed clothes, learned to tie knots, and put up the sail. He was hardworking and diligent, and his good work and attitude caught the eye of the ship's captain who took the young man under his wing. Soon Si Tanggang was not only learning how to lead a sailing ship, but also how to navigate the waters and establish trading ties. Years passed and Si Tanggang matured and grew into a wealthy captain of his own ship. The sultan was so impressed that he agreed to marry his daughter to Si Tanggang.

One day, Si Tanggang decided to take his new bride on a tour of the islands and by sheer coincidence happened to stop at the harbour facing the shores of his old village. At the village, rumour soon spread that Si Tanggang had returned. Si Deruma and Si Dalang held their arms up in the air to thank god for bringing their son home. Si Deruma quickly prepared her son's favourite meal—grilled bananas and fish wrapped in banana leaf. Si Dalang and Si Deruma rowed their old rickety sampan towards the big ship.

'Captain Tanggang, there is an old couple here to see you,' announced a young sailor. Si Tanggang frowned and wondered who had come. He walked with his wife to the side of the ship and saw an old couple dressed in rags holding a tray of food. When the old woman saw him she burst into tears.

'Oh my son, you have finally come back to us. Every day I prayed to God for your safety and good fortune,' cried Si Deruma.

'My son, it is good to see you again,' said Si Dalang with tears in his eyes.

For the longest time, Si Tanggang could not move or say a word. He had been so busy making his fortune that he had not spared a thought for his parents. He looked at their old, weathered faces and the rags they wore, and he felt ashamed of them.

'Husband, who are these people? Are they truly your parents?' asked his new bride. Si Tanggang felt heat rising to his cheeks. He could not let his princess know that this was where he came from.

'I do not know these people,' said Si Tanggang, his voice cold and cruel. 'Take them away. I do not want to see them here again.'

'Tanggang!' pleaded his mother. 'What has become of you, my son? I am your mother. Have you forgotten me?' Si Tanggang swallowed and clenched his jaw.

'You are not my mother,' he spat. 'And you are not my father. Go now, before I sink your sampan.'

Si Deruma felt, as if her world had collapsed. The only thing that kept her going all these years was the thought that perhaps one day, her beloved son would return. She never dreamed he would commit such a sin as this. Si Dalang slowly rowed back to shore listening to his wife's sobs. When they reached land, Si Deruma looked up at the big ship.

'My son has forsaken me. I ask God to punish him for his sin.' Si Deruma's words echoed in the wind and for a moment everything stood still. The sky darkened as a storm approached.

'Look at that cloud! It is coming for the big ship,' shouted someone from the village. Si Deruma and Si Dalang looked up and saw a thick black cloud approaching their son's ship. The wind which had been soft and gentle just moments before, was now fierce and howling. The water churned making the big ship rock and sway. The villagers could hear the sailors screaming and pleading for help. In the sky, the sound of thunder roared and a bolt of lightning hit the sails setting fire to the ship. Just then, a massive wall of water crashed down onto the ship, destroying everything in its path.

When the storm died, the villagers saw that the Si Tanggang's ship had turned into stone. The waves washed up curious objects onto the shore—rock statues of people who looked very much like the sailors on the ship. Si Deruma and Si Dalang walked among the rocky corpses until they found him, their son. Si Tanggang had his arms up in the air as if pleading for mercy which never came.

* * *

This folk tale originates from Malaysia and is one of the most well-known folk tales in Southeast Asia and the Nusantara. The seafaring nature of *Si Tanggang* is a reflection of the way in which this tale has travelled throughout Southeast Asia.

In Malaysia, we know this story as the tale of *Si Tanggang*, but he has different names in other parts of Southeast Asia, although the storyline remains the same. In Indonesia, he is known Malim Kundang (West Sumatra) and Lancang Kuning (Riau). In Brunei, he is known as Mahkota Manis. In other parts of Southeast Asia, the title of this story is taken from the various rock formations which are said to have come from the mother's curse. The same story also takes its name from rock formations such as *The Story of Sampuraga* (in Central Kalimantan), *Supirak* (in Sabah, Malaysia), and *The Origins of Mount Batu Banawa* (in Indonesia). These rock formations include islands, mountains and hills which resemble a ship.

The story of Si Tanggang began as an oral tale, but this story is also contained in Walter Skeat's book, *Malay Magic*. In this book, the story which is called *Charitra Megat Sajobang* was told to Skeats by the Selangor Malays. The main character was originally of Sakai descent (one of the indigenous Orang Asli people of West Malaysia). However, over the years, through movies and books, this character was transformed from an Orang Asli to a Malay, with the name of Si Tanggang. Once again, this is an example of how these stories have changed and adapted over the years.

In the places where these stories are said to take place are rock formations which resemble people and ships. It is said that the Batu Caves in West Malaysia is the actual ship of Si Tanggang. On Supirak island in Sabah, there is a huge boulder in the shape of a ship. In Indonesia, there is a rock formation called Batu Malim Kundang which looks like a man bending down begging for mercy.

The story of Si Tanggang contains an important message which applies to cultures across Asia, and that is this concept of filial piety. The Malay term which describes this concept is 'derhaka', which denotes the act of betraying one's elders. The moralistic ending of these stories shows a cultural disapproval of disobeying your elders. In general, society is on the side of the mother and in all versions of this story (no matter which country it comes from), the punishment faced by the son reflects a universal understanding that a mother's care is not unconditional. At least in this part of the world, children are indebted to their mothers, to their parents, and it is believed, those who disobey will face the consequences.

Chapter 31

Bawang Putih Bawang Merah
and the Magic Swing
(Malaysia, Indonesia)

Once there was a man who had two wives: each gave birth to a beautiful daughter. The daughter of the first wife was called Bawang Putih, and she was sweet and lovely. The daughter of the second wife was called Bawang Merah. She was beautiful, but cruel and lazy. The first wife was a kind, gentle woman who was much loved by her husband. The second one was beautiful, but her heart was dark and filled with envy. All she could think of was how to get rid of the first wife.

'If I were the first wife, my life would be so much better. Bawang Merah would never have to worry about her future.' She was convinced that the only way to survive in this harsh world was to get rid of her rival.

One day, the second wife saw the first wife leaning over the side of the river washing clothes. It had rained all night and the current was fast. *This is my chance to get rid of her*, she thought to herself.

The evil woman crept up to the first wife and without a second thought, pushed her into the river where she was washed away by the strong current. The second wife pretended to faint and grieved for days.

'Oh, if only she had been more careful. How could she fall in? What will we do now? I loved her like my own sister,' lamented the second wife, who was now the first wife.

Bawang Putih was distraught at the loss of her beloved mother but she stayed strong and gave comfort to her grieving father. She vowed that she would help care for her family because she knew this was what her mother would have wanted her to do.

A few weeks passed and slowly, bit by bit, life began to change in the household. The second wife was now head of the household. She got rid of all the servants and ordered Bawang Putih to take over the chores.

'This is how you can repay me for the burden of caring for you.'

She took away all of Bawang Putih's beautiful clothes and jewels, and gave her rags to wear. 'After all, you do not need to wear such nice dresses to cook and clean.'

One day, she ordered Bawang Putih to move out of her room altogether. 'You are so dirty and disgusting from all that cleaning. I do not want you in the house. Go and sleep in the outhouse in the garden.'

Father was still grieving over the loss of his beloved wife and had buried himself in his work, so he did not notice how Bawang Putih was being badly treated by her stepmother. Meanwhile, Bawang Merah enjoyed a lavish and carefree life. She woke up when the sun was high in the sky and demanded a breakfast of coconut rice with sambal and fried eggs. She then spent all day trying on the new clothes and jewels her mother had bought for her. Bawang Merah could see how hard her stepsister was working, but she did not lift a finger to help.

'I am now the daughter of the first wife and I deserve to have a comfortable life,' said Bawang Merah to her sister.

Bawang Putih did not say anything about her mistreatment and continued to work hard for the family. She woke up at the crack of dawn to make breakfast for the family, to collect water from the well and wash the clothes, clean the house, and tend to the vegetable patch. She worked diligently and never complained. At least the work helped take her mind off her troubles.

One day, as she was feeding the fish in the pond just outside the house, she thought she heard the sound of her mother singing an old lullaby.

'Why are you so sad, my love?' said a voice from the pond.

Bawang Putih looked into the water and saw a golden fish peering at her just below the surface. 'I miss my mother. Life is very hard now, but I could bear it if only I could see mother one more time.'

'Do not be sad, Bawang Putih. I am here, and I will always be here for you,' replied the fish.

Bawang Putih looked at the fish and realized that it was her mother. 'Is that really you, mother?'

'Yes, you can come see me every day if you wish. I will help you with all your work and ease your burden. I am your mother after all,' said the magical fish.

Bawang Putih was so happy that she began to walk around with an extra spring in her step. The colour came back to her cheeks making her even more beautiful and no matter how much work the stepmother piled on, Bawang Putih was able to complete it with a smile on her lips.

'Something odd is going on here,' thought the stepmother. One day, she decided to spy on Bawang Putih and found the girl deep in conversation with the fish in the pond. The stepmother could see that the fish was a source of comfort to Bawang Putih and immediately resolved to kill it. When Bawang Putih left the pond, the stepmother caught and killed the fish with her bare hands. She fried the fish and gave it to Bawang Putih.

'Eat this. I fried it just for you.' And because Bawang Putih was always hungry, she ate the fish leaving just the bones which were then scattered underneath the house.

The next day, Bawang Putih went to visit her mother at the pond, but she was not there. Later that night, Bawang Putih had a dream about her mother who told her what the wicked stepmother had done.

'Collect my bones and bury them in the garden. Something wonderful will happen,' said her mother in her dreams. In the morning, Bawang Putih woke up in tears. She could not believe that she had lost her mother once again. She quickly looked under the house and saw the fish bones scattered all around. Just then, an army of black ants crept towards her and began to gather all the fish bones together. Bawang Putih watched in amazement as the ants collected the bones and arranged it in a pile.

'Thank you, my friends. I am forever grateful to you,' said Bawang Putih who took the bones and buried them at the bottom of the garden. The next day, a tiny shoot emerged out of the ground and the day after that, the shoot grew into a sturdy plant. Bawang Putih watered and cared for the plant until it grew into a beautiful tree and one day, the tree produced a golden swing which seemed to be made just for Bawang Putih. As soon as she sat on it, the swing swayed and a song filled the air. Bawang Putih was so happy that she began to sing the song her mother had taught her. Her beautiful lilting voice was carried through the forest and attracted the attention of a passing prince who was out hunting with his men.

Mesmerized by the beautiful singing, the prince followed the sound of Bawang Putih's voice to her house. When he arrived, the stepmother forced Bawang Putih to hide under the house.

'Who is singing that song?' asked the prince.

'Oh, that is my daughter, Bawang Merah,' replied the wicked stepmother. She presented her daughter to the prince who thought that the girl was very pretty indeed, but he had to make sure she was the right girl.

'Please sing that song again,' said the prince.

Bawang Merah cleared her throat and began to sing, but she was not much of a singer and what came out of her lips was nothing but screeches and yelps. The prince had to cover his ears.

'This is not the girl who was singing. Is there anyone else here?' asked the prince.

'No, there is no one else.'

Just then, the swing swayed even though there was no wind. A voice rang out from the tree. 'There is someone. She is under the house. Call her out! Call her out!'

The prince ordered the stepmother to bring Bawang Putih out and then she had no choice but to abide. Bawang Putih smiled at the prince and sat on her swing to sing her beautiful song. The prince was so enraptured by Bawang Putih that he took her back to palace where they were wed and they lived happily ever after. As for the wicked stepmother and Bawang Merah, well, they were never heard from again.

* * *

This tale is also known as *Bawang Merah Bawang Putih*, and in some versions, Bawang Merah is the good sister. There are variations of this tale all over Southeast Asia, but it is most popular in Malaysia and Indonesia where the tale has been adapted into different forms such as picture books, movies, and dramas. *Bawang Putih* means 'garlic' and *Bawang Merah* means 'shallot', which are two essential ingredients in Southeast Asian cooking.

There is some evidence that this type of tale has been in existence since as early as 850 BCE. The story of Ye Xian from China has similar traits with the mother going through various transformations in order to help her daughter. The strength and popularity of this tale is supported by the fact that this story has spread throughout Southeast Asia. Variations of this tale can be found in Indonesia (*Leungli*) and Vietnam (*The Tale of Tam and Cam*), and there is also a similar story called *The Magic Swing* from Malaysia. This story also shares the same theme as *The Tale of the Honey Tree* from Sarawak where the unfair treatment faced by the two main protagonists has propelled them to take active steps in order to secure their future. At the very heart of the story is the issue of conflict and rivalry brought about by limited resources, and made worse by a polygamous marriage. Not only is there rivalry between the two stepsisters, there is also rivalry between the two wives.

Chapter 32

The Three Princesses and Prince Andriamohamona (Madagascar)

Once there were three princess sisters who lived in a small village on the island of Madagascar. The Sisters were all quite pretty but the most beautiful sister was the youngest, and this made the other two jealous. The two older sisters always tried to find a way to put the youngest sister down.

One day, a grand procession arrived in their village and caused quite a stir especially amongst the maidens. A gentleman prince from a neighbouring kingdom arrived bearing a golden staff. His name was Prince Andriamohamona and he was the most handsome man to have ever stepped foot in the village. All the maidens swooned at the sight of the prince. The prince met the king of the village and declared that he would like to find a wife amongst one of the three princesses.

When the sisters were informed of this, they were so excited that they fell into a faint and could not be revived for several hours.

'Please wake up, Princesses. We must get you ready for the prince,' said their servants.

When they were revived, the sisters bathed themselves in perfumed water and put on their best dresses and jewels. The three sisters began to talk about what they would do if they were picked to become the prince's wife.

The eldest princess declared that, 'If I marry the prince, I will make a pretty mat out of little reeds and put it under the mattress so we can both rest there.'

The middle princess declared , 'If I marry the prince, I will make a mat from fine straw to serve as our bed.'

The youngest princess said, 'As for me, the sweet potato I am going to eat will become our child.'

The sisters waited for the prince to come courting. They waited till noon but he was nowhere to be seen. They waited till sunset and still, he had not come. By the time the moon was high in the sky, the sisters had given up and went to bed. The next day, the sisters got ready to receive the prince once more but this time the eldest sister came up with a plan.

'Instead of waiting for Prince Adrianmohamona to come here, we should go to him. He is staying at our father's second home in the village.'

'That is a wonderful idea, sister,' said the middle sister. 'It is not too far to walk there and on the way, we can hold a beauty pageant to see who is the most beautiful amongst us.'

Beauty pageants were very popular on the island, and the maidens enjoyed competing against each other to see who was the prettiest and most accomplished. Unfortunately, the two older sisters had forgotten just how beautiful the youngest sister was. They were beaten by the youngest sister in every category and they both felt very low.

'How dare she beat us?' said the eldest sister.

'She is only the youngest sister. We cannot allow her to win,' said the middle sister.

Together, the two sisters came up with a plan to make sure that the youngest sister was not chosen by the prince.

'Youngest sister, since we are older than you, we have more of a right to marry the prince. Therefore, you must pretend to be our slave,' said the eldest one. Even though the youngest sister did not want to pretend to be her sisters' slave, she did not want to upset them either, and agreed. The two evil sisters shaved off her beautiful long hair, they covered her face in dirt to make her ugly and forced her to wear rags.

'There, you really look like our slave now. We shall call you "Sandroy",' teased the middle sister.

Fortunately, a rat saw what was happening and decided to help the youngest sister. When the two older sisters had left, the rat walked up to her, who was by then crying.

'Tell me girl. Do you want to marry the prince?' asked the rat.

'I just want a fair chance to marry him,' replied the youngest sister.

'Then I shall grant you your wish,' said the rat. The rat used her magical powers to restore the youngest sister's long, beautiful hair. The rat also gave her a magnificent dress and new slippers to wear.

The two older sisters arrived and were so excited to meet Prince Andriamohamona that they did not notice that their youngest sister was beautiful once more. They did not notice that her hair was long and lustrous and that she was wearing a new flowing gown and sparkling slippers. The prince however noticed that a beautiful girl was carrying the bags of the two sisters.

'Prince Adrianmohamona, we have come here with our servants to give you a warm welcome to our village,' announced the eldest sister.

The prince was confused because the beautiful girl did not look like a slave. He immediately called the youngest sister over and asked her, 'Who are you? Are you really the slave of those two sisters?'

'No, Prince Adrianmohamona,' she replied truthfully. 'I am their youngest sister. On the way here, my sisters shaved my hair, gave me rags to wear, and forced me to be their slave. However, a rat came to my rescue and here I am.'

Upon hearing this the prince became angry and banished the two evil sisters from the village.

'You have acted wickedly towards your sibling. I cast you out of this village.' The two sisters were chased out with boos and jeers before transforming into little lizards. 'Sandroy' however, married Prince Andriamohamona, and together they lived happily ever after.

* * *

This story is also known as *The Three Princesses and Andriamohamona* and originates from Madagascar. This tale is included in this collection as Madagascar shares the Austronesian language. This story is contained in the book titled, *Stars and Keys: Folktales and Creolization in the Indian*

Ocean (Lee Haring, Indiana University Press, 2007). The overall theme of this fairy tale is sibling rivalry, in particular the intense competition between the two older sisters and the youngest. In tales featuring sibling rivalry (such as the Indonesian stories of *Molek* and *Tattadu*), the order of birth plays an important role. It can be said that the two older unmarried sisters may have a sense of entitlement over the youngest sister and feel that it is unfair if the younger sister were to win the heart of the prince. In order to avoid 'losing face' the two older sisters collaborate to ensure that the younger sister does not attract the attention of the prince.

Chapter 33

Bawang Putih Bawang Merah and the Magic Pumpkin (Indonesia)

A long time ago in a faraway land, there lived a little girl called Bawang Putih. For many years she lived happily with her mother and father in a small house by the river. Sadly, Bawang Putih's mother passed away, and her father was filled with enough grief and despair that could have filled a whole ocean. With the death of his beloved wife, he too, lost his way.

Sometimes when people are lost, they do strange and peculiar things. And this is what happened to Bawang Putih's father. One day he woke up and found himself married to another woman, a widow with her own daughter called Bawang Merah. The two stepsisters were both beautiful, but whereas Bawang Putih was kind and gentle, Bawang Merah's heart was full of hate and greed. The family lived together in the house by the river; the father worked hard and always managed to provide more than enough for the women in his family. However, the stepmother and her daughter had a lavish lifestyle and were constantly buying some expensive item or another. Bawang Putih being a sensible girl did not care for such trinkets and was happy just to be with her father.

One unfortunate day, the father died after a short illness leaving the stepmother to care for Bawang Putih and Bawang Merah. The woman hated the thought that she would have to once again work for a living, this time not only to support her own daughter, but also the stepdaughter she had come to despise. Resentment filled her heart and she began a cruel campaign against Bawang Putih.

'Bawang Putih, we can no longer afford our servants, so you must now do all the chores. Do you understand?'

'Yes, Stepmother,' replied Bawang Putih, happy to be of any service to her new family.

Every day Bawang Putih worked hard. However, her stepsister Bawang Merah, was lazy and did not lift a finger to help. The girl was vain and spent all day staring at her beautiful image in her looking glass. From dawn to dusk, Bawang Putih cleaned, cooked, mended clothes, chopped wood, and tended to the farm animals and the vegetable garden. The evil stepmother sold all of Bawang Putih's beautiful dresses and left her with only rags to wear. She was even forced to sleep in the servant's small room next to the kitchen where it was always damp and musty.

But the sweet-natured Bawang Putih did not mind. She was heartbroken when her father passed away and she felt happy that she could at least, help care for her stepfamily. One bright morning, Bawang Putih was washing clothes by the river when her stepmother's best sarong batik fell into the water and floated downstream. Bawang Putih followed the batik as it made its way down the river until it finally flowed into a cave. At the entrance of the cave stood a withered grey woman who bent down to pick up the sarong.

'Is this yours, my child?' she asked. Bawang Putih smiled and came forward. 'Thank you, Nenek. It belongs to my stepmother.' Nenek stared into the girl's sweet face and after a while, she spoke.

'Come and help me with some chores. Once you've finished, I will give you the batik, together with a little present.' Nenek gestured for the girl to follow her. They walked into the mouth of the cave which was dark and smelled of jasmine. Bawang Putih reached out to hold Nenek's hand, guiding the old woman as they made their way through the watery cave. Eventually, they emerged out the other end onto a beautiful green field. Bawang Putih could see something growing across the field and after walking for a while, she found out what it was.

'Pumpkins,' she smiled, as she squeezed Nenek's hands. 'I do love pumpkins, especially steamed and dusted with sugar and grated coconut. Father used to bring back the most delicious pumpkins from the market.'

'Come my child, my house is very close by,' said Nenek. They walked through the field and soon arrived at Nenek's house. Without being told what to do, Bawang Putih set to work hanging out laundry to dry in the sun, sweeping the leaves, and cutting some pumpkins to steam. She served it on a plate with a dusting of sugar and grated coconut.

'This is delicious, my child,' said Nenek as she ate the tender sweet flesh of the pumpkin. When she finished, Nenek brought out two pumpkins as a gift to Bawang Putih; a big pumpkin the size of a lantern, and a small one which fit nicely in the palm of her hands. Being a sensible girl, Bawang Putih chose the smaller pumpkin, knowing that its flesh would be tender and sweet. She kissed Nenek's soft cheeks and left for home with her stepmother's batik and the pumpkin.

Stepmother was furious with Bawang Putih for being late and she beat the poor girl with a stick. Feeling scared, Bawang Putih tried to explain what had happened and handed over the small pumpkin, but Stepmother merely flung the pumpkin onto the ground. The pumpkin shattered open and to their amazement, they found treasure spilling out of the pumpkin. There were gold and silver coins, rubies and emeralds, diamonds the size of a large rock. There were so many treasures that Bawang Putih wondered how it had all fit into the tiny pumpkin.

'Where did you get these treasures?' asked Bawang Merah, her eyes wide with wonder and greed.

Once more, Bawang Putih told the story of the old woman who lived at the bottom of the river on the other side of the cave. This time her stepmother and stepsister listened carefully and did not interrupt. When Bawang Putih finished telling her tale, they knew exactly what to do.

Early the next morning, Bawang Merah took the washing down to the river but instead of cleaning the clothes, she simply threw in her mother's batik scarf. It flowed down the river until it reached the mouth of the cave where Bawang Merah saw an old, haggard woman sitting on a rock.

'Is this yours, my child?' croaked Nenek. Bawang Merah nodded.

'Come and help me with some chores. Once you've finished I will return the scarf together with a little present,' said Nenek.

'Very well, take me to your home, old woman,' ordered Bawang Merah. Nenek turned and led Bawang Merah into the dark cave. When they reached Nenek's house, Bawang Merah could see a field of pumpkins and her heart fluttered at the thought of all the treasures. She knew that she had to perform some chores for the woman first, but she felt she was above such menial tasks.

'Old woman, give me the largest pumpkin you have. I want it now,' ordered Bawang Merah. Nenek stared at Bawang Merah for the longest time, not saying a word. And then she turned and shuffled towards the field with Bawang Merah trailing not far behind. Just beyond a tall clump of grass was a large, perfectly round pumpkin which glinted under the light of the sun. Bawang Merah rushed towards it, and even though it was heavy, she heaved it up and without a word of thanks, made her way back home.

'Mother, see here, I have brought even more treasures,' said the greedy Bawang Merah. Stepmother rubbed her hands together and quickly fetched the parang from the kitchen. Bawang Putih excused herself as she wanted to finish cooking their meal and left them to their treasure which is why she did not witness the terrible thing that happened next. Stepmother swung the parang into the pumpkin and cut it in half, but instead of gold and jewels spilling out from its belly, something altogether more sinister slithered out. Snakes! Hundreds and hundreds of poisonous snakes came out and in two breaths covered the stepmother and Bawang Merah and devoured them until there was nothing left.

In the kitchen Bawang Putih thought she heard a hissing sound, but when she looked out the window she saw nothing but a blue bird chirping in the willow tree.

* * *

This is a completely different Bawang Putih Bawang Merah story which features the same core characters of Bawang Putih, Bawang Merah, and the stepmother. Bawang Putih's dead mother is not present in this story and the emphasis seems to be on this idea of good and bad deeds. This version of Bawang Putih Bawang Merah is also popular in Indonesia and Malaysia.

This story falls under the category of tales of good deeds and bad deeds, and recognizes the agency of the wise, respected female figure who has the power to reward or punish in this tale. There is a clear didactic element in this story in the way that it shows how good deeds and good intentions are rewarded to the kind and helpful Bawang Putih. On the other hand, Bawang Merah and the stepmother are severely punished as a result of their greed, cruelty, and unkindness. In the past, these types of exemplary stories were told to children in order to encourage good behaviour. It is clear that these kinds of folk tales reflect desirable social values—being kind and helpful to those in need of help.

This version of *Bawang Putih Bawang Merah* is quite similar to the Grimm's tale of *The Three Little Men in the Woods*, the Thai story of *Phikul Thong* and *The Gift of the Winter Melon* from Sabah which also has been included in this collection.

Chapter 34

The Tale of the Honey Tree
(Malaysia)

Si Jurai was a lonely boy who lived in a longhouse deep in the jungles of Sarawak. His mother and father had passed away a long time ago, and the poor orphan only had his grandmother to care for him. By right, the people of his longhouse were supposed to take care of those who had fallen on hard times, but the chief of the longhouse was cruel and greedy and only wanted to take care of his own family.

One day, a man brought home honey from the jungle and as with the custom of the Bidayuh people, a huge banana leaf was laid down in the front garden. The honeycomb, oozing with sweet nectar, was placed on the banana leaf, and each person from the longhouse came up to enjoy their share of the delicious bounty. All the children squealed with joy as they tasted the sweet treat, but there was one child who did not get his share. Si Jurai stood behind a nearby tree and watched as everyone enjoyed the honey.

'That orphan is skulking around watching us. Maybe we should give him some honey,' said one of the older boys.

'Why should we be bothered by him? He's a nobody. I'm sure he's not interested in tasting something as fine as this,' replied another boy. However, they were wrong. Si Jurai's mouth watered at the sight of the honey and he longed to have a little taste. When the feast was over and everyone had left, Si Jurai crept closer to the banana leaf and to his delight, found a tiny drop of honey left. Gingerly, he scooped the precious morsel with his finger and was just about to put it in his mouth when he remembered his grandmother. Si Jurai wanted to share the honey with his grandmother and immediately raced home to look for her.

'Look Grandmother! I have honey for us to share.' Grandmother saw a tiny drop of honey on the tip of Si Jurai's fingers.

'Why did they give you honey like that? They should put it on a piece of banana leaf. That is the way,' she commented.

'Oh, they didn't share the honey with me, Grandmother. I had to wait till everyone was finished to see if there was any leftover, and I found some. Aren't we lucky?' Si Jurai looked so pleased with himself that it broke grandmother's heart.

'Oh my poor child. How cruel is this world to us? We live in a longhouse where everyone is supposed to share and take care of each other and yet, you are treated so unfairly. Whenever you catch fish in the river, you share it with the whole house for you are a good soul. However, when someone finds honey, they cannot even spare a morsel for you.'

Grandmother looked so sad that it made Si Jurai cry. 'Grandmother, I am fine. I am grateful for even this tiny bit of honey.' Grandmother's face suddenly changed as if an angry spirit had taken over her body. It frightened Si Jurai.

'Something bad will happen to the people in this longhouse. They have forgotten our customs and ways. Si Jurai, one day I will no longer be here to take care of you. My bones are brittle and my body is broken.'

'Oh, Grandmother, don't say that!'

'If I am no longer here, you must come and look for me. I will be at the second bend of the river. Look for me there,' instructed Grandmother.

Si Jurai promised he would, but he was distraught at the thought of losing his grandmother. Over the next few days, he kept close to her and refused to let her out of his sight, but one day, he had to go out to look for food and when he came back to their shabby room, grandmother was gone.

'Please, help me look for her,' pleaded Si Jurai to the chief who simply sniffed and looked away.

'Humph, the sun has already set. Why should I send good men out into the dark jungle to look for that old lady?' said the chief. No one in the longhouse wanted to help Si Jurai, no matter how much he pleaded.

The next morning, Si Jurai remembered his grandmother's words and ran to the second bend of the river. He called out to her and looked everywhere, but all he saw were the morning birds chirping in the branches of the trees. Feeling desperate, Si Jurai fell to his knees and prayed for a miracle.

'Si Jurai, why are you crying? I am right here,' said a voice which blew in from the wind. The boy looked up at the sound of the voice and noticed a tall tualang tree he had never noticed before. He wiped his tears and stood up.

'Grandmother?'

'I am here. I am the tree you see in front of you.' The branches of the tualang tree moved as if waving to him and the breeze brought the sweet warm smell of his grandmother. A faint buzzing could be heard up above and when Si Jurai looked closer, he saw crescent moon shaped beehives filled with the most delicious honey.

'This is how I can protect you, my child. Our longhouse has forsaken us. I can give you the honey you wanted so much. I can give you protection. I can give you my love.'

The tree then whispered her secrets to the boy—the secret of how to harvest the rainforest honey from its branches. Si Jurai was so happy that he decided he would no longer live at the longhouse. He would move to his late mother's longhouse further down the river. 'I will find a new family and a new life.'

Si Jurai left for his new life, and with the protection of his grandmother, he was always blessed with honey from the magic tualang tree which he shared with his new longhouse family.

* * *

This folk tale is also known as *The Honey Tree* and originates from the Bidayuh people of Sarawak, Malaysia. Before the arrival of religions such as Christianity and Islam, the Bidayuhs and many other ethnic groups held animistic beliefs and offered prayers to the natural world. Their way of life was governed by their *adat* (or customary law) which defines and instructs them on how to survive in the challenging environment of the rainforest. Periods of crop failure, illness, and threats from other longhouses meant that it was imperative for the community to be united in order to thrive.

It's not surprising that the core element of this *adat* is a strong sense of communal sharing and equality which encompasses the longhouse cultures of most of the ethnic people of East Malaysia. In this regard, it is common to share whatever food and resources are available, such as the meat from a successful hunt, bounty from the harvest, and jungle delicacies, such as wild honey.

This was not the case, however, in the story of *The Tale of the Honey Tree* when Si Jurai is excluded because he was an orphan and deemed to be unworthy. This story shares the same theme as *Bawang Putih Bawang Merah and the Magic Swing* in that the suffering and unfair treatment faced by the two protagonists have caused them to take active steps in order to secure their future. In the end, Si Jurai undergoes a transformation in his character from a timid, orphan boy to a mature young man able to make rational decisions in his life.

Chapter 35

The Gift of the Winter Melon
(Malaysia)

Once upon a faraway time there lived a kind and handsome man by the name of Anak-Anak. Anak-Anak lived in a small village in the land below the wind.

One day, Anak-Anak went into the jungle to gather some fruits and nuts, but luck was not on his side, and he ended the day empty-handed. He decided to return home but as he passed the river he came across an old lady.

'Where are you going, young man? What are you looking for?' she asked.

'I am looking for a wife,' replied Anak-Anak for he was always joking around.

'Looking for a wife is easy, but finding one is not. I can help you but you must come with me back to my home,' said the old lady.

Anak-Anak felt uneasy and did not really want to follow the old lady, but there was some truth to his words; he did want to find a good wife and settle down. And so, the young man followed the old lady back to her home in the jungle.

When they reached her house, the old lady turned towards Anak-Anak and told him the conditions he would have to fulfil in order to find a wife. 'First of all, you must beat up all my children and beat them proper. Make sure they are battered and bruised. Secondly, you must go to my garden at the back of my house and destroy all my fruit trees and flowers. Burn them to the ground. Do you understand, young man?'

Anak-Anak was surprised at the harsh conditions, but he nodded. The old woman opened the door of her house and told him to enter alone. As soon as Anak-Anak stepped through the door, he could hear the sound of happy children playing and laughing. He saw that there were at least ten small children tumbling and rolling in the middle of the house, looking so joyful that he knew he would not have the heart to beat or injure any of them. He laughed as he watched them play and then he walked to the back of the house and opened the door to the garden.

Outside, he saw a lush green garden bursting with vegetables and fruit trees. He marvelled at the sight of it and once again, knew that he would not have the heart to burn the garden down. Anak-Anak leaned against the tree to enjoy the beauty of the garden.

A short while later, the old woman returned but she did not say anything to Anak-Anak. She could see that he had failed to fulfil the conditions. Instead, she invited the young man to eat dinner with the family which he did. The table was laden with rice and fresh ulam from the garden, ripe sweet pumpkin stew, and fresh grilled fish from the river. The children sang to Anak-Anak and he found that he was having a marvellous time.

'You can sleep here tonight, young man. Tomorrow you can go home.' Anak-Anak spent the night and slept well in the company of the happy children.

The next morning the old woman said goodbye to Anak-Anak and gave him a small winter melon called Labu Kundur with instructions. 'When you reach the river, throw this melon into the water.'

It was a strange request, but since Anak-Anak had failed with the previous day's conditions, he thought he would obey the old lady by throwing the melon in the river. When he reached the river, this is exactly what he did. For a while, the melon simply bobbed up and down in the water but then something began to happen. The melon shimmered and shook and out of it popped the most beautiful girl Anak-Anak had ever seen. Her skin was as smooth as rose petals and her hair as shiny as the dewdrops in his garden.

'Do not be afraid, Anak-Anak,' said the beautiful maiden. 'I am the Goddess of the Winter Melon and if you so wish, I can be your wife.'

Well, Anak-Anak could not argue with that. He knew that the goddess would make a perfect wife and so he brought her home to meet his family.

The story of how Anak-Anak met his wife soon spread throughout the village and one day, a lazy young man by the name of Bongkoron decided he would try his luck at finding a wife. The man wandered into the jungle and after a while came across the same old lady.

'What are you looking for, young man?' she asked.

'I am looking for a wife,' said Bongkoron.

'Looking for a wife is easy, but finding one is not. I can help you but you must come with me back to my home,' said the old lady.

Bongkoron smiled and followed the lady to her home in the jungle but before he entered the house the old woman explained to him the conditions he must fulfil in order to get a wife. 'First of all, you must beat up all my children and beat them proper. Make sure they are battered and bruised. Secondly, you must go to my garden at the back of my house and destroy all my crops. Burn them to the ground. Do you understand, young man?'

Bongkoron nodded and the old woman left him to enter her house. As soon as he entered, he saw the beautiful children playing and singing but without a moment's hesitation, Bongkoron beat up the children with no regret and no remorse.

Then he walked to the back of the house into the garden and set fire to all the beautiful plants and fruit trees until the whole place was charred and smoking.

When the old woman returned home she found that her children were bruised and battered, her garden scorched by the fire. The old woman fixed Bongkoran with a glare that would have frightened the bravest man.

'You will leave this house immediately,' she said. 'Take this winter melon and when you come to the river, throw the melon into the river. You will get the wife you deserve.'

Feeling excited, Bongkoran grabbed the melon and ran to the river. When he reached the bank, he threw the melon in and watched as it bobbed above the water. However, Bongkoron was impatient and instead of waiting for his wife to appear, he jumped into the river in order to retrieve her. His hands found a body and he quickly pulled her up the river bank. What a shock he got when he saw that there was no beautiful maiden for him. The woman from the melon was an old hag, her grey hair reached her knees and her yellow eyes stared at him with hatred.

'I am the *other* Goddess of the Winter Melon. And you will take me for your wife.' The old hag then opened her mouth and laughed.

'No, no!' cried Bongkoran. The man leapt up and raced into the jungle but the other goddess, although old, was strong and she soon caught up with her husband. After that, Bongkoran was never seen again.

* * *

This folk tale is also known as *Dewi Labu Kundur* (The Winter Melon Goddess) and originates from Sabah, Malaysia. This story falls under the category of tales of good deeds and bad deeds, and recognizes the agency of the wise, respected female figure who has the power to reward or punish in this tale. The domestic tasks she sets for Anak-Anak and Bongkoron are considered conventionally female tasks. Anak-Anak passes the test by caring for the children and tending to the garden, and is rewarded with a good wife. The old woman's approval of Anak-Anak's behaviour is an endorsement of family values such as nurturing respect, patience, and diligence. On the other hand, her punishment of Bongkoron reflects society's rejection of the values he represents: greed, laziness, impatience, and selfishness. These are the negative traits which hinder the process of civilization.

However, this tale is problematic as it still conforms to patriarchal ideas in that Anak-Anak's good deeds are rewarded with a 'lovely maiden' whereas, Bongkoran is punished with an 'ugly hag'. The tale suggests that beautiful young women are still seen as the 'reward'. Even though this tale has patriarchal elements, it still goes some way to overturning gender stereotypes and highlights female agency through the wise old woman.

Chapter 36

Phikul Tong
(Thailand)

Once there was a girl who was kind and sweet. She was also beautiful which was a comfort to some, but also a cause of envy to others. Unfortunately for Phikul Thong, she was forced to live with two of the most envious women in her village; her stepmother and stepsister. Day by day, Phikul Thong's beauty blossomed until the very sight of her made the stepmother and stepsister ill. In order to vent out her frustration, the stepmother forced Phikul Thong to do all the chores from dawn to dusk. She dressed the girl up in rags and fed her their leftovers. Even with such a hard life to bear, Phikul Thong never complained but was always happy to help and was grateful that she had a family and a roof over her head.

'Go and fetch water from the river for my bath. And be quick about it,' ordered the stepmother. Phikul Thong smiled sweetly and said she would be happy to help if it would ease her stepmother's burden. For some reason, this irked the stepmother even more.

At the river, Phikul Thong collected the water and began her long walk home. It was hard work but she did not mind. The sun was shining, the birds were singing, and she felt a lightness in her heart. On the way home she met an old lady sitting on a stump of a tree by the side of the path.

'Good morning, Grandma. Are you well?' asked Phikul Thong. The old woman looked at the girl and nodded. 'Oh, I am quite all right my child. I would like a little water to drink though.'

'Yes, of course, Grandma,' replied Phikul Thong. 'I have a bucket of water here. Let me pour you a cup.' She then took a little cup from her pocket and filled it with the clear, cool water from the river.

The old woman gratefully took the cup and after drinking she looked much revived. 'Thank you, my child. You are a kind soul and one day you will be rewarded for your good deeds.' Phikul Thong sat next to the old woman for a while. And then, when the sun was quite high in the sky, she took her bucket and went back to the river to fetch more water for her stepmother's bath.

Unfortunately, by the time Phikul Thong returned home, it was way past noon and she was met by her furious stepmother. 'What took you so long!'

'I am sorry, but on the way home I met an old lady who needed help.' Phikul Thong began to explain but as she spoke, a peculiar thing happened—golden flowers fell from her lips. These flowers were no ordinary flowers for they came from the tanjung or bullet wood tree and were extremely valuable. The stepmother and stepsister began to collect all the flowers that fell from Phikul Thong's lips.

'Mother, we can sell these flowers at the market. We will be rich.' From that day onwards, the greedy stepmother forced Phikul Thong to talk and talk in order to produce more flowers. Phikul Thong was happy to help at first, but she gradually grew weak and one day, she lost her voice completely.

Angered by this, the stepmother told her own daughter to go to the river to look for the old woman. 'Force her to give you this gift so that we may be rich.' The girl grabbed the bucket and walked to the river and on the way she met someone but it was not an old, frail woman. Standing before her was a beautiful, elegant lady in the finest silk robes. Her long, dark hair was braided with golden ribbons. The stepsister was quite jealous of the finely dressed lady.

'Greetings. I need some help. Will you help me, please?' asked the beautiful lady.

'Why should I help you? You look well enough to me.' And then the stepsister whirled around and walked back home again.

'Well, did you meet the old woman?' asked the stepmother. When the stepsister opened her mouth to speak, a wriggly fat worm fell from her lips. Horrified, she screamed and as a result, more and more worms crawled out of her mouth and fell to the ground. The stepmother looked at her daughter, and then she turned towards Phikul Thong.

'You lied to us. There was no old woman who gave this gift to you. I want you out of my house. Be gone from here!' Phikul Thong was forced to leave her home with nothing but the clothes on her back. She ran into the woods feeling quite distraught and wondering what to do. For days she wandered through the woods and lived on fruits and edible leaves. She slept in the high branches of the trees and drank from the river. How long could she survive out here in the wild, she wondered. Then one day, as Phikul Thong was trying to catch fish, she thought she saw a familiar figure across the river.

'Grandma,' she called out, but no one was there. Sighing Phikul Thong got to her feet and walked towards a clearing. As she stepped out from behind a tree, she bumped into a prince who was out hunting in the woods. He was so struck by her beauty that he dropped his bow and arrow.

'Why do you look so sad?' asked the prince. Phikul Thong told him her story and as she spoke the golden flowers fell once more from her lips.

'You have nothing to fear, Phikul Thong, for you are a kind, gentle soul. I will do my best to help you from this day onwards.' The prince took Phikul Thong back to his kingdom where they fell in love and lived happily ever after.

* * *

Phikul Thong is a folk tale from Thailand and has similar traits and qualities to the other good deed–bad deed tales. Once again, the tale highlights the power and agency of the older woman who is able to bestow reward and punishment on the two girls.

In a Grimm's fairy tale called *The Three Little Men in the Woods,* the kind sister is rewarded when gold coins fall from her mouth every time she speaks. In Charles Perrault's *The Fairies* (also known as *Diamonds and Toads*), the good daughter is rewarded when not just flowers, but diamonds and pearls fall from her mouth. It is thought that the Thai version of this story uses flowers because the predominantly Buddhist people in this region place a high value on compassion and kindness. The flowers which fall from Phikul Thong's lips come from the tanjung or the bullet wood tree, which is the same tree in the story of *The Tanjung Blossom Fairy.*

Chapter 37

The Woodcutter's Axe
(Malaysia)

Once upon a time there was a woodcutter who was so poor that he did not even own an axe. Every time he wanted to cut some wood, he would have to borrow an axe from his friends. Most of the time, his friends did not mind lending him their axe because he was very careful and always made sure not to lose the axe.

The woodcutter was ashamed but no matter how much wood he chopped, it was only just enough to pay for his food and clothes. He never managed to save enough money to buy himself an axe of his own and this made him very sad. However, the woodcutter did not give up and continued to work hard every day to try to make enough money so that he could buy himself an axe.

One day, as the woodcutter was busy chopping wood near a lake, his axe slipped from his hands and fell into the water. The woodcutter immediately dove into the water to search for the axe, but it was of no use. The axe had sunk right to the bottom of the lake.

'Oh, this is terrible. How will I explain this to my friend?' said the woodcutter to himself. He felt terrible. He sat on a rock and stared at the water feeling upset. Just then, a strange thing happened. The water in the lake began to bubble and out of it emerged an old man.

'Why are you so sad, woodcutter?' asked the old man.

'I have lost my friend's axe. It slipped from my hand as I was working and it fell into the lake. How will I tell my friend that I have lost his axe?' replied the Woodcutter.

'Is that all? Do not be sad, young man. I will find the axe for you.' The old man dove down into the water and a few moments later, he resurfaced. He was smiling and in his hand, he carried an axe made out of pure gold. It glinted under the sun.

'Is this your friend's axe, woodcutter?' asked the old man. The woodcutter took one look at the axe and shook his head.

'Oh no. My friend's axe is made out of iron. That one is made from pure gold. See how it gleams,' answered the woodcutter. The old man smiled and then dove back into the water. A short while later he resurfaced, and this time he had two axes; one made of gold and the other made of iron.

'Yes, that iron axe belongs to my friend. Thank you, old man,' said the woodcutter who was smiling from ear to ear.

'Woodcutter, you are a good and honest man. As a reward, I will give you both axes. You can return the iron axe to your friend and you may keep the gold axe for yourself. You deserve it,' said the old man.

The woodcutter thanked the old man and ran back to tell his friend what had happened. When his friend heard the story he was surprised and excited. He was also a little jealous and wanted a gold axe for himself. The next day, he went to the lake and threw his iron axe in. He could not believe his eyes when the water started to bubble and out of it emerged an old man.

'Why do you look so sad?' asked the old man.

'Old man, I have lost my axe. Can you help me find it, please?' asked the woodcutter's friend.

Once again, the old man dove under the water and a short while later, he resurfaced carrying a gold axe in his hands.

'Is this your axe, young man?' he asked.

'Oh yes. That's mine!' replied the woodcutter's friend. His eyes flashed as he saw the shiny axe.

The old man frowned. 'No, you are lying. You are not like the other woodcutter.' He threw the gold axe into the river and vanished under the water.

The woodcutter's friend immediately jumped into the river to retrieve the gold axe but in his excitement, he forgot that he did not know how to swim. He vanished, along with the gold axe.

* * *

This story is also known as *The Gold Axe* or *The Golden Axe,* and originates from Malaysia, although there are many different variations of this story across Southeast Asia and the world. This folk tale falls under the category of good deeds and bad deeds but instead of an older woman, it features an old man who has to the power to reward and punish. *The Woodcutter's Axe* is remarkably similar to one of the *Aesop's Fables* called *The Honest Woodcutter* and is often used as a cautionary tale to show that honesty really is the best policy.

The following stories of *Sang Kancil* have been grouped together, with a general commentary at the end of this section.

Chapter 38

How Sang Kancil Tricked Tiger
(Malaysia, Indonesia)

Once there was a clever mouse deer called Sang Kancil who loved to walk through the jungle to look for tasty treats to eat. Although the mouse deer was small, he was not afraid because he knew he was the smartest animal in the jungle. As he passed a cave, Sang Kancil heard a low growl coming from inside and stopped in his tracks. It was Sang Harimau, the ferocious tiger.

'Sang Kancil,' said the tiger as he poked his head out of the cave. 'It's so nice of you to drop by. I was getting a little hungry and you look especially tasty this fine evening.' Naturally, Sang Kancil did not want to become the tiger's dinner. He looked around and saw a muddy puddle which gave him an idea.

'I'm very sorry, Sang Harimau, I would love to stay but the king has ordered me to guard his royal treat. It's his royal pudding.'

'His royal pudding?' asked the tiger.

'Why yes, Tiger. There it is,' said Sang Kancil, pointing to the muddy puddle. 'It is the most delicious pudding in the world. The king has asked me to guard it as he does not want anyone else to taste his precious pudding.'

The tiger looked longingly at the puddle and licked his lips.

'Mmm... I would like to taste some of that pudding,' said Sang Harimau.

'Oh no, Tiger! The king would be very angry if I let you taste his royal pudding,' replied Sang Kancil.

'Just one little taste. The king will never know,' said Tiger.

'Alright then. But first, let me run away from here so that no one blames me,' pleaded Sang Kancil.

'Very well, you may go,' replied the tiger. Sang Kancil gave a little bow and ran off with a smile on his lips.

'Imagine,' said the greedy tiger. 'The king's royal pudding.' He bent down and took in a big mouthful of thick, sticky mud.

'Argh, it's only mud! That mouse deer tricked me.' Tiger roared and ran to catch up with Sang Kancil.

'Sang Kancil! You may have tricked me but I have you now. You will not escape this time,' said the tiger.

Once again, Sang Kancil looked around and this time, he saw a wasps' nest hanging from the branch of a tree.

'I'm very sorry, Tiger but I really cannot stay. The king has asked me to guard his royal drum,' said Sang Kancil.

'His royal drum?' asked the tiger.

'Yes, there it is hanging from that tree. It makes a wonderful sound. The king does not want anybody to beat his special drum,' said Sang Kancil.

'I would like to beat the king's drum,' said Tiger.

Sang Kancil eyes widened. 'Oh no, Tiger! The king would be very angry.'

'Just one hit, the king would never know,' replied the tiger as he stared up at the wasps' nest.

'Alright Tiger, just one hit. But first let me run far away so that no one will blame me,' said clever Sang Kancil.

'Very well, you may go,' said Sang Harimau. Sang Kancil sped off as he laughed to himself.

'Imagine,' said Tiger. 'The king's royal drum.' The tiger leapt up towards the wasps' nest and hit it with his powerful paws. The nest swung back and forth, but there was no drum sound. All the tiger could hear was the sound of loud buzzing as hundreds of angry wasps flew out to attack and sting him.

'Ahhh! That is no drum. It is a wasps nest!' shouted the tiger. He jumped into the river and stayed there until the wasps flew away. Tiger was so angry his whole body was shaking. He sped through the jungle until he finally caught up with Sang Kancil.

'You've tricked me again, but no more. I will make a meal out of you, Sang Kancil,' said the mean old tiger.

Sang Kancil looked around again and this time he saw a sleeping python.

'I'm very sorry Tiger, but I really cannot stay. You see, the king has ordered me to guard his royal belt.'

'His royal belt?' asked the tiger.

'Yes, there it is,' said Sang Kancil as he pointed to the sleeping python. 'It is the most beautiful belt in the world. This belt has magical powers and can cure any ailments. The king does not want anyone to wear it.'

By this time, the tiger was hungry, tired, and covered in wasp's bites. The thought of wearing a magical belt that can cure his ailments was very appealing to him.

'I would like to wear the king's belt,' said Tiger.

'Oh no Tiger! The King would be very angry if he knew someone wore his belt,' replied Sang Kancil.

'I will only wear it for a little while. The king will never know,' said Tiger.

'Alright, Tiger. But first let me run far away so that no one will blame me,' replied Sang Kancil.

'Very well, you may go,' replied Sang Harimau .

Once again, Sang Kancil ran off smiling to himself.

'Imagine,' said the tiger. 'The king's belt!' He grabbed the sleeping python and wrapped its long body around his belly.

The snake woke up. Hisssssssssss! The long snake wrapped its body around Tiger.

'Oh no! This is not a belt, it is a python! Help! Help me, Sang Kancil,' shouted the tiger. But by this time, Sang Kancil was far, far away.

Chapter 39

How Sang Kancil Tricked the Crocodiles
(Malaysia and Indonesia)

Sang Kancil was the smartest animal in the whole forest. Even though he was tiny and weak, he always had a knack for outwitting the bigger animals such as Sang Buaya, the crocodile.

One day Sang Kancil was walking by the river when something caught his eyes: on the other side of the river there was a tree full of beautiful, ripe, delicious mangoes. Well, of course, the sight made Sang Kancil's mouth water and he had a sudden longing to eat the fruit.

Unfortunately, he couldn't cross the river because he knew that it was infested with hungry crocodiles. Any animal who was foolish enough to go too near the edge was attacked and devoured by a bask of crocodiles living there.

Sang Kancil stared at the river for a long time, and then he looked at the delicious mangoes hanging from the tree. He closed his eyes and thought hard until he finally came up with a cunning plan. Clearing his throat, Sang Kancil stood up on a rock and began to speak.

'Attention! May I have your attention please?' At first, nothing happened and the river was still and quiet. Sang Kancil cleared his throat again.

'I am here under the orders of the sultan. His highness will be having a special kenduri feast at his palace tonight and has invited all the crocodiles from this river to attend.'

Slowly, the water began to churn and bubble as beady eyes emerged from the top of the river.

'What did you say, Sang Kancil?'

'The sultan is having a feast and we are invited?'

Sang Kancil smiled to himself. 'The sultan wants to invite all of you for a feast tonight. He has asked me to count your heads so that he knows how much food to prepare.'

By now, the crocodiles became very excited and one by one, their heads popped out of the water.

'What do you want us to do, Sang Kancil?' asked the biggest, meanest crocodile.

'Please line up from this side of the river, and form a straight line all the way to the other side so that I can count your heads.'

Obediently, the crocodiles swam and positioned themselves in a straight line from one side of the river to the other. The line of crocodiles looked like a perfect bridge.

'Thank you, I will now begin the count,' announced Sang Kancil in an official tone. The little mouse deer jumped on the head of the nearest crocodile and shouted, 'One!' He jumped on the head of the second crocodile and shouted 'Two!' This went on till he reached the other side of the river where he gracefully leapt and landed safely on the bank.

Sang Kancil moved a safe distance away from the edge of the water and smiled at the silly crocodiles. 'Thank you for your cooperation. However, I'm afraid, there will be no kenduri feast for you all tonight.'

The crocodiles roared and gnashed their terrible teeth at Sang Kancil. 'What do you mean there will be no feast tonight? Why did you count our heads then?' asked one of the crocodiles.

'I just wanted to get to the other side of the river to eat those lovely mangoes. Thank you all for helping me cross the river unharmed,' said Sang Kancil with a smile.

'You tricked us Sang Kancil! Prepare to die!'

Sang Kancil laughed for he knew that he was too far away from the water for the crocodiles to attack him. After a while, the crocodiles gave up and slunk down into the depths of the river hoping that one day they would get their revenge on Sang Kancil.

Chapter 40

How Sang Kancil Helped Man
Escape From Tiger
(Malaysia, Indonesia)

One day, it came to be that Sang Harimau, the tiger, found himself caught in a tiger trap made by the hunter. Sang Harimau was wondering what to do when he spotted a man walking past.

'Hey, you,' he called out. The man turned towards the voice and was shocked to find a huge tiger caught in a trap.

'Are you speaking to me?' asked the man nervously.

'Yes, of course I am. Who else would I be speaking to?' replied the tiger. 'Can you lift the latch on this trap and let me out?'

The man couldn't help but notice the tiger's great big jaws and sharp claws. He didn't think it was a good idea to let tiger out of the trap.

'I'd like to help you Sang Harimau, but I'm afraid that if I let you out, you will kill me and eat me. That's what tigers do, you see.'

The tiger looked shocked.

'Why would you think of such a thing?' he replied. 'If you help me out of here, you will be my saviour. Of course, I wouldn't harm a hair on your head.'

'I still don't think it's a good idea,' said the man.

'Please, if you were trapped in here, I would definitely come to your rescue. Please help me,' said the tiger. And because the tiger looked so forlorn and because this particular man was a kind-hearted soul, he decided to help the tiger.

'Very well then, Tiger. I will help you but you must remember your promise not to kill me,' said the man after a long pause.

'I promise,' replied Sang Harimau .

The man reached out and opened the door of the trap and soon, the tiger walked out with a smile. The great animal stretched his back and let out a great breath.

'Ahh! Thank you. That feels much better. It was rather cramped in there,' said the tiger.

'Well, good day then,' said the man as he went on his way. Tiger watched him walk away and he suddenly felt quite hungry. He hadn't eaten for a while now and the man looked mighty tasty. Tiger leaped towards the man and blocked his way.

'Where are you going, Man?' he asked.

'I must go home now,' replied the man nervously. He didn't like the look in the tiger's eye.

'Well, you see, I know I promised I wouldn't kill you if you helped me out but I haven't eaten for days and I'm famished,' said Sang Harimau.

'Tiger, you promised! How can you go back on your promise?' said the man backing away.

'Well, I am a tiger after all and this is my nature–I kill and eat prey,' said the tiger licking his lips and creeping closer.

'No, this is unfair! Let us ask someone for their opinion,' said the man.

'Very well,' replied the tiger. 'Let's walk together for a while and if we see anyone on this road, we can ask them for a verdict,' said the tiger.

Man and Tiger walked along the road but they didn't see a single person or animal there. All they saw was the road, and so Man bent down and asked the road for its verdict.

'Road, I helped Tiger out of a trap and in return he promised not to kill me. Now he wants to go back on his word and eat me. Is it right for Tiger to kill me after I've helped him out?' asked the man.

'I agree with Tiger. Look at me. Even though I am useful to people, they do not reciprocate and take care of me. All they do is walk over me with their dirty feet,' replied the road.

'You see, Man. Just because you helped me, doesn't mean I should repay you. It is my nature,' said the tiger as he got ready to pounce on him.

'Wait, let's ask another person for their verdict,' pleaded the man.

The two walked on but once again, they didn't see a single person or animal. All they saw was a tree growing by the side of the road. Man walked up to the tree and asked for its verdict.

'Tree, I helped Sang Harimau out of a trap and in return he promised not to kill me. Now he wants to go back on his word and eat me. Is it right for him to kill me after I've helped him out?' asked the man.

'I agree with Tiger. Look at me. Even though I am useful to people, they do not reciprocate and take care of me. All they do is cut off my branches and use me as firewood.'

'You see, Man. Just because you helped me, doesn't mean I should repay you. It is my nature,' said the tiger as he got ready to pounce on the man.

'Wait, let's ask one last person for their verdict,' pleaded the man.

The two walked on once again and this time they met Sang Kancil, the mouse deer.

'Sang Kancil, I helped Sang Harimau out of a trap and in return he promised not to kill me. Now he wants to go back on his word and eat me. Is it right for him to kill me after I've helped him out?' asked Man.

Sang Kancil listened carefully to the man. He frowned and looked confused.

'I don't understand. You say that the tiger was caught in a trap? Where is this trap? How was the tiger caught in it?'

By now Sang Harimau was ravenous and wanted his meal. 'Why are you so stupid today, Sang Kancil? Come follow me, I will show you the trap.'

So Sang Kancil, Sang Harimau, and the man walked all the way back to the trap. 'Here is the trap,' said the tiger triumphantly.

'But I don't understand. How did a big, strong predator like you end up in such a trap?' asked Sang Kancil.

By now, the tiger had had enough. 'You really are being stupid today, Sang Kancil. Here, I'll show you exactly how I was caught in the trap. You see, I was walking along and not paying much attention when I accidentally walked into this trap,' explained Sang Harimau as he entered the trap.

As soon as Tiger was inside the bamboo cage, Sang Kancil yelled to the man, 'Close the trap door now!' Which is exactly what the man did.

Sand Kancil looked at the tiger and said, 'You ungrateful creature! This man took pity on you and was kind enough to help you but you wanted to repay that kindness by killing him. You deserve to be sentenced to death.'

Chapter 41

How Sang Kancil Helped Buffalo
(Malaysia, Indonesia)

One day, it came to be that Sang Buaya, the crocodile, found himself trapped under a huge log by the side of the river. He was wondering how he would get out of this predicament when he happened to see Sang Kerbau, the buffalo, passing nearby.

'Hey, Buffalo. Help me out, will you? I'm stuck under this heavy log and I cannot get out,' said the crocodile to the buffalo.

Buffalo looked at the crocodile and slowly shook his great, big head. 'No, I will not help you. As soon as I release you, you will attack and kill me.'

The crocodile was shocked. 'That is the most ridiculous thing I have ever heard! If you help me out, I promise I won't attack you.'

And because the buffalo was kind and a bit dim-witted, he believed the crocodile and began to push the log off the crocodile's back.

'Ahh! Thank you Buffalo, that's much better,' said the crocodile. He stretched his great big head and moved his great big tail from side-to-side, and then he looked at the buffalo and his stomach began to rumble. He hadn't had a decent meal in days.

'You know how I said I wouldn't attack you?' said the crocodile.

'Yes, you promised not to attack me if I helped you,' replied the buffalo.

'Well, I've changed my mind. I haven't eaten in days and being trapped under that heavy log has made me extremely hungry. I think I will kill you after all.'

It was lucky that just at that moment, Sang Kancil, the clever mouse deer, came strolling past. He had seen what had transpired between the two and thought he had better step in.

'Good morning, Crocodile! Good morning, Buffalo! How are you two today?' asked Sang Kancil.

'I helped him trapped under a log and now he wants to eat me. Do you think that's fair, Sang Kancil?' asked the buffalo with great big tears in his eyes.

'Well, it is my nature to attack such creatures,' said the crocodile defending himself.

'I don't understand. You said that crocodile was trapped under the log? Which log? Where?' asked Sang Kancil pretending to be dumb.

'That one there,' said the crocodile.

'I don't believe you. How could you, a big strong crocodile, get caught under a log like that,' said Sang Kancil. 'You will have to show me.'

'Very well,' replied the crocodile who foolishly crawled back into the position. 'Buffalo, you may place the log back on me so we can show Sang Kancil how I was trapped.'

Buffalo picked up the log and placed it on the crocodile's back. 'There, you see, Sang Kancil. This was how I was trapped. Now take this off again so I can have my meal.'

'Come Buffalo, let's go for a nice walk. Sang Buaya is so mean that he doesn't deserve to be rescued,' said Sang Kancil. Then, Sang Kancil and Sang Kerbau turned and left the crocodile.

* * *

There are many stories of Sang Kancil throughout Malaysia and Indonesia, each story complete with a host of familiar characters such as Sang Harimau (the tiger), Sang Buaya (the crocodile), Sang Kerbau (the buffalo), and others. This mouse deer is considered to be one of the most well-known folklore characters in the Nusantara region. In addition, Sang Kancil makes a regular appearance in the folk tales from the Orang Asli people of West Malaysia, and the different ethnic groups in East Malaysia.

It is believed that the Sang Kancil stories come from the *Jataka Tales*, which is a body of literature concerning the previous lives of Buddha.

A collection of stories known as the *Panchatantra* (from 300 BCE) also comes from this source. In fact, there is a Buddhist stupa (a monument) in Bharhut, India, which is carved with beast stories not only from the Sang Kancil stories, but also from the *Aesop's Fables*. According to Sir Richard Winsted in *A History of Classical Malay Literature*, these stories had spread out of India, westwards towards Africa and eastwards towards Indonesia and Malaya.

Sang Kancil is considered to be a trickster figure, much like the trickster figures of Anansi the Spider from Africa, the Brer Rabbit from North America (which features the stories of the African American people) and Reynard the Fox from Europe. In some stories, Sang Kancil acts as a judge or a mediator. These stories often represent a commentary on the abuse of power by those in authority with Sang Kancil representing a symbol of resistance and change.

The following are two different versions of the story of *The Owl and the Moon*, with a general commentary at the end of this section.

Chapter 42

Why the Owl Loves the Moon
(Malaysia)

A long time ago, there lived a prince called Putera Pungguk who lived in a magnificent palace on the moon. At that time, the moon was a lovely place to live as it was high in the sky above the earth. During this time, all sorts of plants and vegetables could be grown on the moon and Putera Pungguk had the most beautiful garden where he liked to take long walks and look down on the earth. Putera Pungguk was content and happy to live on the moon with his family.

One night, Putera Pungguk could not sleep and decided to go for a walk in his garden. As he passed the sleeping flowers he came upon a beautiful girl sitting under a tree humming to herself. Putera Pungguk bowed graciously and introduced himself.

'Good evening, my name is Putera Pungguk.'

'Good evening, I am Puteri Bulan. I am the Princess of the Moon,' she replied, smiling so sweetly that it took his breath away.

From that night onwards, Putera Pungguk and Puteri Bulan would meet in the palace gardens to gaze at the sky and walk amongst the flowers. They loved to look down at the earth. At that time, the earth was an empty mysterious place.

'I wonder what is down there on Earth?' asked Puteri Bulan. 'Are there any beautiful flowers like we have here on the moon?'

'If there are any, I would gladly go down to earth to gather them for you, my love,' replied Putera Pungguk.

One night, Puteri Bulan looked down at the earth and saw a beautiful silver flower with golden sparkles. She became mesmerized by this flower and could not stop thinking about it.

'Oh, how I wish I could see that flower. How I wish I could hold it in my hands,' she said.

'Your wish is my heart's desire,' replied Putera Pungguk, for he would have given his life just to make her happy. 'I will fly down to earth and bring back this special flower for you, my love.'

'And I promise I will wait for you, my prince. No matter how long it takes,' she replied.

Putera Pungguk immediately went to his father and asked for permission to fly down to earth.

'You must not go to earth, my son. Our place is on the moon,' said his father. 'Once we leave the moon, our bodies will change and we may not be able to come back.'

Putera Pungguk was distraught, but he knew he could not disappoint Puteri Bulan for he loved her with all his heart. Even though he knew it was dangerous, he still wanted to fly down to earth to search for the silver flower which captivated Puteri Bulan's heart. He said goodbye to his sweetheart and flew down to earth.

As Putera Pungguk got nearer to earth, he could feel his body changing. It became smaller, his skin turned into soft feathers and his arms turned into wings. His eyes became round and he found that he could see in the dark.

When Putera Pungguk arrived on earth, he wasted no time and began to search for the silver flower with the golden sparkles. He flew all around the earth and found flowers in every shape and colour but sadly, he could not find the silver flower with golden sparkles which Puteri Bulan longed for.

One night, Putera Pungguk perched himself onto a branch and stared up at the moon. He hooted a love song to the moon and wept, for he missed Puteri Bulan. And this is why the owl loves the moon.

Chapter 43

The Owl and the Moon
(Malaysia)

This tale takes place a long, long time ago when the earth was wild and empty.

Once upon a time, Puok, the owl, forced Moon to marry him because she was the love of his life. Moon, however, did not feel the same way. She did not love Puok the way he loved her and she certainly did not want to marry him. Moon decided to think of a way to get rid of Puok.

One day, she took her comb and threw it down to earth. She pretended to be upset and cried her eyes out all day and all night. Puok was heartbroken to see that the love of his life was so distraught.

'Do not cry, my love. Tell me why you are sad and I will do everything I can to make you happy once more,' said Puok.

'Oh Puok, what shall I do? My favourite comb has fallen down to earth. I love that comb and I cannot live without it,' said Moon through her tears.

At this time, the earth was an unknown and dangerous place. No one had ever been down to Earth and Puok was not keen to go there. However, Moon continued to cry. She begged and pleaded until he finally relented.

'Hush now, dry your eyes. If you make a rope and lower me down to earth, I will go down there and find your comb,' said Puok to Moon.

Moon used her magical powers and wished for the bark of the tree that the Idahans call 'baloh'. She then made a rope out of the bark and when it was ready, she called out to Puok.

'The rope is ready. Hurry now, Puok, I will lower you down to earth so you can search for my comb.'

Puok took the rope in his hands and began to climb down to earth. It was hard and his hands kept slipping but he loved Moon and would not give up. Finally Puok reached the ground and looked all around. Earth was so different to his home. It was a cold, barren land with dark skies and it frightened him. Puok looked around and by some miracle found Moon's comb lying on the ground.

Delighted, he picked up the comb and called out to Moon. 'I have found your comb, my love! You can pull me up now.'

Puok waited but Moon did not respond.

'Moon, I have found your comb. Please, pull me up, my love,' he shouted again but once more, he was met with silence.

Moon had heard Puok's call but instead of pulling him up, Moon released the rope and left Puok stranded on earth. To this day, whenever she appears in the night sky, Puok always calls out to his beloved Moon.

* * *

These two 'Owl and Moon' stories come from Malaysia. 'Pungguk' is the Malay word for owl, whereas 'Puok' also means owl in the Kadazan-dusun language, which come from the ethnic people in Sabah. The first story is a tender love story that seeks to explain the owl as a nocturnal animal. Some owls have a tendency to hoot at the moon which may have inspired the original tale.

The second story is an oral tale which was recorded by the author of the book, *A Cultural Heritage of North Borneo: Animal Tales of Sabah*, P. S. Shim (2002). This particular folk tale takes an alternative and perhaps more realistic view of the relationship between the owl and the moon. Oral tales typically depend on the life experience of the storyteller. As such, while the first story is framed as a tender love story, the second one highlights the obsessive and abusive nature of the owl, and how the moon deals with this problem. It can be said that the storyteller in the second tale may have added their own spin to the story in order to highlight a particular issue. Once again, this is an example of how these tales have been adapted to suit the needs of a particular society.

Chapter 44

Cunning Cat and the Two Silly Monkeys (Malaysia)

Long ago there lived two monkeys who were friends on some days, but enemies on the others. One day the first monkey saw a fine-looking fish lying by the side of the river bank. The fish had just leapt upon the shore and was still fresh.

'Oh my! Look at that fine fish,' said the first monkey, but before he could lay his paws on the fish, the second monkey raced to the river bank and grabbed the precious fish. Both were excited at the prospect of such a fine breakfast, but the two monkeys soon broke out into an argument, each claiming the fish as his own. They argued from morning till noon when the rumbling of their hungry stomachs finally stopped them.

'Let's ask Cat who is entitled to this fish,' said the first monkey, scratching his head.

'Why must we ask Cat?' asked the second monkey scratching his ears.

'Because Cat likes fish and is therefore a good judge on these fishy matters,' replied the first monkey scratching the back of his neck.

So the two silly monkeys brought their fish to Cat who lived at the farmer's house at the edge of the jungle. They told Cat their problem.

'This morning, I saw this fine fish by the river bank first, but my friend ran towards the bank and grabbed it. It is mine, I am sure of it, but my friend claims it is his too. Who shall have the fish, Cat?' asked the first monkey, as he scratched his elbow.

'I can help you my friends. We can divide the fish in two equal parts so that you both have some,' said Cat.

The two monkeys began to dance and squeal in delight. They both thought this was a fine idea.

'First let me fetch the weighing scales from my master's house.' Cat left the two monkeys and then reappeared with a pair of scales in which to weigh the fish. Cat gently took half the fish in her mouth and bit it in half. There was now a head and a tail. Then Cat placed the two pieces on the scales and found that the head was heavier than the tail.

'Ah, the head is heavier than the tail, but do not fret my friends, I can fix this.' And he nibbled at the head, eating the delicious flesh of the fish. She licked her lips and smiled at the two silly monkeys. Then he weighed the two portions again. This time the tail was heavier than the head.

'Oh dear, the tail is now heavier than the head, but worry not, I will soon fix that problem.' And he once again nibbled on the fish tail.

'That should do it. Let's weigh the fish again,' said Cat, but this time the head was heavier than the tail again, so Cat was forced once again to eat a bit of the head to solve the problem. The two monkeys waited patiently as they scratched their armpits and chests and legs, and every part of their bodies.

Cat kept weighing the two parts of the fish and nibbling away at this and that until nothing was left but bones.

'There! You see my friends, I have solved your problem. Both of you silly monkeys have got exactly what you deserved.' And with a swish of her furry tail, Cat sauntered away to have her afternoon nap after a delicious lunch.

* * *

This tale is also called *How the Cat Became a Judge*, and comes from Malaysia. This kind of short narrative can be classified as a fable and features animals with human characteristics. Usually, these types of fables convey wisdom, and helps us understand human nature and human behaviour. These stories were originally passed down through oral tradition and were eventually written down. This particular fable teaches us the foolishness of trusting others blindly.

Chapter 45

Hitam Manis and the Tualang Bees
(Malaysia)

Once upon a long time ago, in the land of mountains and green lush woods, there lived a beautiful maiden called Hitam Manis. Her skin was as dark and smooth as the night, and her smile as sweet as honey. So stunning was her beauty and pure her intent, that she captured the hearts of many who wanted to marry her. However, Hitam Manis loved her job of tending to the beautiful flowers at the palace gardens and did not wish to settle down just yet. She had magic in her hands and the garden flourished under her loving care.

One day, one of the royal servers fell ill and could not perform her duties.

'Hitam Manis, you must serve the sultan and prince their dinner tonight,' ordered the royal housekeeper. Hitam Manis was happy to help, although she had never served the royal family before and was nervous.

That evening, the sultan was in an ill temper with his son who he thought was not fulfilling his royal duties. The prince was young and would not settle down, preferring instead to go hunting in the woods.

'You are going to become sultan one day, my son. You must take your duties seriously.'

'Yes.' The prince looked down at his feet and wished the meal would end soon. He wanted nothing more than to flee the room and the constant nagging of his father which burned his ears.

Just then, Hitam Manis walked in bearing a tray of food and all thoughts of his father slipped out of his mind. His breath caught in his throat and he felt as if he had been hit by an invisible bolt of lightning. Forgetting his station and his manners, the prince stared open-mouthed at the beautiful girl whose face was as sweet as honey.

Hitam Manis cast her eyes down to the floor, too afraid to look at the royal family. But as she served the young prince, she peered up and saw a pair of warm eyes and a ghost of a smile at the corner of his lips. His smile lit up his face which was so lovely that Hitam Manis forgot herself and smiled back.

The smile, the look, was as brief as a touch of a mother's kiss on the cheeks of her slumbering child. But it changed everything. Hitam Manis felt the earth quiver under her feet and the prince felt as if he was floating.

That night, sleep eluded the young prince. His mind was filled with visions of the beautiful girl, and although his head told him it was an impossible situation, his heart knew that he had found his one true love. Next morning, the prince wasted no time in finding out more about the girl and by the time evening approached, he knew where she would be.

Hitam Manis was in the garden watching the sun set over the mountains. Although the appearance of the young prince surprised her, she was happy to see him. As the sun set over the palace walls, the prince confessed his love for her and all was as it should be.

Later that night, the sultan discovered that the prince was in love with Hitam Manis for he had spies in every corner of the palace. He knew what he must do.

The next morning, Hitam Manis floated to the palace on a cloud. She felt like her feet would never touch the ground, such was her happiness. She danced and twirled around the garden picking flowers and arranging the sultan's bouquet, much to the delight of her friends.

Soon, all her friends gathered in the garden to watch Hitam Manis twirl and move around the beautiful flowers. They clapped and laughed, and joined Hitam Manis in her dance of joy and love.

Unbeknownst to the girls, the royal guards had crept into the garden bearing daggers of steel, for the evil sultan had given the order of death to the girl who had stolen the heart of his only son. As the girls danced, the guards silently surrounded them.

Hitam Manis leapt through the air, and in that moment a steel dagger appeared, stabbing her in the heart. Hitam Manis fell to the ground clutching the dagger. The guards did not know what to do with the other girls, and so they were killed as well, each of them with a stab through the heart.

After the massacre, the guards lowered their weapons, but at that moment something peculiar happened. The bodies of the dead girls shimmered under the morning sun, and then vanished into a black mist which floated up in the air. Shocked, the guards ran away, but not before they saw a swarm of bees fly off into the woods.

The young prince was heartbroken over the sudden disappearance of Hitam Manis, but the sultan ordered his royal shaman to cast a forgetting spell on his son and soon, the prince was back to his usual jovial ways.

Many, many moons later, the prince found himself in the woods when he came upon a magnificent tualang tree. Its silvery bark stretched high into the canopy of the forest, and nestled up in its branches were crescent-shaped beehives, filled with the most delicious rainforest honey. The prince gazed up at the hive and was suddenly overcome by a craving for something sweet.

'I wish to climb this tree and taste some of that honey,' he told his men. The men protested, each volunteering to retrieve the honey, but the prince refused. With a wink and a smile, the prince climbed the tree and being young and agile, reached the top in no time at all carrying nothing but a pail tied to a rope, and his steel dagger. Up near the honeycomb, he could smell the sweet aroma and he immediately began to cut off large chunks—his mouth watering at the sight of the thick, golden honey as it fell into the pail.

The men were anxious for their prince for he was so high up in the tree. Finally, the prince dropped the rope, signalling for his men to bring down the pail. Relieved, they slowly pulled the rope, but when it reached the ground they found a grisly sight. The prince had been killed, his body cut up into pieces and stuffed inside the pail.

The tualang tree began to softly vibrate and hum, and a strange, echoing voice came from the top of the tree, whispering at first, but gradually growing louder.

'We are the bees of the tualang tree and hear our words. Heed our warning. No man shall cut our honeycomb with blades of steel, for you can see what will become of him.'

The men began to tremble and someone cried out.

'Oh, what will we tell the sultan? The prince is dead.'

When the bees heard this lament, they flew down in an angry swarm surrounding the prince, covering him with their honey. The men tried to protect the body of their dead prince, but they were attacked and stung mercilessly. All they could do was watch helplessly as the bees appeared to massacre the body of the prince.

Gradually, the bees flew away and the men could finally see their prince lying on the ground. To their great astonishment, he was whole again. The prince opened his eyes and looked up as a voice spoke from the high branches of the tualang tree.

'My prince, I am Hitam Manis. I loved you with all my heart, but I was killed for that love.'

The prince closed his eyes and remembered everything. He leapt to his feet shaking and crying.

'Hitam Manis! Please come back to me. I fear someone has cast a spell on me, for how else can it be possible that I have forgotten my true love!'

There came a sound from the top of the tree which was like the soft weeping of a broken heart.

'I can never be as I was, my love. But you can always find me here. We are the rainforest bees, and we will always have our honeycombs on the tops of the tualang tree. Our honey is the sweetest in the land but take heed, never, ever use a metal knife to cut my honeycomb for this is how I was murdered by those who despised my love for you.'

The prince felt like his heart would break a thousand times.

'I will my love, my sweet Hitam Manis. That, at least, I can promise you.'

* * *

This oral tale is also known as *Hitam Manis*, and originates from Malaysia. 'Hitam' means black, and 'manis' means sweet, and this is a reference to the rainforest bees and the sweet honey which these bees produce.

In the state of Perak, Malaysia, these tualang trees are owned by individuals and during the honey-harvesting period, the whole family climb the tree on a moonless night to collect the honey. They gather the honey at night and use fire to lure the bees away from the hive. It's interesting to note that these honey-gatherers still follow the warning contained in the fairy tale, and will only use knives made out of buffalo bone (and not metal) to cut the honeycomb.

This fairy tale has been passed on from one generation to the next, which is why the current honey-gatherers know about the taboos related to this. It is not only a story that seeks to pass on valuable information, it is also a cautionary tale about the dangers of love.

Chapter 46

The Snake King of Antah Berantah
(Malaysia)

The enemy was at the gate, ready to plunder the wealth of the kingdom of Antah Berantah. The king watched from his tall tower as the walls surrounding his once mighty kingdom fell to the ground. Angry flames licked the wooden houses of his beloved people. The king let his tears fall.

'Your Highness, you must take the queen and your baby son and flee to the Dark Mountains. Go now before it is too late,' implored the Court Bendahara. Horses were ready to take the royal family away.

'I will not flee. I will face my enemies and die defending my kingdom.' The king's voice was soft but etched in iron. It was clear that he would never leave his palace.

'Take the queen and my son to safety,' ordered the king.

'Leave my home? Never,' said the queen who was equally, if not more, stubborn. 'Why should you be the only one to have the satisfaction of facing our enemy? Just as I have pledged to live with you as your wife, so it will be in death.'

The king was upset with his wife's decision, but he knew that once she had made up her mind, nothing would change it. And so, he ordered his Bendahara to take his newborn son into the mountains. 'Keep him safe. See that he lives on so that he may avenge our deaths.'

With the prince tied securely in a sarong around his chest, the Bendahara galloped away on the back of the royal steed and headed towards the Dark Mountains. He knew that the enemy would never follow them to this dangerous place, full of other-worldly creatures and strange animals. At the foot of the mountain, the old Bendahara turned around and watched as the great kingdom of Antah Berantah burned to the ground.

As the Bendahara made his way further and further into the mountains, he felt a heaviness in his limbs, his breathing became laboured, and his head dizzy. Unable to go further, the Bendahara collapsed under a banyan tree.

'I fear this is my end,' he said to the young prince. 'Forgive me, may God protect you in this cursed place.' A sharp stab of pain pierced through his heart. Using his last strength, the Bendahara carried the baby and placed him in a dry hollow at the bottom of a banyan tree. He bent down and whispered into the baby's ear.

'My prince, you are heir to the throne of Antah Berantah. May you return to your country one day so that you can avenge the death of your parents.' The man took his last breath and slumped down to the ground. The only witness to his death was the full moon which smiled at him from the night sky, and a curious creature who happened to be curled up in the branches of the banyan tree. Her forked tongue slithered out of her mouth as she listened to the old Bendahara. Her dark eyes glistened as she sat still and watched. In the dead of night, she slithered down from the branch and slowly wrapped her long body around the dead man. Moving swiftly and silently, she took the body away. Her babies would have a hearty feast that night.

The next morning, the forest was awoken by the sound of a low hiss in the wet undergrowth of the woods. Dead branches and twigs moved on the forest floor. The creature headed to the same banyan tree where the previous night she had found food for her babies.

Ssssss… a forked tongue emerged from the undergrowth tasting the air. The snake, for this was the creature which had caused the forest floor to move, lifted her head and peered into the hollow of the banyan tree. The baby, as if sensing danger, opened his eyes, but instead of crying out, gurgled and smiled at the She-snake.

'Well, you do not look so bad. A prince, are you?' She spoke to him in the language of her kind. 'Yesss, you are rather special, aren't you?

I will not eat you , not today at least. Let us see what is to become of you first,' hissed the snake who then proceeded to wrap her long scaly body around the baby. She carried the child back to her home in a nearby cave. As the She-snake emerged from the undergrowth it was clear that this was no ordinary snake for she was the length of the tallest tree in the jungle.

The cave was her domain, the mother of all the snakes in the world. She was the one who gave life to, and who nurtured and cared for these creatures. The baby snakes shivered and shook in excitement when they saw what they thought would be their meal, riding on the back of their mother.

'No, my children, this is not your meal. This is the prince of Antah Berantah. For now, we are to care for him as if he was one of us. This child is your brother. Show him our ways and perhaps in the future, he will take care of you in return,' said the She-snake.

The years passed and for one reason or another, the She-snake and all the baby snakes did not kill the young prince. He was left to grow and flourish into a strong, young man capable of speaking in the snake tongue. He had the respect and love of all his brother and sister snakes, and knew their secrets which he pledged to guard to his death. Often, the boy would sit atop the mountain and look upon his lost kingdom, now ruled by an imposter. His snake mother had told him the story of how he came to the Dark Mountain and what his father, the old king of Antah Berantah wanted from him.

'I will take back my kingdom, Mother. I swear it.'

'And we will help you my son,' she replied.

Finally, the day came when the prince was ready to take back what was his. He strode down the mountain wearing a coat made out of the scales of his many brothers and sisters. In his hand, he carried a spear topped by the sharpest viper tooth covered in venom. Travelling with the prince were hundreds and hundreds of snakes ready to take up arms with their brother.

The imposter king took one look at the prince and the hundreds of snakes slithering and weaving into every hole and crevice of the palace, and he fled, never to return.

'My brothers and sisters,' said the new king to the snakes. 'You are always welcome in my kingdom.'

'Thank you, brother,' they hissed in unison in a language that only the new king could understand. 'Thank you, but our place is in the Dark Mountains. We bid you farewell.'

* * *

This tale is also known as *The Prince and the Snake*, and comes from Malaysia. This story is contained in a children's book of Malaysian folk tales and has all the elements of a thrilling epic; a deposed prince brought up by a family of snakes, who eventually grows up to take back his kingdom. There are many stories about snakes in Malay folklore due to the early cultural and religious influence of Hinduism. In many of these fairy tales from Indonesia and Malaysia, there is a reference to a place called Antah Berantah, which is roughly translated as the 'middle of nowhere' and refers to a fictional place.

Chapter 47

The Snake Prince
(Malaysia)

Once there was a young woman called Asmah who lived with her poor parents by the edge of the jungle. Asmah's mother and father loved their daughter and were worried about her future.

'We must marry Asmah off to someone who is rich, so that he can take care of her,' said her mother.

'But who will marry her? We are so poor and lowly that no one in the village will welcome us into their family,' said her father.

'We may be poor, but our daughter is kind and clever. She would make an excellent wife,' replied her mother who had a little more faith in Asmah.

Asmah shook her head in disgust and said, 'Why should I marry someone who will not accept us just because we are poor? No, that will not do. I would rather live here with you for the rest of my days.'

'You are a silly child. How do you expect to live?' asked her mother.

'How are we living now, Mother? We have a little paddy field to give us rice. Our lovely hens provide us with eggs, and I can catch fish from the river and pick fresh ulam and herbs from the woods every day. I do not need a husband, unless I want one.' Before her mother could say another word, Asmah skipped down the steps of their wooden house and vanished into the woods to gather some fresh herbs for their dinner. There was a patch of wild herbs growing in the middle of the woods which had the most delicious ulam raja.

'Oh, what will we do with that girl?' cried Mother.

Deep in the woods, Asmah thought about what mother had said and frowned. 'Why must I marry a man? He will just tell me what to do and get in my way. Worse of all, any man I marry will look down upon us,' she grumbled, as she bent down to pick the delicate leaves of the wild herbs.

'That's very true. If you marry a man, he will probably tell you what to do, get in your way, and look down upon your family,' said a low, hissing voice from behind a tree. Asmah was so startled that she dropped her bundle of herbs. She quickly grabbed a big branch and held it up like a knife.

'Who's there? How dare you sneak up on me like that?' She looked all around, but could not see the source of that slippery voice. All she could here was a slither in the bushes followed by a hissing sound.

'Do not be afraid, Asmah. I would never hurt you,' said the voice.

'How do you know my name?'

'I've seen you before, many times. You always come to my garden to pick my herbs.'

'Oh, I did not know that this was your garden.' Asmah suddenly felt guilty for stealing someone's food, although she did not do so intentionally. 'I'm sorry.'

The voice broke into a merry laugh. 'Don't be silly, Asmah. I planted the herbs for you. I don't really eat such things you see.'

'Oh.'

'Do you like my herbs?'

'Oh yes, my favourite is the ulam raja. It's delicious and sweet.'

'Just like you,' said the voice. Asmah felt herself blush.

'If you agree to marry me, I promise I will plant all your favourite herbs. I promise never to tell you what to do, or get in your way, or look down upon your family. What do you say? Will you marry me?' asked the strange voice.

Asmah thought about it for a while. She did like the herbs this man had planted, and it would be nice if her future husband never told her what to do or look down upon her family.

'Very well. I agree to marry you,' she answered and ran home to tell her parents that she had found a husband.

'Asmah! What have you done?' cried her mother when she heard the story. 'You have agreed to marry a snake. Didn't you hear him hissing and slithering?'

'Oh, so that was the strange sound I heard. But Mother, he had a lovely voice and he did promise to plant my favourite herbs.'

Asmah's parents were sad that their daughter was to be engaged to a snake, but they knew they had no choice. Poor people seldom do. And so they cleaned up their little hut and got ready for the wedding thattook place that evening. No one came to the wedding of course, and the groom was nowhere to be seen although they did hear him slithering in the bushes outside their house.

That night Asmah lay down on her wedding bed and wondered whether she would finally meet her husband. After a while, she got tired of waiting and dozed off, but sometime in the middle of the night she was awoken by a cold, tickling sensation around her feet and ankles.

'Oh! What is that feeling?' She could feel her toes tingling and something soft running up her legs. Asmah covered her legs with a blanket and went back to sleep, but a short while later she felt something move from the tip of her fingers and up her arms.

'Ooh!' she exclaimed for she had never encountered such a feeling as this. The tingling crept up her back and reached her neck where it tickled her ears and made her laugh.

The next morning Asmah woke up to find herself alone in bed.

'Oh,' she said feeling a little disappointed. However, when she got out of bed, she found beautiful jewels around her ankles, wrists, and neck. Gifts from her husband.

'Mother, look at these wedding gifts from my husband,' said Asmah, showing her parents a pair of gold anklets around her feet, jewel encrusted bracelets around her wrists, and a glittering diamond necklace hung around her neck. Her mother almost fainted from the shock.

'I must find my husband to thank him,' she said, as she ran off into the woods towards the little herb garden. When she reached the place, she did not see her husband but did find a long piece of snake skin on the ground. Asmah quickly made a small bonfire and threw the snake skin into the fire.

'I want to see my husband,' she declared to the wind.

A short while later a tall man appeared out of the river. 'Asmah, there you are. I was waiting for you.' He laughed and when she heard the sound, she knew that she had made the right decision.

'I've cut some ulam raja just for you, Asmah. Would you like to try it?' His eyes danced under the light of the sun. Asmah could not help but smile at her handsome new husband.

'Yes, I think I would like some, Husband.'

* * *

This folk tale originates from Malaysia and falls under the category of stories of animal husbands. Variations on this theme appear in other stories around the region such as *Molek* from Riau, Indonesia, (where the husband is a fish) and *Tattadu* from South Sulawesi, Indonesia, (where the husband is a caterpillar).

Presumably the curse on the prince was broken either when he married Asmah or when she burned his snake skin. This is similar to the earlier story of *The Crocodile Princes* (when their crocodile skins were burned, the two princes had to remain in human form and could not transform back into crocodiles). Other myths around the world, such as stories of the mythical creatures called the Selkies in Ireland, have a similar theme.

Chapter 48

The Tale of Princess Khamariah and the Male Fish (Malaysia)

Princess Khamariah was in her private garden one day when she happened to come upon gardener Yusof. When the gardener saw the princess, the world seemed to stop. When the princess looked at the gardener, she thought her heart might just burst from her chest. As one can imagine, this was an impossible situation because Princess Khamariah was a member of the royal family and was already married to Raja Adnan. And Yusof was, well he was just a gardener.

The gardener knew his place and tried to forget about the princess, but she could not do the same. She became obsessed with the gardener and began to think up ways in which they could be together.

One day, the princess came up with a cunning plan. She told Yusof that she could not possibly marry him for he was but a mere gardener, but there was a way for them to be together. She ordered the gardener to disguise himself as a woman and seek work as her handmaiden. 'You might get caught and be killed for no man is allowed in my quarters. However, you must do this for me,' she said.

Donning a dress and covering his head with a veil, Yusof transformed into '*Kalthum*' and obtained the position of handmaiden to Princess Khamariah. From that moment on, the princess and the gardener spent every waking moment together. The two were deeply in love and because the princess was so entranced by the gardener, she did not pay any attention to her own husband who also loved her.

One day, Raja Adnan decided to send his wife a gift of two fine chickens, but failed to notice that one of the animals was a rooster. Princess Khamariah promptly returned the rooster, offended that the sultan would send a male animal to live in her private quarters. Naturally, the sultan was filled with great admiration for his wife's sense of modesty and purity of heart. He decided to send her another gift, this time of two beautiful goldfish.

Once again, one of the goldfish was returned to the sultan with a curt message. 'If I do not allow a rooster to reside in my residence, what would make you think I would allow this male fish to stay here?'

The sultan was astounded and wondered how his wife could tell the difference between a male and female fish. Puzzled, the sultan asked his royal adviser, Johari, to investigate. The Royal Adviser searched through all the books and scriptures, spoke to the fishermen and gardeners and travelled the country but alas, he found no answer to the Sultan's question. One day, as he returned from another useless trip, his wife, Siti Zabedah noticed his low spirits and asked if she could help.

'I must find out how Princess Khamariah can tell the difference between a male and female fish,' he said. Siti Zabedah immediately suspected that something was amiss.

'Husband, there is a way to tell the difference between a man and a woman and that is by their physique. Men are usually stronger in their bodies, although women can be stronger in their minds. Why not hold a competition to find the most athletic man and woman in the kingdom?'

'How would that help?' asked Johari.

'It might reveal the secret between men and women.'

Feeling desperate, Johari advised the sultan to hold a competition for both the men and women of the kingdom. On the day of the competition, the men were lined up on one side of the field and the women on the other. Throughout the day, competitions were held to see who could run the fastest and longest, who could throw the furthest, who could lift the most coconuts and other games. Siti Zabedah sat next to her husband and watched the princess like a hawk. She noticed that the princess had her eyes on her pretty handmaiden, Kalthum. The princess was not at all interested in watching the men compete, but instead clapped and cheered as Kalthum won each and every race. Siti Zabedah could not help but observe that the handmaiden was exceptionally tall and strong and quite physically gifted.

'Husband, I believe I know the answer to the sultan's question,' whispered Siti Zabedah to her astonished husband. She explained that the princess only pretended to be able to identify the male fish in order to show the purity of her character but in actual fact, her lover had been living in her quarters all this while.

When all was revealed, the sultan had Princess Khamariah and the unfortunate gardener Yusof sealed in a barrel and thrown out to sea and that was the end of that.

* * *

This folk tale is also known as *Ikan Jantan* (which means male fish) and originates from Malaysia. It is an oral tale which was collected by Malay cultural figure and scholar, Zakaria Hitam who is known for his collection of Pahang folklore. This tale is unique in that it features a scheming and manipulative princess who exploits her position of power in order to fulfil her desires. Through emotional manipulation, she is able to continue to live under the protection of her husband while at the same time enjoying the company of the handsome gardener. Her lies are uncovered by another woman which ultimately leads to her downfall.

Chapter 49

The Princess With The Trailing Hair Knot
Puteri Sanggul Berjuntai
(Malaysia)

Once upon a time, there lived a king and queen who were cursed with misfortune after misfortune which eventually led to their deaths. One dark night, greedy relatives crept into the palace with evil etched in their hearts; they wanted to kill the king's two daughters and take over the throne. Fortunately for the two princesses, their loyal handmaiden helped them escape into the forest where they lived a simple life in a cottage near the river.

The eldest sister, Puteri Gunung Balai, was used to life in the palace and could not bear living in such poverty. The younger sister however, loved her new life under the canopy of the rainforest trees with the sound of the birds and crickets to keep her company. Puteri Sanggul Berjuntai (for that was her name) was so content to live in the forest that when Puteri Gunung Balai eventually married a court official and invited her to rejoin society, she refused.

'I am happy here, Sister. I have fruit and nuts to eat, and the best tasting water from the river. Why would I want to go back to a place that destroyed our family?' said Puteri Sanggul Berjuntai. The princess continued her life in the forest and eventually her smooth, fair skin became sun-kissed. Her active life made her body strong and she grew tall, much taller than the other girls in court. Her long dark hair, which was usually worn in an intricate 'sanggul' or hair knot, kept getting caught in the branches and began to unravel until she gave up on her hair knot altogether, and wore her hair loose like a wild thing. And this is how she eventually got her nickname—Puteri Sanggul Berjuntai—which meant the princess with the trailing hair knot.

The princess had no care for courtly fashions and left her wild hair to grow until it reached her ankles. With her hair unravelled and blowing in the wind, Puteri Sanggul Berjuntai was the most ravishing of creatures. Unfortunately, it was her beautiful wild hair which eventually brought about her troubles.

One day, Puteri Sanggul Berjuntai found a basket of mangoes outside her cottage and assuming that her sister had sent her the fruit, she ate it all. The next day, a strange man appeared at her door.

'Princess, you have taken the offering I left here. I am here to collect my payment,' he said in a gruff voice. The man was huge and looked as if he could wrestle a hundred buffaloes. The princess could see a sharp *keris* dagger tucked in his belt and she knew she had to be wary.

'I did not know the offering was from you, sir. Had I known, I would never have touched it,' she said holding her head up high for she would not be bullied by such a man.

'You know the laws of this forest. Any offerings taken must be paid for and the payment I seek is your hand in marriage. Although you are too tall and dark to be considered a beauty, I saw you walking in the fields with your hair unravelled, and I was enchanted,' he said in a low but dangerous voice. The princess could see that she could not avoid the terms and instead, began to think of a way to outwit the man.

'Very well,' she said. 'I will follow you, but first let me pack my things.' She rushed into her room and began to wrap up her hair in a long cloth making sure that it would not unravel for she realized this was the cause of her problems. Then she packed some clothes, her jewels, and some food, and followed the man to the river.

'Get into the sampan,' he said pointing to the small boat which was tied up by the edge of the river.

'A sampan! Oh no, I do not know how to swim. I shall drown in that thing,' she exclaimed.

'Get in, you silly girl.' And because she looked so helpless and meek, the man began to relax his guard and simply shoved Puteri Sanggul Berjuntai into the boat. He untied the rope and pushed the boat into the river intending to jump in, but the princess was too quick for him. She grabbed the oars and began to row the sampan down the river. Living in the wild had made her strong and agile and she easily steered the sampan away.

'Come back here!' he shouted, but the princess merely laughed as she made her escape. Since she was already packed and ready for a trip, the princess decided to travel further down the river. After rowing a day and a night, she came upon another girl dressed in rags who was waving at her from an island in the middle of the river.

'Ho! Are you in distress? Are you in need of a rescue?' asked the princess.

'Oh yes, I thank the stars and the moon that you arrived here just in time. I have been on this island for weeks and weeks waiting for someone to rescue me,' said the girl who was called Paku Mayang. 'Please help me, I ran away from my village. My parents wanted to marry me off to a horrible old man.'

The princess helped the girl into the boat. She gave the girl some nourishing food, and clothed her in her very own fine garments made of the best silks. She braided and pinned up Paku Mayang's hair using her own jewelled clips and before long, Paku Mayang looked very decent and lovely indeed.

'Oh thank you, Puteri Sanggul Berjuntai. How can I ever repay you?' cried Paku Mayang.

'It is a small matter,' laughed the princess and she continued to row the sampan down the river. As they travelled, the Princess told Paku Mayang her story and the girl listened carefully. In fact, if truth be told she listened a little too carefully.

The next day, the little sampan went around the bend of a river and came upon a magnificent royal party on the banks. There were dancers in colourful dresses swaying to the sound of a gamelan orchestra. A picnic lunch of roasted meats, fresh ferns, and fruits of every colour lay on a low table filled with wild flowers from the forest. As the little sampan came to rest by the side of the river, a handsome man who was actually the crown prince stood looking thunderstruck at the two ladies who had mysteriously arrived out of nowhere. For the last seven nights, the prince had been haunted by a dream that his one true love would come to him in a sampan on the river. He had been so anxious that his mother, the queen had arranged the royal picnic to ease his mind.

As Puteri Sanggul Berjuntai and Paku Mayang stepped out of the sampan, the prince knew in his heart of hearts that one of these two maidens was to be his future wife. *But which one?* The first maiden was dressed in old clothes which had seen better days. Her hair was wrapped up in a batik cloth, her skin was sun-kissed, and she wore a grave expression on her face. The second maiden was dressed in fine silk and jewels, her hair was pinned up in a beautiful sanggul hair knot, and she had a sweet smile. Surely, the second maiden was his future wife.

Paku Mayang looked around and quickly got the measure of things. She saw how the others treated the man and surmised that he was of importance. She glanced at Puteri Sanggul Berjuntai in her old clothes and quickly made her move.

'Thank goodness, you have found us. My servant and I have been stranded on this river for days. I am Puteri Paku Mayang. I was forced to flee my kingdom when my parents died and cruel relatives came to seize the throne.'

Puteri Sanggul Berjuntai was surprised to hear Paku Mayang telling her very own story, but she kept quiet. She could see that the prince believed every word.

'Princess, you are most welcome to take sanctuary in my kingdom. I will take you to my palace this instant,' said the prince and just like that, Puteri Sanggul Berjuntai found that her identity had been snatched away. Paku Mayang gave the princess a long look.

'Thank you, my Lord. My servant will stay in your servant quarters. You may do with her as you will,' ordered Paku Mayang who was beginning to sound very regal indeed.

Puteri Sanggul Berjuntai was taken to the servant quarters where she was given the job as the bird chaser. Every day, she would go to the paddy fields to chase the birds away which, considering that she loved being outdoors under the open sky, was not a bad life for her.

Meanwhile, Paku Mayang worked quickly and soon convinced the prince to marry her. A big celebration was held and everyone rejoiced that the prince had finally found his true love. However, after a while, the young prince began to notice that his bride lacked a certain refinement. She was greedy and mean to those around her. He began to think that he had made a grave mistake.

One evening as the prince wandered alone in the fields, he came upon Puteri Sanggul Berjuntai as she ran and chased the birds away. Hiding behind a tree, he watched as the princess spun around in the air laughing. She reached up and took off her hair wrap to let her long hair flow down and in that very moment, the prince recognized the girl from his dreams. So, this was his one true love.

When Puteri Sanggul Berjuntai saw the prince she smiled.

'You are the real princess. Why did you not tell me?' he asked.

'I do not want to be a princess. My parents died in court and I do not want that kind of life. I want to live out here in the fields under this beautiful sky,' replied Puteri Sanggul Berjuntai.

'There is no reason why you cannot do both,' said the prince as he took her hands. He took her back to the palace to confront Paku Mayang who refused to confess to her crimes. After a while, the prince ordered Paku Mayang to be put to death for impersonating the princess and the very next day, he married Puteri Sanggul Berjuntai and they lived happily ever after.

* * *

This story is known locally as *Puteri Sanggul Berjuntai* and originates from Malaysia. 'Puteri' means 'princess', and 'sanggul' refers to 'hair bun' or 'hair-knot', while *berjuntai* means 'something that is hanging loose or trailing'. 'Puteri sanggul berjuntai' therefore means the 'princess with the trailing hair-knot'. This image of a messy princess does not conform with the usual perception of what a princess should be like—neat and proper. This particular princess takes it even further as she loves to live in nature and despises life in the palace. Puteri Sanggul Berjuntai rejects a comfortable life in court in exchange for freedom to live her life the way she wants.

Wronged by an imposter, Puteri Sanggul Berjuntai does not seek justice or revenge. Instead, she once again retreats into nature (by working in the paddy fields as a bird-catcher) and is eventually restored to her rightful place when the prince finally recognizes her as the girl from his dreams.

There is a similar tale from Indonesia called *Putri Bunga Telur* (or Princess Jasmine Flower) which has magical elements. In this story, the princess, who is no bigger than a stalk of jasmine, goes on a journey in a banana boat and meets an ugly 'thumbling' called Tuntung Kapur from the wild lilies. The princess invites the thumbling onto her boat and they sail away. Later, they arrive at a kingdom where the prince is the size of a thumb and is destined to marry a woman in a banana boat. Like Paku Mayang, Tuntung Kapur takes over Putri Bunga Telur's identity with disastrous consequences.

The following *Pak Pandir* stories have been grouped together with a general commentary at the end of this section.

Chapter 50

Pak Pandir and his Unfortunate Child
(Malaysia)

Once there was a villager called Pak Pandir. Unfortunately, Pak Pandir was not very clever and was always getting himself into trouble. Fortunately for Pak Pandir, he had a clever wife called Mak Andeh who loved him and was always there to help him. However, because Pak Pandir was not clever, Mak Andeh had to be careful about what she said to Pak Pandir because sometimes, he got even the simplest instructions wrong. This is what happened on a particular occasion.

One day, Mak Andeh was in a rush to check on their paddy field. She wanted to see if the paddy was ready to be harvested but at the same time, was busy taking care of her baby son. She looked at Pak Pandir who was daydreaming under the tree outside their house and called him in.

'Pak Pandir, I need some help. I want to check if our paddy field is ready to be harvested. Please stay home and look after our baby son,' instructed Mak Andeh handing him the baby.

'Yes, dear. I can do that. I can look after our son,' replied Pak Pandir as he smiled at his wife. Even though he was not clever, Pak Pandir was confident that he could take care of their son. All his son needed was food and a safe place to sleep.

'I've already fed the baby but he needs a warm bath before he takes his nap. Boil some water in the cauldron and fill up his bath tub to make a nice warm bath for him. Make sure the water is warm, Pak Pandir.

I do not want our son to catch a cold,' said Mak Andeh as she rushed out of the front door.

'Yes, dear. I will bathe the baby in warm water. I'll remember that,' replied Pak Pandir as he waved to his wife.

Pak Pandir played with his son for a while and then suddenly remembered that he had to give him a nice warm bath.

Pak Pandir tried to recall his wife's instructions. 'Mak Andeh told me to boil some water and to fill up the tub to make sure the water is nice and warm,' said Pak Pandir to himself. He took a big cauldron which Mak Andeh used to boil water in and filled it up with fresh water. Then he lit a fire and waited for the water to boil.

'I must not let the baby catch cold. The water should be nice and warm,' repeated Pak Pandir as he waited for the water to boil. As he stared at the bubbling water, a sudden thought popped into his mind.

'Boiling water and filling up the tub will take far too long. It will be faster and easier if I simply boil the water in this cauldron and bathe the baby here,' he said to himself. He was pleased with himself for coming up with such a clever idea.

'Come now, my son. It's time for your bath.' The baby gurgled and cooed as Pak Pandir carried him to the cauldron of boiling water.

'Mak Andeh wants you to have a nice warm bath,' he said as he lowered his son into the boiling water. The baby kicked and splashed, but silly Pak Pandir thought that his son was happy to have a nice warm bath.

'Mak Andeh will be happy when she sees what I've done,' he thought as he sang to his son.

Just then, Mak Andeh walked through the door. When she saw her baby being scalded by the hot water, she let out a piercing scream.

'Pak Pandir! Oh, what have you done to our son?' she screamed

'What do you mean, Mak Andeh? Our son is enjoying a warm bath.' But by then, it was too late, and the baby was gone.

Chapter 51

Pak Pandir's Bag of Salt
(Malaysia)

One day, Pak Pandir had a terrible day working under the sun in his paddy field. He complained to his wife that he had to wake up early every morning to plant his paddy and make sure the field is watered and to chase away all the mice and birds when the paddy was about to harvest.

'This is too hard. There must be an easier way to make a living,' said Pak Pandir.

Mak Andeh just shook her head and laughed. 'Pak Pandir, at least we have a plot of land and we can grow our own rice. If we work hard now, we can live an easy life later.'

Pak Pandir disagreed. He was tired of working in the paddy field and decided that he would open a new business in order to make money.

'I know! I am going to get salt from the sea and sell it to the villagers,' he told his wife. 'Everyone needs salt for their cooking. This is a good idea. My best idea till date! We will be rich.' Mak Andeh just shook her head. She did not say anything because sometimes it was better just to let Pak Pandir carry out his silly ideas.

The next day, Pak Pandir woke up early and told Mak Andeh that he was going to the seaside to collect salt. He grabbed a big sack and took a pleasant walk under the shade of the coconut trees.

'Ah, this is more like it. Walking to the beach on a beautiful morning is so much nicer than working in the paddy field,' said Pak Pandir to himself. The sun was shining, the breeze was cool, and Pak Pandir was feeling pleased with himself.

When he arrived at the seaside, he dug a small hole in the sand and poured seawater into the hole. Then, Pak Pandir sat under a cool shade and took a mid-morning nap. He chuckled to himself. 'I never get a chance to take a nap when I'm working in the paddy field but look at me now!' He dozed off dreaming of making lots of money in his new business.

A few hours later, the hot sun had evaporated the seawater leaving clumps of sea salt in the hole. Pak Pandir was very excited when he saw the salt.

'Oh, look at all this salt. I will take this salt and keep it safe in my sack. Tomorrow, I will sell the salt at the market and we will be rich! Mak Andeh will be so proud of me,' said Pak Pandir to himself.

Pak Pandir scooped up all the salt into his sack and with a happy heart, made his way home. After walking for an hour, Pak Pandir felt sleepy and decided to have another nap by the river. However, he was worried that someone would come and steal his sack of salt, and so he hid the sack under a rock in the river.

'I am very clever. No one will find my salt here,' he said to himself as he settled down for his second nap of the day. An hour later, Pak Pandir woke up, took his sack of salt, and continued his journey home.

'Mak Andeh, look how much salt I've collected.' Pak Padir opened the sack and poured out the contents into a bowl, but to his surprise, nothing came out.

'What are you talking about, Pak Pandir? I do not see any salt,' said Mak Andeh peering at the empty bowl.

'Mak Andeh! I think someone has stolen all my salt.' Pak Pandir told his wife how he had stopped for a nap on the way home and had hidden the sack of salt in the river.

'Pak Pandir, you are a silly old man. All the salt in your sack is gone now. The river water has taken it.' Pak Pandir felt silly indeed. The next day, he decided it was easier to go back to work on his paddy field.

Chapter 52

Pak Pandir Repairs His House
(Malaysia)

One day, after a heavy downpour, Mak Andeh discovered that there was a leak in the roof of their house. The roof was so old that there were several holes which let in the rain water. As she mopped up the water on the floor, she also saw that the back door was broken and the window could not be closed properly. She crossed her arms and shook her head.

'This house is falling apart. I need to ask Pak Pandir to repair the roof and fix the back door and window.' She looked around for Pak Pandir but he was nowhere to be found. Finally, she found him lying down in bed even though the sun was high up in the sky.

'Pak Pandir, there are several holes in the roof of our house. Please get up and repair the roof before it rains again,' said Mak Andeh.

'Yes dear, I will fix the roof when I get around to it,' replied Pak Pandir as rubbed his eyes.

'Pak Pandir, please repair the broken door and the window at the back of the house also,' said Mak Andeh. 'I'm worried that burglars may come into our house at night.'

'Yes dear, I will fix the door and window when I get around to it,' he yawned, ready for his mid-morning nap.

Mak Andeh crossed her arms and shook her head. She knew that Pak Pandir would simply sleep all day if she didn't do something about it. She had to come up with a clever plan to get Pak Pandir finish the repairs around the house. Mak Andeh looked out of the window and was struck by an idea. While Pak Pandir napped, Mak Andeh cleared a path from the back of their house into the jungle. The path passed three tall trees and looped back to their house.

When Pak Pandir woke up, Mak Andeh told him about an exciting well-paying job. 'This lady wants you to fix her house. She's willing to pay you quite well.'

'Where does she live, Mak Andeh?' asked Pak Pandir who was getting quite excited.

'Mak Andeh took Pak Pandir to the back of their house. 'Do you see that path over there?' she said, pointing to the path she had just cleared. Pak Pandir nodded.

'Just follow that path which will lead you pass three tall trees. The path is not straight and you will loop around slightly, but you will eventually come to the back of the lady's house. She wants you to fix the leak in her roof, and repair her broken door and window,' said Mak Andeh.

'Yes, dear,' replied Pak Pandir. He gathered his tools and made his way down the path. Pak Pandir passed one tree, and then another, and then another.

'Aha! I have passed three trees. I must be near the lady's house,' he said to himself. True enough, he soon arrived at the back of a house.

Pak Pandir worked hard over the next three days to fix the lady's roof, door, and back window. During all that time, he never saw the lady who lived in the house but around noon, a tray of food and drink was left for him on the porch. When Pak Pandir finished his work on the third day, the lady left him some money on the porch.

Pak Pandir was so happy about the fact that he had made some money, he ran home to tell his wife. However, when he reached home, he was puzzled to see that his own roof was no longer leaking. The door and window had also been fixed.

'Mak Andeh, who repaired our house?' he asked scratching his head.

'Pak Pandir, you are a silly man. You are the one who repaired our house.' She smiled and told him what she had done. Pak Pandir laughed and said that she was a very clever wife.

Chapter 53

Pak Pandir and the Hungry Giants
(Malaysia)

Pak Pandir loved his wife dearly not only because she was clever and had helped him out of many sticky situations, but also because she was the best cook in the village. One day, Mak Andeh asked Pak Pandir to invite Tok Penghulu, the village head, over for dinner.

'Tok Penghulu? Who is Tok Penghulu?' asked Pak Pandir, who never paid attention to people's names.

'Haish! You are so forgetful, Pak Pandir. Tok Penghulu is a very important man. He is the head of our village. Please go to his house and invite his family over for dinner. I will cook up a feast,' said Mak Andeh.

'Yes, dear,' replied Pak Pandir. 'Just tell me where he lives and I will go and invite him for dinner.'

Mak Andeh took Pak Padir out the front door and pointed to the path outside their house. 'Listen carefully, Pak Pandir. Walk straight along that path and when you get to the end of it, turn right. Tok Penghulu's house is the big house made of stone at the end of that road.'

'Yes, dear. I must walk straight along that path and then turn right,' repeated Pak Pandir. As he walked along the path he mumbled under his breath, 'Go straight, turn right. Go straight, turn right.'

Pak Pandir was concentrating so hard that he did not look where he was going and stumbled over a rock. He fell down in the middle of the path and got so muddled that he forgot whether he was supposed to turn right or left.

'Oh dear,' he said to himself as he scratched his head. Pak Pandir got up and decided to take one of the paths which eventually led him to a big stone cave. 'Oh, this must be the house. It is big and made out of stone.' Pak Pandir was quite pleased with his cleverness and began to call out to Tok Pengulu.

'Greetings Tok Penghulu! I have come to invite you and your family over to my house for dinner. Mak Andeh has cooked up a feast,' said Pak Pandir. 'Hello? Tok Penghulu, are you there?'

At first the cave was silent and still. Pak Pandir thought that perhaps no one was home. Just as he was about to leave, he heard a low, angry growl coming from inside the cave.

'Tok Penghulu? Is that you?' asked Pak Pandir.

Pak Pandir heard a grunt and suddenly, a huge man appeared at the entrance of the cave. He was as tall as Pak Pandir's coconut tree and his chest was as wide as Pak Pandir's buffalo. He did not smile and looked very hungry. The man's appearance frightened Pak Pandir, but he remembered Mak Andeh's instructions.

'Tok Penghulu, you and your family are invited to my house for dinner. Please follow me.' At first the man looked confused, but after a while he grunted and nodded. He yelled out for his wife and son to join him, and together they made their way back to Pak Pandir's house.

Stomp, stomp, stomp! Tok Penghulu's family were so huge that they made a loud thumping sound as they walked along the path. *Tok Penghulu is so big and strong, no wonder he is the leader of the village*, thought Pak Pandir to himself. When they arrived home, Mak Andeh went out to greet them. She got quite a shock when she saw that Pak Pandir had brought home a family of giants!

'Welcome to our home, please come in,' she said inviting them in. The giants came in and sat down. They were so big that they filled up the entire house.

Mak Andeh took Pak Pandir into the kitchen and whispered. 'Pak Pandir, you silly fool! That is not Tok Penghulu. That is Tok Gergasi, and if we're not careful he might eat us.'

'Oh, then we better feed them your delicious food,' said Pak Pandir. Luckily for them, Mak Andeh was the best cook in the village. The family of giants enjoyed eating her steamed coconut rice, beef rendang, and fresh vegetable stew. After dinner, the family of giants thanked Pak Pandir and Mak Andeh, and returned back to their cave.

Chapter 54

Pak Pandir and the Tiger
(Malaysia)

Since Pak Pandir was so silly, Mak Andeh sometimes liked to tease and play tricks on him. However, sometimes her tricks produced an unexpected result which is what happened on this occasion.

One day, Pak Pandir and Mak Andeh decided to go to the next village to visit Mak Andeh's sister who was ill. The next village was across a hill and in the past, it took several days to walk around the hill to reach there. Pak Pandir was not looking forward to the long journey.

'How will we travel to your sister's house? She lives far away,' asked Pak Pandir, forgetting that there was now a short cut which led to the next village. At that moment, Mak Andeh was cooking some snacks to bring on their trip and she decided to play a trick on her husband.

'Well, if you can find a zebra in the jungle tomorrow, we can ride on the back of a zebra,' replied Mak Andeh.

Pak Pandir was surprised because he had never heard of a zebra. He wanted to know more about this strange creature.

'A zebra? Tell me, Mak Andeh, what does a zebra look like,' asked Pak Pandir scratching his head.

'Well, a zebra is an animal,' replied Mak Andeh. 'We can sit on its back and it will take us to my sister's house.'

'How wonderful! What does a zebra look like?'

'Well, it has four legs, two eyes, and two ears.'

'I see,' replied Pak Pandir.

'Oh, and it has stripes on its body,' added Mak Andeh.

'I see,' said Pak Pandir, nodding his head. He tried to picture an animal which had four legs, two eyes, and two ears, with stripes on his body, but he just couldn't imagine it in his mind.

'I will go out first thing tomorrow morning to find us a zebra, Mak Andeh,' said Pak Pandir who was excited at the prospect of riding on the back of a zebra.

The next morning, Pak Pandir set off into the jungle to see if he could find a zebra. He saw a squirrel and a few birds, but he couldn't find any animal with stripes on its body. Pak Pandir decided to walk deeper into the jungle. He walked so far into the jungle until he finally caught sight of an animal which fit the description. This creature was huge and it walked slowly in between the trees. Pak Pandir could see that the animal had four legs, two eyes, and two ears, and its body was covered in black and yellow stripes.

'Aha! This must be a zebra,' thought Pak Pandir to himself. He approached the animal and held up his hands.

'Come now zebra, we must go home now. Mak Andeh and I need you to take us to the next village' he said to the animal. The *zebra* slowly turned its yellow eyes towards Pak Pandir. The animal licked its lips and then let out a ferocious roar which made Pak Pandir jump. The creature leaped towards Pak Pandir who screamed and ran away as fast as he could. He was so terrified that he did not stop until he reached his house.

'Mak Andeh! Mak Andeh! I went into the jungle and I found the zebra, but it roared at me and chased me,' said Pak Pandir to his wife. He told her exactly what had happened and Mak Andeh fell down from the shock.

'Oh Pak Pandir! I was only teasing you about the zebra. A zebra is an animal that lives far away in another country. What you found in the jungle wasn't a zebra. It was a tiger, you, silly old man.'

Pak Pandir was so shocked that he fainted on the spot.

Chapter 55

Pak Pandir and the Golden Pot
(Malaysia)

Even though Pak Pandir was not very clever, he was always cheerful and liked to help around the house. One day, Mak Andeh asked Pak Pandir to fetch some water from the river.

'I need to clean the house today and I need lots of water,' she said.

'The river is so far away, Mak Andeh. It will take me a long time to go back and forth in order to get enough water for you. I know! I will dig a well near our house so that we will always have access to water,' said Pak Pandir. Mak Andeh was surprised because for once, Pak Pandir had a good idea. She smiled and patted him on his back.

Pak Pandir took his shovel and began to dig the well just outside their house. He worked all morning digging and shovelling the soil. Suddenly, his shovel hit something hard which was buried in the ground. Pak Pandir bent down to take a closer look and was surprised to find a beautiful pot made out of gold.

He carefully dug out the pot and stared at it feeling thrilled. The pot was so shiny that it gleamed under the sun.

'I am rich! I have found a pot made of gold.' Pak Pandir began to dream about what he would do with his new-found wealth. He would buy some land and build a huge house for Mak Andeh. Then he would get people to dig a well near his house so that he would never have to fetch water from the river again. He would also use the money to buy Mak Andeh new clothes and jewellery. It went on and on. He was having such a fine time daydreaming that he didn't realize that several hours had passed.

Pak Pandir was suddenly aware that he was sitting outside his house holding the golden pot and he became worried that someone might try to steal his new-found treasure.

'I must hide my treasure in a safe place,' he said to himself.

Pak Pandir decided to dig another hole under a nearby tree and placed the golden pot inside. He covered the hole with soil and then took a piece of chalk from his pocket and wrote on the tree trunk in big letters—THERE IS NO GOLDEN POT BURIED HERE.

'There. No one will ever find my golden pot here,' he said to himself as he walked away. He was quite pleased with his cleverness.

Unknown to Pak Pandir, Mak Andeh was watching him from behind a tree. She saw the sign he wrote and shook her head.

'What a silly old man.' Mak Andeh then dug out the golden pot and hid it in the house. She waited for Pak Pandir to return.

'Have you finished digging up the well?' she asked him, when he returned to the house.

'I don't have to dig a well, Mak Andeh. I am rich now,' he replied, looking pleased with himself.

'Rich? What do you mean "rich"?' she asked.

'When I was digging the well, I found a golden pot. We can sell it and then we will have lots of money. I can buy you a bigger house and we can pay other people to dig a nice, big well for us. Doesn't that sound nice?' Pak Pandir was so happy that he started dancing around the house.

'So where is this golden pot? I don't see it here,' asked Mak Andeh.

'Come, I will show you. But you must keep it a secret.' Pak Pandir took his wife to the tree with the sign and began to dig. He dug deeper and deeper but he couldn't find the golden pot.

'Oh no! My golden pot is gone! Someone has stolen my treasure.' Pak Pandir looked so sad that Mak Andeh felt sorry for him.

'Don't worry, Pak Pandir. I've taken your pot and hidden it somewhere safe in the house,' she said. Mak Andeh pointed to the sign Pak Pandir had written on the tree.

'Next time, I suggest that you do not write anything to show where you've hidden your treasure.'

* * *

The stories of Pak Pandir are said to have originated from the state of Perak, in Malaysia, and were originally oral tales narrated by the headmen of the village who played an important role as narrators of Malay folk stories in the past. These stories were also told by the 'penglipur lara', a term used to describe the professional oral storyteller whose trade was to entertain the village folk with traditional tales. These oral tales were eventually documented and written down by people such as Raja Haji Yahya, who worked closely with R.O. Winstedt, who was actively collecting and publishing reading materials in Malay while he was working in the Federated Malay States Civil Service around 1920–40. The Pak Pandir are popular comic tales that have been an integral part of Malay folk tradition and focuses on the life of the ordinary person in a village setting. Although these tales are presented in a comic and farcical manner, they also contain some elements of social criticism and moral lessons.

Chapter 56

The Story of Pak Kadok
(Malaysia)

Once there was a king in a country called Seri Gading. The king loved games and his favourite pastime was to watch cockfights. Every week, the palace would hold a royal cockfight competition and people from all around the country would come with their best birds in order to place bets and see the fights.

In that land, there lived a man named Pak Kadok who lived with his wife, Mak Kadok. Pak Kadok was famous for being the village fool. However, even though Pak Kadok was but a mere simpleton, he happened to own a very fine cockerel. One day he said to Mak Kadok, 'Shall we enter our prized bird at the royal cockfight? He is strong and clever, and will surely win.'

'Our bird will surely win, but we are poor and we have nothing to wager,' replied Mak Kadok.

'Do not worry. I am confident that our bird will be the champion. We can wager our house and our village.' Pak Kadok wanted to go to the cockfight in style and so he asked his wife to make him new clothes.

'Make me a set of clothes out of white cloth for the cockfight,' said Pak Kadok.

'We do not have any white cloth, Pak Kadok,' replied Mak Kadok.

'Then make it out of white paper. I need to look impressive for the king.'

'Why are you so silly, Pak Kadok? If I make your clothes from paper, it will easily rip. Will you not be embarrassed if your clothes are torn in front of the king?' asked Mak Kadok.

'What do I care of such things! Make me clothes out of paper, wife. I need to make a fine impression when I walk into the palace.'

Even though Mak Kadok thought it was a bad idea, she did as he requested and made him a pair of trousers and a shirt out of white paper. Her needlework was so good that Pak Kadok looked rather striking as he strode into the palace carrying his prized cock.

The king and all the people were gathered in the cockpit to watch the competition. Pak Kadok approached the king and asked for permission to enter his cockerel.

'What can you offer as a wager?' asked the king.

'Your Highness, I am a poor man and have no money or gold, but I am confident that my bird will win today. I am willing to wager my house and my entire village,' answered the silly Pak Kadok. While Pak Kadok was busy talking, the king could not help but admire Pak Kadok's bird. The greedy king came up with a plan to trick Pak Kadok and win the competition.

'Very well, Pak Kadok. You may enter this competition on one condition. My cockerel is a great fighter. I think you should take my bird and I will take yours. That is a fair exchange,' said the king.

Pak Kadok was so excited to be allowed in the competition that he immediately agreed to the king's terms without thinking. 'I agree to your terms, Your Highness!'

Soon the cockfight was underway. At first, both birds were evenly matched and both fought valiantly. However, after a while, the king's bird became tired and at that moment Pak Kadok's bird delivered a powerful kick which made the other bird fall to the ground. Pak Kadok's cockerel had won the fight! Alas, poor Pak Kadok. He had completely forgotten that he had traded his bird with the king and he thought that he had won the fight. In his excitement, Pak Kadok jumped up and down and waved his arms vigorously in the air. He was so happy that he couldn't stop jumping.

Unfortunately for Pak Kadok, he also forgot that he was wearing clothes made out of paper. His shirt tore apart and his trousers ripped into shreds and before he knew it, he was standing completely naked in front of the king and all the people in town. At first, everyone was shocked to see a naked man standing in front of the king, and then the crowd broke out in laughter. How they laughed at the silly Pak Kadok! Feeling embarrassed Pak Kadok ran all the way home to tell Mak Kadok what had happened.

Mak Kadok could not believe her ears when she heard the story.

'How could you be embarrassed because you stood naked in front of the king! What is worse is that you have lost our house and village because you gave your prized cock to the king!'

Pak Kadok could do nothing but regret his foolish decision. Poor Pak Kadok.

* * *

Pak Kadok is one of the five comic characters embodied in Malay folklore, which also includes the tales of Lebai Malang, Pak Pandir, Pak Belalang and Si Luncai. There are many stories of Pak Kadok which falls under the category of the village simpleton. These comic tales not only have high moral values, they also act as a form of accepted social criticism. In the past, the Malay feudal society demanded unquestionable loyalty from its subjects and any form of criticism would be punished and dealt with severely. As such, these tales developed in order to give a voice to the people's grievances and dissatisfaction towards the rulers. These cleverly written tales were presented in a comic way to make them acceptable to the authorities.

Chapter 57

Tun Jana Khatib
Sulalat al-Salatin
(Singapore)

Once there was a merchant and a powerful ulama by the name of Tun Jana Khatib. Tun Jana Khatib had heard that the Paduka Seri Maharaja, the king of Temasek (Singapore), was a Hindu and he decided to go to the island kingdom to preach.

When Tun Jana Khatib arrived in Temasek, he found the people of Temasek to be hard-working and friendly. He enjoyed watching the children play in the market and he loved to eat the bikang cake seller's delicious local treats. There were so many wonderful sights and sounds to take in, and Tun Jana Khatib marvelled at the beauty and magnificence of the city. However, he was sad that he was unable to carry out his mission. One night, he dreamt of the palace which stood on a hill in the city, and when he woke up the next morning, Tun Jana Khatib decided to try to gain an audience with the king. Perhaps if he could speak to the ruler, he would be able to persuade the king to convert to Islam.

'Cake seller, can you tell me how to get to the king's palace?' asked Tun Jana Khatib.

'Why do you want to go to the palace?' asked the cake seller.

'I need to speak to the king,' replied Tun Jana Khatib.

The cake seller laughed and patted Tun Jana Khatib on the back. 'Follow that road and it will lead you to the place. However, be careful, my friend. Our King has a very bad temper so you must not do anything to anger him.'

Tun Jana Khatib thanked the cake seller and set off towards the palace. As he walked along the road, he did not realize that he was being observed by the Permaisuri, the queen and her court ladies. The ladies were in the royal garden enjoying some fresh air when they noticed the young man walking towards palace gates.

It was obvious from his clothes and mannerisms that Tun Jana Khatib was a foreigner and the ladies were curious to see what he was up to. Tun Jana Khatib reached the front gate of the palace and suddenly stopped. He turned around and began to pace outside the gate until he stopped beside a beautiful areca palm tree which was growing nearby. The queen and her ladies looked at each other feeling puzzled. They wondered what was so special about the tree when all of a sudden, a flash of lightning followed by a booming clap of thunder erupted from the sky. The tree, suddenly and without warning, split into two and crashed to the ground frightening the ladies. The queen screamed and fell into a faint as her court ladies ran around in a state of panic.

Unfortunately for Tun Jana Khatib, the king was looking out of his window at this precise moment and saw the whole incident. The king saw the queen taking an interest in the stranger as he walked towards the palace. He noticed how Tun Jana Khatib lingered by the areca tree and using some unknown power, split the tree into two. In the king's mind, Tun Jana Khatib was showing off his magical powers to the queen and this enraged him. The king immediately ordered his men to seize Tun Jana Khatib.

'How dare you come to the royal palace to perform your magic tricks in front of the queen,' said the red-faced king. 'I sentence you to death.'

Tun Jana Khatib was swiftly taken to the execution ground which was near the house of the seller of bikang cakes.

'Please, I am innocent! I did not mean any harm,' pleaded Tun Jana Khatib but his pleas fell on death ears. Tun Jana Khatib was tied up and stabbed in the heart, and as the blood touched the ground, his body vanished into thin air. The bikang cake seller rushed forward and covered the blood with her *tudung saji,* a dish cover made from pine leaves. For some mysterious reason, the tudung saji immediately turned into stone.

No one could explain the mysterious disappearance of Tun Jana Khatib's body, but according to another tale, at the exact moment when his body vanished from the country of Singapore, it appeared on the coast of Langkawi Island in the north. The people of Langkawi brought his body and laid it to rest in a cemetery called Makam Purba.

* * *

This is a literary tale and concerns events which took place on the island of Temasek. Temasek (or Temasik) is an early recorded name of a settlement on the site of modern Singapore. Unlike most fairy tales and folktales, this story is not an oral tale and has actually been recorded and written down in a book called *Sulalat al-Salatin* or *Sejarah Melayu.* The *Sulalat al-Salatin* is one of the earliest Malay literary work and is regarded as the finest and most famous of all the Malay classics.

The main objective of the *Sulalat al-Salatin* is quite clear; the author sought to provide an account of the Malay Sultans of the Melaka line. It was written to provide a memorial for the rulers to remind them of their duties, and to provide the succeeding Malay generations with the history of the genealogy of the Melaka sultans, together with a chronicle of the Malay royal ceremonies. However, unlike most history books, the *Sulalat al-Salatin* contains a of mixture of historical facts, myths, legends and folklore such as the story of Tun Jana Khatib.

Chapter 58

The Swordfish Attack of Singapore
Sulalat al-Salatin
(Singapore)

A long time ago on the island of Temasek all was not well. The Paduka Seri Maharaja, the king had just sentenced an innocent man to death and the gods were angry.

Strange things were happening around the island; the cockerels refused to crow at dawn, the fish suddenly vanished from the waters around the island and hard rocks fell from the sky. The people of Temasek began to wonder whether their island was under a curse. They were worried that the king had gone too far and that they would soon be punished for the king's cruel reign over the country.

One evening the skies over the island of Singapore darkened and the sea began to churn as if there was a monster underneath. A fierce howling wind uprooted the trees lining the seaside and sent them tumbling to the ground.

The people huddled together in their homes and prayed. Some of the more curious villagers gathered at the beach and were shocked to see a huge wall of water coming towards the island. A storm was coming. But this was no ordinary storm. A colossal wave moved closer to the shore and out of the water emerged thousands of ikan todak, or swordfish. Their dagger-like snouts glimmered and sparkled under the setting sun. Without warning, a wave of swordfish came flying towards the shore. One of these creatures flung itself through the air and impaled a man with its razor-sharp snout. The man died instantly, his blood spreading across the sand. Men, women, and children screamed as they tried to run away.

'The swordfish are attacking us!'

The unlucky people on the beach did not have time to run away as the swordfish were swift and deadly. The attack was relentless and soon, the beach turned red with the blood of the people.

When news of the attack reached the king, he sent his men down to the shore, but they were powerless against the might of the swordfish army. There were too many. It was as if all the swordfish in the entire ocean had gathered to attack the tiny island.

In a state of panic, the king ordered his people to form a human shield around the island in order to stop the swordfish from moving further inland towards the palace. The king did not once think of the safety of his people. He just wanted to save his own life.

'Every man, woman, and child must stand in a line across the shoreline. The people must sacrifice themselves for their king,' he ordered. Soldiers were sent to every house. They dragged out whole families and forced them to stand in a line on the shore. The frightened people screamed and tried to run away. Parents hid their children and tried to fight off the soldiers. The people could not believe that the king could be so cruel as to sacrifice his own people.

Finally, a young boy stepped forward and spoke up to the king.

'Your Highness, there is no need to sacrifice the people. I know how to defeat the swordfish,' said the young boy.

'Tell us then, boy. How can we stop this slaughter?' asked one of the ministers.

'It is simple. All we have to do is cut down all the banana trees on the island and plant the trunks along the coastline to form a barricade. The swordfish will be impaled on the soft bark and will not be able to escape,' replied the boy.

Everyone was stunned by the boy's brilliant idea.

'The boy is right! We can trap the swordfish with banana trunks,' said the minister. The king agreed and immediately ordered everyone to build the barricade of banana trunks. All across the island, the soldiers and villagers worked together to cut down all the banana trees. They then replanted the trunks around the entire shoreline to form a barricade in order to stop the attack from the swordfish. When the next wave of swordfish came from the sea, the fish were impaled on the banana trunks and were quickly killed by the people. Everyone rejoiced and cheered for the young boy who had saved their lives.

* * *

This is a literary tale which is contained in the *Sulalat al-Salatin* or the *Sejarah Melayu*, and concerns the events which occurred on the island of Temasek. This is one of the most famous legends from the *Sulalat al-Salatin* and has spawned many oral versions, books, and even a movie (*Singapura Dilanggar Todak*, 1961). *Tanjong Pagar* (which means 'fenced headland' in modern-day Singapore), takes its name from the barricade of banana trunks used in this tale. In the actual text of the *Sejarah Melayu*, the swordfish story is situated right after the story of Tun Jana Khatib, but it is unclear whether the two stories are connected.

Chapter 59

The Tale of Hang Nadim
Sulalat al-Salatin
(Singapore)

It was said that a long time ago, the island of Temasek was under attack from an army of swordfish. The swordfish congregated around the island and began to kill the people with their sharp snouts. No one knew what to do and the cruel king only thought of himself and ordered all the people to stand in a line around the island in order to form a human wall.

Fortunately, a young boy stepped up and saved the day with his idea of using banana trunks to form a barrier around the island. After the people of Temasek had successfully defeated the swordfish, they rejoiced and cheered for the boy who had saved the day. The boy, who was called Hang Nadim, was declared a hero by the people of Temasek.

'Summon Hang Nadim to the palace,' ordered the Seri Paduka Maharaja, the king. 'He has saved Temasek and I want to reward him for his good deed.'

All the ministers agreed that Hang Nadim deserved to be rewarded for saving the country. Unfortunately, there were some who were jealous. They did not like how popular Hang Nadim had become and they were worried about their positions in court. One of these men was the Bendahara, the prime minister, who had great ambitions to succeed the throne one day. He could see that Hang Nadim had the intelligence and talent to become ruler of Temasek.

One day, the Bendahara met the king and casually remarked on Hang Nadim's popularity. 'Hang Nadim is only a boy and yet he has more insight than most of the ministers in court. I can only imagine what he will be like when he is an adult. I must say that I am worried that when he grows up, he will have more power than the king himself.'

Upon hearing these words, the king became anxious about the boy. He could not eat or sleep for days. The thought of Hang Nadim taking over his kingdom worried and angered the king until finally, he made a decision to sentence Hang Nadim to death.

'The boy must not be allowed to gain more power. My position as king is at risk,' thought the king to himself.

That night, the king's soldiers crept up to the humble home of Hang Nadim on a green hill outside town. They waited in the dark until morning and when Hang Nadim came out of his house, they attacked and killed the boy. The blood of Hang Nadim spread across the green grass. It is said that because of the cruel act of the king, the hill became stained with blood and was later named Bukit Merah, or Red Hill.

* * *

This is a literary tale which is contained in the *Sulalat al-Salatin* or the *Sejarah Melayu*, and concerns events which occurred on the island of Temasek. In the *Sejarah Melayu*, the youth who came up with the idea of using banana trunks to catch the swordfish is unnamed. It is only in later retellings of this story, that the youth is identified as Hang Nadim. Again, it is interesting that the names of these places still exist today. Hang Nadim was said to be killed on a green hill which turned red with his blood. Today, this place is called Bukit Merah, or Red Hill. In another version of this story, Hang Nadim is tied up in chains and drowned at Batu Berhenti (Stopping Stone) in the Straits of Singapore.

Chapter 60

How The Kingdom of Melaka Was Discovered
Sulalat al-Salatin
(Malaysia)

It came to be that the island kingdom of Temasek was attacked and defeated by their more powerful neighbour, the kingdom of Majapahit. By this time, Temasek was ruled by the son of the Seri Paduka Maharaja who was called Raja Secandar Shah. The young Raja decided to leave Temasek with his royal entourage in order to set up a new empire.

Raja Secandar Shah left his island city and crossed the narrow straits. They followed the river to the north until he reached a place called Moar. The Raja was impressed with this town and thought that perhaps this would be a good location for his new empire. He ordered his men to set up camp near the river and then settled for the night. However, in the middle of the night, the men were awoken by strange noises coming from outside their camp. It sounded as if a million small feet were trampling on the ground around them. Suddenly, a foul stench wafted in from outside the tent. The smell was so pungent and vile that it made some of the men quite ill.

The next morning, they discovered the source of the strange noise and the foul smell. The place was overrun by thousands of lizards. The Sultan and his men killed the creatures and threw them into the river, but that night, thousands more appeared. The stench of the lizards was so awful that Raja Secander Shah named this place Bewak Busok, or 'stinking lizard'.

Unable to stand the horrible smell, the royal entourage decided to move on. They searched for many days, trekking through thick jungle, until they reached a place high on a hill. Raja Secander Shah liked being on a hill and ordered his men to build a fort. The men worked hard to put up the walls of the fort and by evening, there was shelter for Raja Secander Shah. Feeling satisfied, the young raja went to sleep but in the morning, he was surprised to find that the walls of the fort had crumbled around him. Raja Secander Shah named this place Cotaburu or 'rotten fort'. Once again, the royal entourage was forced to move on in order to look for a more suitable place.

One day, feeling listless and dull, the raja decided to release his dogs and hunt the area for game. The sound of barking, loud and thunderous, echoed through the jungle and soon, the dogs caught the scent of an animal and began the chase. Raja Secander Shah felt his blood pumping with excitement as he ran after the dogs through the thick, dark jungle. The animal that was being chased was fast and strong. However, the prey was eventually cornered by the river, surrounded by the hunting dogs. Raja Secander Shah was surprised to see that it was a tiny kancil, a mouse deer no bigger than a cat.

'Your Highness, it is a white kancil. This is a good omen,' cried one of the guards, for the Kancil was revered as the wisest of all animals. Raja Secander Shah ordered his men to hold back from the hunt.

'I want to see what the white kancil will do,' said the raja. He sat under the shade of a tall tree and watched as the ferocious hunting dogs, their jaws quivering with the anticipation of a kill began to surround the small animal. Silence filled the air for a brief moment and then, there came a low growl like the rumble of thunder. Raja Secander Shah was surprised to find that the sound came not from the dogs, but from the white kancil.

The small animal shook, not from fear, but from rage. Then all at once, the dogs leaped upon the creature and all was lost in a sea of teeth and claws. The raja thought he saw a flash of white, under the grey pelt of his dogs but then it vanished. Soon, one by one the dogs were thrown into the air whimpering in pain. Terrified and ashamed, they ran off into the dark of the jungle, their heads hung low at their defeat.

Raja Secander Shah watched as the white kancil kicked the last dog who flew through the air and landed in the river. The men stood frozen to the spot but the raja knew this was the sign he had been praying for. He laughed and then bowed his head to the white kancil who simply blinked at him and then vanished into the undergrowth.

Raja Secander Shah asked his men for the name of the tree he was resting under.

'Your Highness, this is the melaka tree,' replied one of the men.

'Then I shall name my new kingdom, Melaka.' The kingdom of Melaka went on to become the most powerful and influential kingdom in the whole region.

* * *

The legend of how the Melaka empire was discovered is written in the *Sulalat al-Salatin* or the *Sejarah Melayu*. At this time, Temasek was ruled by the son of Seri Paduka Maharaja, who was named in the *Sejarah Melayu* as Raja Secander Shah, or Sultan Iskandar Shah. However, since Temasek was under Hindu influence, it is unlikely that its ruler bore this name when Melaka was founded. There is some evidence that a prince named Parameswara is the same person as the Raja Secander Shah referred to in the *Sejarah Melayu*. According to the book, Parameswara ruled Temasek from 1389 to 1398. However, after a naval invasion from the Majapahit empire, the king fled the island kingdom and founded his new stronghold on the mouth of the Bertam river in 1402. Within decades, this city expanded to become the capital of the Melaka Sultanate.

Chapter 61

The Malay Tale of The Pig King
Hikayat Raja Babi
(Indonesia)

Once there was a great king by the name of Seri Sultan Tahir Shah who ruled over the kingdom of Rantau Panjang Tebing Berukir, which stood on a magnificent volcano. One day, the king decided that he needed a son to inherit his great kingdom, and so he sent his minister out to find him a suitable wife. The minister returned not with one princess, but with forty-one princesses who were all stunning and lovely. The king decided that he would marry all forty-one princesses, and that was how all the trouble began.

Even though the king had many wives, not one of them could give him a son. Then one day, Puteri Indera Suri announced that she was going to have a baby. Overjoyed, the King decided to send all his other forty wives away.

The other wives were naturally quite angry and came together to curse the King. 'May your son be born a pig,' they cursed. 'A "haram" or forbidden animal.'

Puteri Indera Suri was pregnant for seven long years. The king called in his royal doctors and astrologers to find out why. After examining the queen and consulting the stars, they announced that the king's son was under a powerful curse and that he will be born in the body of a pig. This was a shock to the king but there was nothing he could do.

On the night the prince was born strange things happened. A cannon sounded from beyond the mountains, and a gong began to play on its own accord. The flags outside the palace danced and waved even though there was no breeze.

When the baby was born, the first thing they noticed was that his tusks were the colour of golden ripe bananas. His fur sparkled and his beautiful eyes gleamed. As predicted, the child was very definitely, a pig. By some miracle, the child leaped gracefully up in the air and started to recite a pantun, a poem. Everyone was shocked to hear the little Pig King speak with such sweet eloquence. They were even more shocked to find that he was a magnificent and beautiful creature (even though he was a pig). They cried and praised the Pig King, but they knew they could not keep a 'haram' animal in the palace. The king and queen cried as they placed the little Pig King onto an elephant.

'Do not worry,' said the Pig King. 'I will go off into the world and find a way to break this curse.'

The Pig King was taken to the far edge of the forest where no man had ever stepped foot. There, he met the King of the Boars, Raja Babi Hutan, who had an army of a thousand wild boars.

'How dare you come onto my land?' roared the King of the Boars.

'Is this your land?' asked the Pig King. 'Well, we shall have to see about that.'

The two ferocious pigs entered into an epic battle. Even though the Pig King was still young, he fought with the power of a thousand men against the might of the Boar Army. The ground shook and the trees fell down like matchsticks as the two pigs battled for three days and three nights.

This fight was witnessed by the fairy of Pucuk Puding who lived in that forest. She was impressed by the Pig King's strength and his fine looks and she knew that this was no ordinary pig.

'Pig King! Do not fight with that forbidden animal. Here, take my magic sword. It will fulfil your wishes,' she said, as she threw a magic *parang* sword towards the pig. He caught it with one arm and with one swift blow brought it down upon the head of the King of the Boars, cleaving it in two!

The Fairy took the Pig King into her enchanted garden. She washed the blood of the wild boar off his skin with rose water mixed with musk. She gave him food and drink and cared for the Pig King until he was fit and fine once more. Then she taught him the ways of war with animals, djinn, fairies and gods. Most important of all, she taught him the tricks of men.

After a while, the Pig King told the fairy that he no longer wanted to be a burden on her. 'I wish to see the world and find a way to break this curse.' The fairy was sad, but she let him go. As a gift, she gave him a magic knife. 'This is Si Parang Puting who will help you and grant your wishes. If you are ever in need of help, just call out to her.'

Feeling sorrowful, the Pig King left the fairy of Pucuk Puding and set off into the forest, up the hills and tall mountains, through the undergrowth and caves to see the beauty of god's creation. The Pig King felt humbled by what he saw. He walked on and on until he felt quite exhausted and decided to rest under a big tree near a cave. As it happened, a djinn by the name of Kilat Angkasa passed by and saw the sleeping Pig King.

'What an extraordinary little pig. He is so beautiful that I must bring him to the djinn princess, Tuan Puteri Indera Kemala,' said the djinn to himself. Kilat Angkasa took the sleeping pig and flew him to the country of Syaharastan Yunan, to a place called Padang Berantah Cahaya. They arrived at the palace of the djinn princess, Tuan Puteri Indera Kemala.

The princess was just at that moment passing by with her handmaidens when they spotted the Pig King. They were surprised to see his handsome face and his fur which sparkled with seven colours.

'How lovely! He is so precious!' cried the handmaidens. The djinn presented the Pig King to the princess and when the pig saw the princess he was overcome with love. He had never seen such beauty in all his life and he fell deeply in love.

The Pig King smiled and bowed gracefully to the ladies. He then recited poetry to the princess which impressed them even more. The ladies fussed over the Pig King, and presented him rice with 'gulai' to eat. They praised his fine speech, good manners and handsome looks.

The princess was rather impressed with the Pig King and secretly admired him, but she kept her distance as she was already engaged and would soon be married to a powerful prince.

'Our princess will soon marry a handsome, wealthy prince, Seri Sultan Alam Shah Dewa. He is the mightiest prince in all the land,' said one of the handmaidens to the Pig King. The Pig King did not like this and turned towards the princess.

'Princess, I will wage a war against your prince for your hand in marriage.' The princess did not say anything, but smiled which the Pig King took as an indication of her assent.

That night he called upon his magic knife, Si Parang Puting who appeared spinning in the air. He told Si Parang Puting of his wish and all at once, she created a magical Golden City for the Pig King, filled with his own people and armies of djinn kings, fairy gods, and ferocious warriors. She placed this city in Padang Berantah Cahaya and then went to meet the enemy Prince.

'I have a message from the Pig King. Tomorrow we will go to war for the hand of the princess. We will meet at Padang Berantah Cahaya.'

The prince was angry that the Pig King was trying to stop his marriage to the Princess. He immediately called his generals and army to prepare for war.

When Si Parang Puting returned, the Pig King asked his magic knife if she could bring the princess's palace to his Golden City. 'Why, of course. I can even bring seven mountains here.' Si Parang Puting vanished and reappeared at the princess's palace where she used her magic dagger to stab the walls of the palace. Almost immediately, the palace spun and flew to the Golden City. The princess and her handmaidens were frightened because their palace had moved of its own accord, but the Pig King calmed the princess down. 'As long as I am alive, you will be safe. You are the queen of my heart.'

Then he left his Golden City on a magnificent elephant wearing steel armour with chains and a golden crown. His men followed riding on the backs of great dragons, flying lions, giant birds, some floated in the air under magic umbrellas and on flying chairs. It was a grand sight.

The fairy gods, djinn kings and their ministers, commanders, warriors, and armies were dressed in their finest clothes; jewelled tunics and silk trousers, nine layers of armour and, finely crafted shoes. Some wore seven bangles around their arms and seven necklaces wound around their necks. Their fingers were adorned with golden rings and some wore a Dragon Crown upon their heads.

In their armoury, they carried with them a metal mace on their left shoulder and a sword adorned with precious stones on their right shoulder. Some had arrows made of emeralds and an opal sheath. The Pig King's army marched to meet their enemy at Padang Berantah Cahaya accompanied by the sound of the gendang and serunai.

The Battle of Garuda Bayu was about to begin. The Pig King was surprised to see the might of the prince's army for he too, had the support of his own fairy gods, djinn kings and warriors. The sky became dark from the fighting as blood spilled on the earth until it flooded the land. One by one, the fairy gods and the djinn kings from each side began to confront each other. One fairy god threw an arrow to the sky and made the rain pour down on his enemies. To stop him, the other fairy god created a typhoon to blow away all the rain to the sea.

One djinn king shot an arrow into the sky which turned into a volcano spewing out fire and ash onto his enemies. The other djinn king shot his arrow and made heavy rain to put out the fire.

One warrior shot an arrow and turned it into a thousand dragons which swooped down on its enemies. The other warrior shot an arrow and turned it into a thousand giant Garuda birds which chased the dragons away.

The battle waged on and on until Padang Berantah Cahaya turned into a churning sea. It was soon clear that the Pig King's army was winning the battle. The Pig King sat on his golden saddle and searched the battle field for the prince.

As the Pig King approached, the prince's army surrounded him and showered him with a rain of arrows, but not one could penetrate the Pig King's skin. The Pig King swung Si Parang Puting and killed all his enemies. He spun around and around like a great tornado until fire lit up the sky. He spun closer to the prince and with one move, killed the prince with his magic sword. The war was over.

The Pig King returned to his Golden City and married the princess. He hoped that this was enough to break the curse but unfortunately, he remained in the body of a pig. Disheartened, he knew he must once again make his way into the world to look for another way to break the curse. He called upon Si Parang Puting who appeared spinning in the air.

'Hide my Golden City and keep my princess safe. I will find a way to break the curse and return to her one day.' Then the Pig King set off into the world once more, this time feeling dejected and angry. He soon arrived at a country called Tebing Bunga where he found an orchard full of fruits. Still feeling angry, the Pig King destroyed the trees and frightened the farmers who tried to stab him with their spears. The Pig King chased them to the walls of the royal city and found that it was locked. This infuriated him even more and he shouted, 'Tell your king that the Pig King is here!'

He knocked down the walls of the city and ran amok, destroying shops and houses, injuring people and frightening the villagers.

'Tell the king, there is a vicious animal on the loose! He is headed for the palace!'

The king's warriors attacked the Pig King. They shot a thousand arrows at him but not one penetrated his skin. They then sent forty elephants to try to stop the Pig King but he merely glared at the elephants and the animals began to cower. They lowered their heads and bowed to the Pig King.

The Pig King arrived at the palace, crashed into the throne room and surprised the poor King and his seven daughters who were cowering in fear.

'Please come and have a seat, Pig King,' said the king.

The servants brought huge trays of rice and gulai which the Pig King devoured making a huge mess. Then he jumped towards the Princesses and accidently knocked down a pillar. The seven princesses ran screaming into the garden as the Pig King chased after them. The princesses were all so frightened that they all fell into a faint and did not stir for seventy days.

The king called in the doctors and the astrologers but no one could wake the sleeping princesses. Finally, he was told that the only person who could wake them up was the Pig King himself. Reluctantly, the king asked the Pig King if he could save his daughters. By then, the Pig King regretted losing his temper and was sorry for what he had done.

With the help of Si Parang Puting, the Pig King woke up all seven princesses with magic rose water and everyone rejoiced. Then he apologised to the King and the seven princesses and left the palace for good. As he walked, he felt calm and happy. Had he done enough to break the curse?

The Pig King stopped and asked Si Parang Puting to bring his Golden City to him. All at once, the city appeared and in the distance, the Pig King saw his beloved princess coming towards him. They embraced and that night as he slept on her lap, the curse was finally broken. The Pig King transformed into a handsome young man. The Pig King returned to his father's kingdom to tell him of the news and together, the Pig King and the princess lived happily ever after.

* * *

This story is known as 'Hikayat Raja Babi' and was written in the year 1775 by a Javanese merchant called Usop Abdul Kadir. It is a unique story as it was not commissioned by the palace and was therefore written for the pure entertainment of the author, and his friends, and family. For many years, the original manuscript of 'Hikayat Raja Babi' was kept at the British Library, but in 2015, Malaysian publisher Fixi transliterated the text from Jawi script and made it far more accessible to the public. This story is considered to be an epic. It is a classic coming-of-age story where the protagonist must go on a journey through life to find a way to break the curse and find his happily ever after.